PRAISE FO

Be prepared to do nothing until you've finished reading this masterful suspense novel! I took a peek at the first page and couldn't stop until the last sentence.

DIANN MILLS, bestselling, award-winning author of *Lethal Standoff*, on *Every Deadly Suspicion*

A thrilling read full of heart-stopping tension and great twists. An awesome blend of suspense and romance. Don't miss *Every Deadly Suspicion*.

DARLENE L. TURNER, *Publishers Weekly* bestselling author of the Crisis Rescue Team series

At some point in our lives, everyone needs a hero. In *Every Deadly Suspicion*, Jared is Hanna's. From fighting fires to rescuing children and dogs, to tracking a serial killer, they find themselves once again drawn to each other—and learn a few lessons along the journey. Janice's books are always something I look forward to reading. She hooks you from page one. I highly recommend you hide somewhere fun to read this book because you won't want to be interrupted.

LYNETTE EASON, bestselling, award-winning author of the Lake City Heroes series

This timely police procedural from a twenty-two-year veteran of the Long Beach, Calif., police satisfies.

PUBLISHERS WEEKLY on *Code of Courage*

In *Breach of Honor*, Janice Cantore tells a complex tale of deceit and backroom deals that leaves you wondering who the good guys actually are. . . . I could not wait to get to the end and see how it all tied together.

HALLEE BRIDGEMAN, bestselling author of the Love and Honor series

Janice Cantore has crafted an adventure filled with brutal crimes, heartbreaking injustice, shocking twists, a gentle romance, and hard-won faith. Words like *page turning*, *breath stealing*, and *pulse racing*, while accurate, don't begin to do it justice.

LYNN H. BLACKBURN, award-winning author of the Dive Team Investigations series, on *Breach of Honor*

A complex tale of murder, deceit, and faith challenges, complete with multifaceted characterizations, authentic details, and action scenes, even a subtle hint of romance . . . [all] well integrated into a suspenseful story line that keeps pages turning until the end.

MIDWEST BOOK REVIEW on *Lethal Target*

EVERY DEADLY SUSPICION

EVERY DEADLY SUSPICION

JANICE CANTORE

Tyndale House Publishers
Carol Stream, Illinois

Visit Tyndale online at tyndale.com.

Visit Janice Cantore's website at janicecantore.com.

Tyndale and Tyndale's quill logo are registered trademarks of Tyndale House Ministries.

Every Deadly Suspicion

Cover designed by Sarah Susan Richardson

Published in association with the literary agency of Books & Such Literary Management, 52 Mission Circle, Suite 122, PMB 170, Santa Rosa, CA 95409.

Scripture quotations are from The ESV® Bible (The Holy Bible, English Standard Version®), copyright © 2001 by Crossway, a publishing ministry of Good News Publishers. Used by permission. All rights reserved.

The URLs in this book were verified prior to publication. The publisher is not responsible for content in the links, links that have expired, or websites that have changed ownership after that time.

For information about special discounts for bulk purchases, please contact Tyndale House Publishers at csresponse@tyndale.com, or call 1-855-277-9400.

Library of Congress Cataloging-in-Publication Data

A catalog record for this book is available from the Library of Congress.

979-8-4005-0129-6 (HC)
978-1-4964-8793-3 (SC)

Printed in the United States of America

30	29	28	27	26	25	24
7	6	5	4	3	2	1

Let all bitterness and wrath and anger and clamor and slander be put away from you, along with all malice. Be kind to one another, tenderhearted, forgiving one another, as God in Christ forgave you.

EPHESIANS 4:31-32

Why do you pass judgment on your brother? Or you, why do you despise your brother? For we will all stand before the judgment seat of God; for it is written, "As I live, says the Lord, every knee shall bow to me, and every tongue shall confess to God." So then each of us will give an account of himself to God.

ROMANS 14:10-12

What we are, and where we are is God's providential arrangement— God's doing, though it may be man's misdoing; and the manly and the wise way is to look your disadvantages in the face and see what can be made out of them.

WILL SCHWALBE

PROLOGUE

"Joe, I'm pregnant."

Those three words had set Joe Keyes's world spinning. The prospect of becoming a father changed his perspective on life. He and Paula had been married for two years and never talked about having kids. When she told him four days ago that she was pregnant, he'd fainted, cutting his head open when he fell.

Later at the hospital, while the doctor stitched him up, Joe felt as if the world had shifted, and he was leaning over the precipice of an abyss. If he pulled himself upright, he'd be the husband and father Paula needed. If he didn't, if he went back to cooking meth, he'd fall straight down into the abyss. And the abyss was bottomless.

"You can't go to jail again, Joe. What will I do with a baby if that happens?" Paula had pleaded with him.

She was right. He shoved his hands in his pockets. *"I do not want to go to jail again."*

It was a cold December in California, and Joe could see his breath as he hurried along the path. Around him loomed snow-covered pines, branches drooping under the weight of new powder.

The place he and Paula rented sat at the edge of the forest, and his favorite shortcut wove through the trees. He was on his way home to give Paula some news. It was the classic good news/bad news. He had a plan, and once he explained, she'd have to see that it made sense.

Since Paula had told him about the baby, Joe did a lot of thinking. As he adjusted to the idea, he liked it. At first, Joe hoped for a boy. He'd be able to teach a boy to be a good man. He'd certainly make sure his son got past the sixth grade. Yes, Joe would raise a good, strong boy who people would respect.

His stomach churned with butterflies when he considered the second option. What on earth could he teach a little girl? He considered a daughter. She'd be pretty, like Paula, with long, soft chestnut hair and warm green eyes the color of priceless emeralds. Eyes that would make a fella's heart stop.

I'll protect her, I'll provide for her, and I'll keep her safe. She'll grow up smart and strong, and she'll be a daddy's girl. He smiled at the thought. He didn't care if it was a boy or a girl. He just wanted to be a good dad, not like the man who'd raised him. That guy had been drunk all the time and rarely home. No, Joe would not be like his dad.

He arrived at home and hurried into the warmth, through the kitchen and into the living room. Paula sat on the couch with a book, bundled up in a blanket.

"I've got news." He sat on the coffee table in front of her.

"You got a job?" Her eyes sparkled with hope.

He tilted his head. "Good news and bad news. Yes, I got a job."

"What's the bad news?"

"It won't start full-time until spring. Ben Hodges hired me to do landscaping. It's only odd jobs right now, like clearing driveways and stuff."

"What will we do until then?" Her gaze darkened.

He held up both hands. "I've got a plan. Hear me out. I've still got the trailer. No one knows about it, not even Blake and Sophia." He threw his partners into the mix because sometimes Paula complained to him that they got too big a cut when Joe did all the work. "I'll cook one last batch of rocks. If it's just us, and I don't have to split anything with them, I should make enough money to tide us over."

Surprisingly, Paula didn't object right away. He could tell she seriously considered the idea, tapping on the book in her lap with a fingernail while she thought. "Promise you'll quit for good?"

"Cross my heart and hope to die."

❧

Two days later, Joe finished his last batch. He figured in his head that the amount of meth he'd made should net him about twenty grand. He broke it up into small rocks to fill individual packets: quarters, eight balls, and teeners. The quarter was the smallest and cheapest, weighing in at a quarter ounce; the eight ball the biggest at 3.5 grams. He weighed each bit and packed everything into separate little baggies. Once finished, he filled his backpack with the product.

Stretching, looking around his favorite kitchen, he admitted it felt good to be done. He shuffled around the empty battery-acid container and ignored the putrid pile of residue that accumulated during the cooking process. He'd let it all pile up inside instead of packing some of it outside.

The trailer was toast when he finished today. It was all going to burn.

He ran his hand through his hair, trying to clear his thoughts.

It was late afternoon; he'd been busy here all day inhaling noxious fumes. Cooking meth did nothing to help a man think straight. Stopping now would be a good thing. When his child was born, Joe wanted a clear head and a clean slate. He slung the backpack over his shoulders and stepped toward the door.

Movement outside the sliver of a window next to the front door caught his eye and he froze. Craning his neck, he peered through the slit.

There it was again.

Stiffening, his heart rate spiked and his pulse pounded. No one else should know about this place. Not even Blake and Sophia.

He never had trusted them with his cooking spot. Blake had a big mouth, and he hung out with untrustworthy dweebs. Joe tiptoed to the bigger window, peeled back a bit of the foil that blacked out the light, and eyeballed what he could of the outside terrain. On the far right, he saw a blue hood and car door. A Jeep. Only a four-by-four would get up here. Chase Buckley drove a blue Jeep.

Joe had been betrayed.

Somehow Blake and Sophia had found him. And they told Chase.

Sure enough, Chase came into view. He walked to the front of the Jeep and stood, staring at the trailer, hands on his hips. Buckley's presence threw Joe for a loop. The guy's family practically owned the whole county, cops included. What did he want here?

"I know Joe's in there." Blake stepped up to Chase's side.

"Is he armed?"

It took a minute for the second voice to register. It wasn't Blake; it was geeky Marcus Marshall of all people. Joe caught Marshall flirting with Paula once and punched him out. A total loser, he hung out with Buckley purely for protection.

"Naw, Joe wouldn't be dumb enough to have a gun," Blake said.

Joe slapped his forehead. Marshall. Joe remembered seeing the geek at the 7-Eleven when he'd picked up some water. Marshall followed him.

That's what Joe got for not being more careful. All he was thinking was that he'd be done with this for good. They'd found him and they'd want a cut of what he'd just cooked. He couldn't go back to Paula and tell her he'd lost half of the money from this batch. Now what was he gonna do?

Muttering under his breath, Joe tried to figure a way out.

"We know you're in there, Joe," Chase called out. "Come on out. I've got a proposition for you. It could make us both a lot of money."

Joe looked around the trailer's kitchen, which had served him so well. He'd done a lot of stupid things in his life, but getting involved with Chase would be the stupidest. The guy was a loose cannon, a wild card, and Joe wanted no part of the spoiled, rich jerk.

"Joe, we found you. Other people will, too." Sophia spoke now.

"You've been holding out on your partners," Blake yelled. "You deserve to be spanked."

"We'll forgive you. But the only way out is to make a deal with us." Chase again.

There was another way out. Joe already had planned to destroy the kitchen. The people outside would witness the destruction. The booby trap was dangerous for those standing too close to the trailer, maybe even deadly. Joe refused to consider the consequences. He didn't invite them here. He flicked the booby-trap switch and hurried for the back of the trailer. With all the caustic chemicals, it would not take much to level the place.

He lifted a hatch in the floor and dropped to the ground as he heard the front door get kicked in. Lying flat, his breath fled as the frigid air hit. He pushed himself out from under the trailer, stood as soon as he could, and then ran. Slipping and sliding in the thin layer of snow on the ground, Joe didn't dare look back.

He'd just reached his motorcycle when the trailer exploded. Joe flinched and looked back, saw the plume of smoke billowing. He shivered in spite of the exertion. At least Blake and Sophia were together. He could care less about Chase and Marshall.

Joe collapsed in a fit of coughing. That always happened after he cooked and then came out into the fresh winter air. For a minute he struggled for breath, his lungs burning.

One day all this cooking would be the death of him.

Slowly his breath returned to normal, and Joe hopped on the bike and sped away, heading for Dry Oaks, Paula, and his new life.

�֍

DEA Agent Gilly surveyed the burned-out trailer site. In the week since the explosion and fire, all the evidence had been collected by local police. Brett kicked through what remained in case they'd missed anything important. He found nothing. Rubbing his hands together, he regretted not having worn gloves.

The explosion was textbook meth-lab booby trap. Gilly could see it in his mind's eye—the cooker in the trailer was surprised, his lab had been discovered. He flipped the trap switch and fled as the lab blew.

Tuolumne County was fortunate the fire had been knocked down quickly. Light snowfall and cold temperatures had helped. Deep in the forest, on county land, the trailer fire could have caused lots more damage. As for the two people injured, they were lucky as well. Sophia Carson got the worst of it, with second- and third-degree burns on her hands and arms and a serious case of smoke inhalation. Blake Carson was barely singed.

Deputies arrested him at the hospital where his wife was admitted for burns and smoke inhalation. They didn't believe his story, and because of his record, they wanted to charge him with the lab and the fire. He'd been in custody during their investigation, but ultimately they had to kick him loose because they didn't have enough evidence to hold him over for trial.

He was guilty, though. Gilly's instinct told him that. Carson had a rap sheet filled with drug crimes. He'd claimed he and his wife had wandered upon the trailer while hiking and made the mistake of opening the door. Neither one was dressed for hiking, and no hiking trails appeared anywhere near the trailer. The Carsons were driven to the hospital by Chase Buckley, who said he was in the area trying out his four-wheel drive. He heard the explosion, drove over to investigate, and rescued them.

Gilly didn't believe any of them.

He hated liars and he hated meth. Somewhere in this county his little brother had bought the first dose of meth that hooked him. Now he couldn't kick the habit, his life was wasted. Gilly was on a mission to put as many cookers out of business and in jail as possible. This burned-out trailer was half the prize—it would no longer produce—but he had to find the cook and put him behind bars.

There was evidence that someone else had been at the scene and fled. Not far from where the trailer was parked, tire tracks were found from a motorcycle. The bike had left in a hurry, digging a deep rut. The rut froze and left a perfect track.

Buckley and the Carsons knew more than they were saying, Gilly was certain. He also had a hunch that the cooker was Joe

Keyes. For Gilly, it was simply putting two and two together. Keyes and Blake Carson were known associates. They'd been arrested twice together in the past. Keyes was known to own a motorcycle, but so far, the local cops had not been able to locate it. Gilly had met Sheriff Peterson, and he had to wonder how hard the guy had searched. He didn't appear to be very motivated.

The two closest towns to the trailer's location were Twain Harte and Dry Oaks. Carson and Keyes stayed in Dry Oaks. Buckley's family owned most of Dry Oaks.

While Gilly couldn't figure how Buckley fit in the puzzle, his thoughts drifted back to his interview with Keyes the day before. He'd found him at the small one-bedroom cabin he and his wife shared. Surprisingly, neither Keyes nor his wife had the look of drug users. Keyes was tall and lanky with a bushy handlebar mustache. His eyes were clear and his teeth good. Meth often destroyed the teeth of users. Keyes's hands were the only thing that gave him away. They were rough, stained, and scarred, most likely from the caustic chemicals he'd worked with.

Paula Keyes was easy on the eyes. A brown-haired classic beauty, almost elegant—until she opened her mouth. Then you saw the hardness in the woman. She'd be difficult to live with, Gilly thought. He concentrated on Joe, but Paula stayed in the room, arms folded, watching the interview while she leaned against the kitchen counter.

They both admitted they knew the area of the forest where the trailer fire had occurred, but that was all they would admit.

"Joe, you've been arrested with Carson, so don't pretend like you don't know the name."

"He's bad news." Keyes looked away and gave a disinterested shrug. "I stay away from bad news."

"He wasn't in the forest hiking."

"You know everything. What was he up there doing?" Keyes smirked.

Gilly looked him in the eye and knew that behind the bravado was fear, and guilt. Keyes was his man. If only there were enough evidence to get him in an interview room.

"Cooking meth with you."

Keyes forced out a nervous chuckle. Then his wife stepped in.

"Joe was here with me. I just found out I'm pregnant. We were celebrating. If you had anything on him, you'd arrest him. But you don't, so leave now. Please."

Gilly didn't believe the story of domestic bliss. He decided that Keyes would be his project. Heaven knew the DEA didn't have the manpower to cover all the Northern California forest and meth cookers and marijuana growers therein, but he could cover one person he was certain was guilty.

He'd be all over Keyes, that was for sure.

CHAPTER 1

Monday morning Chief Hanna Keyes was in her driveway, ready to climb into her police vehicle, when she heard the faltering plane. Her gaze shot up by reflex. It was flying awfully low. The motor sputtered and didn't sound good, but Hanna didn't know anything about small-plane motors. It was Scott Buckley's plane; she did know that. When the weather was nice, he flew his plane around the area at least once a week. And today was a beautiful late-spring day.

Vroom, sputter, vroom, sputter . . . It almost sounded like a car when you accelerated, then took your foot off the gas, then accelerated again.

That couldn't be right. Hanna stood with her door open, her eyes tracking the plane's trajectory. The single-engine plane made a lazy circle, seemed to drop, then stabilize. The engine sounded normal now, yet the flight path was anything but.

Scott was losing altitude.

The closest airport was Columbia, about sixteen driving miles away, and he was headed that general direction. *He's way too far*

10

from the airport to land. She began to feel anxious for Scott. He was a prominent figure in Dry Oaks, a vocal supporter of police and financial supporter of many charities in town.

She got in her SUV and started the engine. As she backed out of her driveway, she leaned forward and looked up for another glimpse of the aircraft. She watched in horror as the plane pointed almost straight down, then looped up slightly and swung back down again. Scott would not make it to the airport.

He was going down.

Hanna activated her SUV's light bar, then picked up her radio mike to contact dispatch as she accelerated down the street. "It's Chief Keyes. I think there's a plane going down. It's headed toward the field at Pine and Baseline."

"10-4, Chief. We're getting calls on that as well. Fire is rolling."

Hanna replaced the mike and concentrated on her driving. The plane dropped below the tree line, and her heart sank. She rounded the corner just in time to see it pull up slightly, then list to the left and come down at an angle so the left wing hit the ground hard, causing the plane to cartwheel across the field. It broke apart as it did so, pieces flying everywhere. The fuselage skidded to a violent stop in the middle of the grassy field. Smoke and dust swirled up, but Hanna didn't see flames yet.

She jumped the curb and angled her SUV across the field from the north as a pickup truck crossed from the south. They met at the plane. Hanna jammed the vehicle into park and leapt from the front seat as the driver of the truck got out.

Jared Hodges. He was a firefighter-EMT, but he was obviously off duty. His presence set her back a bit. Their history together reared up in her thoughts like a wild stallion.

"You have a fire extinguisher?" he called out to Hanna.

She nodded, jolted from her memories, then hurried around her vehicle to the back hatch. She opened it and jerked the extinguisher from its clips.

Jared arrived at her elbow, grabbed it from her, and jogged to the plane, where tongues of flames started to lick at the dry grass underneath.

Hanna followed, just now hearing the blare of the approaching fire truck sirens.

Jared expertly aimed the suppression liquid at the flames. A spurt here and a spurt there as he doused all the flames. The acrid odor of airplane fuel assaulted her nose, causing a grimace. Could Scott have survived such a horrendous impact? Hanna looked back to where he'd first hit the ground. The plane's debris stretched at least a hundred yards across the field.

Jared got down on his hands and knees and peered into the wreckage. He peeled away what would have been the door, and Scott's body was exposed. Hanna knelt next to Jared and gasped at the sight of poor Scott. He was still strapped into his seat, his body completely limp. Blood smeared the instrument panel and was dripping from his head.

"Scott, can you hear me?" Jared asked.

No response.

All she could think was *How am I going to tell his father?*

The arriving fire truck cut its sirens, leaving the rumble of a diesel engine and the pop of air brakes to announce its arrival. Uniformed firefighters exited the rig and set about preparing their equipment for the task at hand.

Jared pressed his fingers to Scott's carotid artery. She doubted he would find a pulse, but the step was necessary. She pulled back, stabilizing herself on her knees.

Jared sat back as well. "I got no pulse."

"It was quite an impact." Hanna coughed as the smoke and fumes seared her nose.

Jared coughed as well and swiped the back of his hand across his mouth. "Saw it on my way to work. He flew straight into the ground."

"You checked it out, Hodges?" Paul Stokes, a senior firefighter, jogged up and asked.

Jared faced Stokes. "I couldn't find a pulse. We need to move him. I think the fire may flare up again."

Stokes signaled for the men manning the hose to start the water flow before returning his attention to Jared. "Okay, stand back. You're not geared up."

"Yes, sir."

Hanna stood and moved back with Jared to let the on-duty firefighters finish their work. Two of them brought up a hose and began to work on the fire, which as Jared had warned was already flaring back up. The ambulance had been on the heels of the pumper, and the medics climbed out, pausing only to remove their rescue equipment from the sides of the truck. Once on the ground next to Scott, they carefully cut the harness holding him in the crumpled plane and then gently removed him from the fire danger.

They did their assessment and began CPR. In a few minutes, they put him on a gurney, slid it into the rig, and drove away code 3, using lights and sirens. The closest trauma center was in Sonora.

Maybe there was hope. Scott was engaged to be married. She prayed that he'd live to see his wedding day.

A crowd started to gather along the fringes of the field. The chatter on her radio told her a patrol unit was almost on-scene. She got on the air and requested mutual aid from the sheriff's department. Hanna's department was competent but small. And the size of the area they needed to contain would keep all her personnel busy. They needed help.

"Half the town probably saw the plane go down," Jared noted, following her gaze.

"I wonder how many people filmed it."

Jared let out a rueful laugh. "That's kind of a given nowadays, isn't it? How are you, Hanna?"

She turned away from the wreck and the crowd to face Jared. Her feelings for him were complicated. They were close friends from seventh grade through college, then Jared left town ten years ago—breaking Hanna's heart. He'd only recently returned, and he was immediately hired by the county fire department. The four-month-long fire academy had kept him busy.

Jared was several years older than most fire department rookies, and she'd wondered how he'd do. From everything she'd heard, he'd done well. While she'd made no effort to rekindle their friendship, when he'd been assigned to the only station in Dry Oaks, well, it was a small town. Hanna's hearing gossip about him had been unavoidable. She still didn't know what to make of his return.

When he'd first left, she prayed and prayed that he'd come home. With time, her hope had faded and she'd moved on. At least she thought she had.

I'm thinking about him an awful lot for someone who has moved on.

"I'm fine, Jared. How's the job?"

"Suits me, I think."

Stokes called out to Hanna, and she stepped toward him.

"We need to make the wreckage safe," Stokes said. "Clean up the fuel, make sure nothing flares up."

She knew what he was asking. Scott was seriously hurt; this crash would be investigated by the NTSB. If Scott didn't make it, the plane and all of its parts would be considered evidence.

"If you have to move the wreckage to make it safe, move it," she said.

Stokes nodded and instructed his men. His radio crackled, and he held it to his ear. He then walked to where Hanna stood, keeping his voice low. "Chief, Buckley didn't make it. They tried to revive him, but he flatlined."

"Thanks." Hanna's heart fell as hope was dashed.

Sergeant Asa Parker and Officer Jenna Cash, Hanna's day-shift people, had just arrived. From the radio she knew some county deputies were also on the way. All personnel were needed. Since this was a fatal crash now, the scene needed to be kept secure until federal investigators arrived. Dry Oaks had one investigator, Terry Holmes, and he would be called out as well.

The Buckleys were a wealthy and influential family in Dry Oaks, indeed in all of Tuolumne County. If something was amiss in the crash, Hanna wanted to know.

"Secure the scene," Hanna told her officers. "Jenna, move your patrol vehicle to the north end of the debris field, tape off the area. I can see gawkers already walking through debris."

"On it." Jenna turned and jogged to her car.

Hanna turned to Asa and pointed to the people approaching the main wreckage. "Tape this off now so we get as little contamination as possible."

A county deputy joined them. Hanna acknowledged him with a nod. "I'm not sure how long it'll take the NTSB to respond. Every bit of the wreckage is evidence. Secure it all." She sighed. "This will be a long day."

"You got it, Chief."

Commotion to the left of the field caught her eye. Marcus Marshall appeared, walking up the field along the debris path. Hanna groaned inwardly. She'd known Marcus since she was in the first grade. Back then he confused her; now he simply irritated her. In the ensuing years, he'd hopped from job to job in Dry Oaks, from newspapers to radio stations to a local news feed. At one time he'd aspired to become a bestselling author. Despite three self-published books, his aspirations had never been achieved.

Currently he wrote a crime blog, assisted at the local paper, and usually drove law enforcement crazy by following the scanner and trying to get a "scoop." A tall man, he stood out in a crowd. Over the years, he'd lost most of his hair, save for a long gray braid that went halfway down his back. He held up his phone, recording the activity, no doubt. He'd want gory pictures for sure. She was glad Scott was no longer on-scene.

"Chief, can I get a statement?" Marcus yelled.

Asa took off across the field to intercept him before he encroached any more on the scene around the main wreckage.

Hanna ignored Marcus and turned to speak to Jared, but he was gone. Sadness bit with sharp teeth, bringing on a sigh of loss. Was it for Scott or for Jared?

There was no time to ponder the question. She'd have to try and get to Everett, Scott's father, before Marcus or any news media did, and tell him what had happened. The bright spring day had suddenly turned very dark.

CHAPTER 2

Driving to the Buckley home always made Hanna think of Hearst Castle. The home was not a castle, but it was at the highest point in Dry Oaks, and the road that took you there wound up an incline like a grand drive. The Buckleys were, in a way, Dry Oaks royalty. Their home occupied a historical spot where a high-producing gold mine once stood, and a marker at the beginning of the drive explained the significance.

Beecher's Mine, like most mines during the California gold rush, had burned brightly for a short time, enough to build a thriving town in the area, and then thinned out. About two hundred acres of Buckley land was originally a claim mined by Dale Beecher.

When Beecher's Mine went bust, Everett Buckley's great-grandfather purchased the mine and surrounding acres for pennies on the dollar. The family became the backbone of Dry Oaks. Because they stayed, invested in real estate, and helped preserve local mining history, the town did not dry up like other mining towns did. Why Dry Oaks hadn't been named Buckley, she didn't know.

Hanna turned right onto the drive and headed toward the main residence. While she loved her job, she hated death notifications. She'd had to do them too many times in her career to suit her.

She approached the gate, which was a mile and a half before the residence, and was surprised to find it crowded with workmen. Then she remembered that Scott was into the latest technology. Everything at the entry was to be upgraded, with underground electrical wire and digital cable. The Buckley compound would likely be the most technologically advanced property in the county. Well, at least in Dry Oaks.

Cameras and smart technology were the order of the day here. Along with heavy-duty gates and fencing. One of the workmen pointed to the right. "You can use the access road there. It's rough and winding, but you have a four-wheel."

Hanna nodded. They'd removed a portion of the fencing off to the side of the entry gate. She turned right and clicked on her four-wheel. She doubted she could outrun the telephone and fully expected that by the time she got to the house, Everett would already know about his son's death.

The old rutted road wound up the hill, with tall pine trees standing sentry on either side. It was no problem for her vehicle. The driveway eventually cut to the left, and as Hanna reached the top of the hill, the house came into view on her right.

The main residence was a sprawling ranch-style log home with a wraparound porch boasting a view of the valley below. Built over the site of the main mine, it had a beautiful rustic, historic look to it, but the residence was equipped with alarms for fire and earthquake safety, and even had a fully equipped panic room in case of an emergency.

Across the parking area from the front of the house was a large barn and stable area including an exercise ring. Everett and several of his nephews raised champion quarter horses.

Hanna spied Everett at the rail of the exercise ring, watching his great-grandson Braden taking a riding lesson. Standing next to Everett was Grover, his right-hand man, and Timmons, his ranch foreman. From their smiles and joviality, Hanna guessed no one had answered a phone call about Scott's accident. Scott's mother had passed just after Hanna graduated from high school, and Everett never remarried. Hanna hated to be the bearer of more bad news to the man.

Where was Chase? Scott's younger brother had been seriously injured the year Hanna was born and seemed to live in the background. Though Everett and Scott always took the lead and the limelight, she'd heard through the grapevine that the horse ranch was Chase's responsibility.

She parked the car, got out, and walked toward Everett. Timmons saw her first and tapped Everett on the shoulder.

Everett turned as she approached, his smile fading, eyebrows arched in surprise. "Chief. What on earth brings you up here today?"

Grover also turned to watch her approach. The only thing that continued was the riding lesson.

"I'm afraid it's not good news."

Everett stiffened and let go of the railing.

Hanna didn't believe he'd appreciate if she beat around the bush. "I'm sorry, Everett, there is no easy way to say this. It's Scott. His plane crashed just now into the field on Baseline. He didn't make it."

"What?" Everett blanched and seemed to totter.

Grover frowned and grabbed his boss's arm to support him.

"You're sure?" Timmons asked.

"I saw it happen. It looked as if he just flew into the ground."

"Where is he?" Everett asked, his voice a whisper.

Hanna sucked in a breath. "They took him to Sonora. They tried to resuscitate him, but he's gone. I'm not certain how long it will take for the NTSB to respond. As you know, they will investigate the likely cause of the crash." She stopped, feeling as though she were rambling.

Everett nodded almost imperceptibly. He turned to Grover. "Take me there. I want to see the plane. Then I want to see Scott."

It would not have been Hanna's choice to send Everett to the crash scene, but she'd been a cop long enough to know that everyone handled death and grief in their own way. She stepped aside as Grover and Everett hurried to the ranch SUV.

"You sure it was an accident?" Timmons asked.

"I'm not sure. The plane dropped fast. The NTSB will have the final say. You don't suspect foul play, do you?"

Timmons shrugged. "Scotty loved that plane, babied it. He was a great pilot. How could he crash?"

"Does he have enemies? Had he received threats?"

"He did have his share of enemies in business. But the past few months, he's been over the moon about his engagement. Everything has been going smooth."

"Ah, his fiancée, is she here? Do you want me to tell her?"

"Valerie's in Corte Madera. I expect Grover will tell her." Timmons hooked his thumbs in his belt and spit. "This just sounds strange to me. And if it was because of some error on Scotty's part, the old man will have a hard time swallowing that."

Hanna could understand. Everett had retired from running the business a few years ago. Scott had taken the lead with gusto. This was a tragic event on so many levels. If the NTSB found evidence of foul play, she'd go after it like any other crime.

Just when she thought the day couldn't get any darker, it did, with the shadow of murder hanging over it.

CHAPTER 3

IT TURNED OUT THAT EVERETT was one of the few people in town who had not seen the crash. Several videos of the incident went viral overnight on social media. Marcus Marshall uploaded the one that got the most clicks. As a result, national media picked up the story, and by Tuesday morning, Dry Oaks Police Department was inundated with media and media requests.

"Can we have a statement?"

"Was the crash pilot error?"

"Chief Keyes! Are you any relation to Joseph Keyes?"

The reference to Joe Keyes surprised her, though she wasn't sure why. Her entire life she'd lived under the shadow of Joe Keyes and what he'd done. Thirty-five years ago, he killed two people and seriously injured a third. He was also implicated in the disappearance of a DEA officer.

Local news often brought up the incident on anniversary dates. Marcus Marshall wrote a book about it. Joe was in prison for life, and Hanna had never met him. But today was about Scott Buckley, not Joe Keyes, so she ignored the reference and hoped the press would drop the old news.

"Mayor Milton will give a statement as soon as possible."

Hanna pushed through them into the station and then headed to her office, closing the door for a minute of quiet.

The PD didn't have a dedicated press office. Thankfully, Mayor Evelyn Milton liked talking to the media. Dry Oaks had not had this much attention from the outside world for as long as Hanna could remember.

A knock sounded at the door, and Terry Holmes poked his head in. "Got a minute, Chief?"

"Yes, come on in."

He entered and closed the door behind him. "Wow, it's a circus out there. Must be a slow news day." He handed her a folder. "Here's everything from yesterday. The good news about the media coverage is I think things will move faster. The NTSB investigator saw some of the posted videos. He doesn't think the plane's path to the ground was indicative of engine problems with the plane."

Hanna took the folder and opened it, skimming the contents. "He's already got preliminary findings here."

"Yeah. The fire was extinguished quickly, and all the wreckage was moved to a hangar at the airport. He had a lot to work with and didn't find anything that showed mechanical malfunction."

"So that leaves us with pilot error or pilot sickness."

"Right." Terry nodded. "And the coroner called. He'll move the autopsy up as soon as possible."

"You talked to the airfield personnel at Columbia. Did they see anything out of the ordinary?"

"It was a normal day. No visitors or unusual people at the field. Scott had a mug of coffee and planned a survey of some property he was considering buying. He did the usual precheck, and his takeoff was smooth. He was in the air for thirty minutes before he crashed."

She closed the folder. "I wonder if he had medical issues he didn't know about."

"It's possible."

"Good work, Terry. We'll both attend the autopsy when it's scheduled."

He nodded and left Hanna alone with her thoughts. She scrolled through social media to see what was trending. Videos of the crash were still getting clicks. To her dismay, Joe and his crimes were also trending, and in the top ten. If people searched *Dry Oaks* for the crash video, they also found Joe Keyes.

Hanna should be used to it, though. Joe had been in jail as long as she'd been alive. It was part of her morbid history.

As tragic as Scott's death was, so far it looked as if it had been a medical emergency. Hanna prayed it would be that simple and that news would trend away from Dry Oaks.

And her father's sins of the past.

❋

Two days later on Wednesday, thoughts of *simple* were demolished by the autopsy. Scott's crash was not a medical emergency: It was murder. The county coroner, sitting behind his desk across from Hanna and Terry, listed the probable cause of death as "poisoning by cyanide."

"I can't make it official until after I get the toxicology results back from the state lab," he said. "But his stomach contents tested positive for cyanide. Most likely it was in his coffee. If you have a mug or carafe for me to test, I can be more definitive."

"As far as I know, there was no mug or thermos with the wreckage," Terry said.

"We'll have to do another sweep of the crash site." Hanna looked down at her notes. "Personnel at the airfield were clear Scott had a travel mug in his hand when he boarded the plane."

"He hadn't eaten. Coffee was all he had in his stomach," the coroner summarized. "He had a seizure at some point. Then his heart stopped. The paramedics tried hard, but essentially Scott was dead when he hit the ground." The coroner put down his paperwork and took off his glasses.

"Who stood to gain from killing Scott Buckley?" he asked, and Hanna had no answer. She did know that she would pull out all the stops to find out.

CHAPTER 4

BESIDES THE CORONER'S REPORT, Hanna also had a preliminary report from the NTSB. It confirmed what Terry had learned the day of the crash. All the plane's mechanical parts were sound and working within normal limits.

It didn't surprise Hanna. She'd read up on small planes and found that it was nearly impossible to sabotage one. Pilots, good pilots, did a preflight check of all their systems. Any sabotage was likely to be discovered there. By all accounts, Scott was a careful pilot. And if the engine did fail because of tampering, odds were good that a pilot could make an emergency landing. Scott could have landed in the field where he crashed—there had been room—but he never made the attempt.

The cyanide was the big surprise.

"Who had motive and opportunity to poison Scott's coffee?" Investigator Holmes asked as he and Hanna left the coroner's office.

"It's a method of murder that indicates planning. And historically, poison is a woman's weapon. At least that was what they taught us in the academy." Hanna knew there were few women in Scott Buckley's inner circle, other than his fiancée, Valerie Fox.

She had not been in Dry Oaks the day of the crash. In fact, she rarely stayed in town. She lived on the coast in Corte Madera. Ms. Fox was wealthy and privileged—murder didn't seem a likely fit.

As if reading her mind, Terry said, "Fox could have paid someone."

Hanna shook her head. "I don't see it. Calling off the wedding would make more sense than murder. And everyone we talked to said they were crazy about one another. She'll be here for the memorial. We'll get a better sense after talking to her then."

From there they drove up to the airfield and collected Scott's coffee maker and coffee supply. On the drive back to Dry Oaks, they returned to the Buckley home and retrieved Scott's laptop in the hopes it would shed some light on the incident. E-mails, online communications could possibly give them leads. They also had a warrant to search the house and outbuildings for cyanide. Hanna dealt with Timmons. Neither Everett nor Chase was on the premises.

"They're in Corte Madera with Scott's girlfriend," Timmons told her. "You won't find any cyanide here; we have no use for it."

He was right. Scott's room was neat and organized. There were no diaries, only the laptop. Hanna was sorry they'd missed Everett and Chase.

"I need to talk to both of them when they get home," she told Timmons.

"I'll tell 'em."

Hanna followed up on leads as soon as she got them. The laptop was no help. There was no indication that Scott had been threatened, worried, or anything but happy about his engagement.

Friday she and Terry caught up with Jeff Smith in Sonora. He was the airplane mechanic Scott had fired two weeks prior to the crash for sloppy maintenance work. He now worked at a small garage called Abel's Automotive. He was underneath a beat-up Toyota Camry when Hanna and Terry walked up.

"Jeff Smith?"

"Yeah?" He slid out to look up at them. Surprise, then annoyance flashed across his face. "Let me guess why you're here." He sat up, then stood, wiping his hands on a greasy rag. "I had nothing to do with that crash."

"Scott wasn't a fan of yours. Want to tell me why he fired you?" Hanna asked.

"That snooty girlfriend of his. The last time he took her for a flight, she got grease on her dress, blamed me."

"Seriously?" Terry asked.

"Yeah." Smith spit on the ground and leveled a disgusted look at her. "I haven't been back to the airfield since I got canned."

"I need you to account for your whereabouts for the past two weeks." Hanna's gut said he was telling the truth, but she had to have something concrete to prove it.

"Here, mostly." He pointed down at the dirty floor. "I make half of what I made as a plane mechanic. And thanks to Saint Scott, I got no references. I work seven days a week. I didn't like Scott, but that don't mean I killed him."

"I can vouch for him."

Hanna turned to see an older man leaning on a cane had exited the office. "You are?"

"Abel Martinez. I own the place. I had a stroke, can't work much. Jeff's been here every day, mostly all day, helping me keep up with the work."

"What about at night? You keep track of him then?" Terry asked.

Martinez shook his head. "He's been a big help to me."

Smith shrugged. "I live alone. But I have neighbors. Look, there are cameras all over that airfield. If you'd seen me on one of them, I'd probably already be in cuffs."

Hanna had viewed hours of video from the airfield. The security system where Scott kept his plane was state of the art. Jeff hadn't shown up on any of the video feeds since he was fired. Still, he would know how to avoid them.

"We'll follow up with your neighbors, Jeff." Hanna turned to leave, then stopped. "If you didn't do it, who do you think did? You worked for Scott for two years, and you didn't like him. Who else felt that way?"

Smith leaned against the car and sighed. "Look, Scott was hard to work for. He was demanding, a perfectionist. Especially when he took his girlfriend up in the plane. I was too unorganized for him. My mind doesn't go to murder. I'd like to have punched him out, though . . ." He gave another half shrug. "The only person I seen him really argue with was that blogger."

"What blogger?"

"You know, Marcus the Muckraker. They got into it really good a few weeks ago at the airfield."

"What about?"

"I don't know. Couldn't hear. There was just a lot of arm waving and Scott poked the guy's chest." Smith held his index finger up and jabbed the air by way of example.

"What do you make of that?" Terry asked Hanna as they drove back to Dry Oaks. They'd followed up with Smith's neighbors and found his alibi solid.

"No one else at the airfield mentioned that fight?"

"Not a word."

"Go back, talk to them again."

"Will do. You ever heard the nickname Marcus the Muckraker?"

Hanna nodded. "He got that nickname years ago. My mom gave it to him after he published his first book. It died out for a bit but was revived a couple of years ago when Bobby Fairchild overdosed."

"Right! I remember that. Marshall posted a list of all the burglaries he thought Bobby was responsible for, then declared Dry Oaks safe again because Bobby OD'd."

"Yeah. Marcus can be a jerk."

"How about a murderer?" Terry asked.

"Marcus has always struck me as a talker not a doer, though. A keyboard warrior I'd call him now. We still need to find out about the argument and check the camera footage again. Make sure we didn't miss anything."

Terry nodded. "I'd also like to talk to Chase. Do you know if the brothers were close?"

"I think they were." Hanna considered the question. Scott's younger brother had been seriously injured thirty-five years ago in an incident that had changed Dry Oaks forever. It had changed Hanna's life as well.

Her father murdered two people and maimed Chase for life. Time had not numbed her to that reality. The knowledge about what Joe Keyes had done still made her sick to her stomach.

"I've always heard that when Chase was injured, Scott became his caretaker. The first time I saw Chase I think I was fifteen years old," she told Terry. "I hiked up to the murder scene with a friend."

"Beecher's Mine cabin?"

29

"Yeah. It was kind of a thing kids did back then. There was nothing to see there. What didn't burn down the night of the murders had been bulldozed by the Buckleys."

"Still, it was a draw?"

"Yeah. While I was there, Chase came roaring up on an ATV. My friend and I hid from him, then watched. He didn't have a prosthetic leg back then. He was on crutches, drunk, and yelling something I couldn't understand. Scott came and got him. I didn't see anger between the brothers; I saw the older taking care of the younger."

"Seems as if he'll want to talk to us then, find out who killed his brother."

"It's odd that he hasn't made himself available." Hanna considered Chase and all that she knew about him. Was it possible he had poisoned his own brother? She hoped not, for Everett's sake.

When Hanna and Terry arrived at the station, Marcus was there, obviously filming something for his blog. Hanna had to suppress the smile that threatened when the name Marcus the Muckraker came to mind. He'd hated it, and it brought her mother no small joy to have been the one who hung it on him.

He pointed his camera at her as she and Terry walked toward the station. "Chief, can we have a statement on the deadly plane crash of Scott Buckley?"

"Sure, after we get a statement from you."

"From me? About what?"

"We have witnesses who saw you and Scott arguing. Do you want to be interviewed on your podcast?"

Marcus lowered the camera and sputtered, "W-w-what are you talking about?"

She pointed to the station. "We can talk in there."

Marcus glanced from her to Terry. "You're serious?"

"Yes. You were seen arguing with Scott, rather heatedly, a couple of weeks ago. What was the fight about?"

His face reddened. "Who's your witness?"

"What was the fight about?"

His eyes narrowed and he waved a hand in irritation. "It was a misunderstanding."

"About what?"

He tossed his head back and huffed. "Personal stuff. Look, he was mad at me. I had no beef with Scott. Your witness can probably testify that Scott was the aggressor." Shoving one hand in his pocket, Marcus looked Hanna in the eye.

"Everyone thinks Chase was the hothead. But Scott had a temper too."

CHAPTER 5

SCOTT'S MEMORIAL SERVICE took place on a stifling day at the end of May. Hanna's mother would have called it "earthquake weather": windy, hot, and dry. Dust devils formed here and there, clothes rippled, and hats needed to be held.

A lot of people attended. The Buckley business empire was large. From the number of rental cars in the parking lot, many people flew in from San Francisco and other big cities. Hanna saw that most of the town was here as well.

At one point she spied Jared in uniform with personnel from the fire department. They were county firefighters, and the one station in Dry Oaks had been built and donated by Buckley Enterprises. She had no chance to talk to him. Marcus Marshall was also there, filming. He'd been crowing all over town about how he'd gotten the best video of the crash. That man was so annoying.

"Big crowd," Hanna's steady guy, Detective Nathan Sharp, commented as they exited the car. He'd given her a ride. The small local cemetery just outside downtown was packed, a line of black limos stretching a long way along the road. The Buckleys weren't churchgoers, so the only public service was graveside.

Many large, ornate headstones belonged to pioneers, Civil War vets, and gold miners. The place attracted a lot of history hunters, and parts of several western movies had been filmed here. The Buckley plot was in the oldest section of the cemetery. Scott would be buried next to his mother, Hattie, and his grandfather, Alphonse Buckley, or Big Al as everyone called him. Hanna's mother was also buried in the cemetery, not near the Buckleys, but being in this place reminded Hanna of her.

"Hanna!"

She turned and saw that Amanda Carson, her grandmother Betty, and Edda Fairchild were heading toward the service as well. Hanna and Nathan stopped and waited for them to catch up. Betty had recently had hip replacement surgery, and Mandy pushed her in a wheelchair.

They shared hugs all around. Two years older than Hanna, Amanda had been her best friend since grade school. They used to pretend that they were sisters. Mostly Hanna pretended. As a child she sometimes prayed that she could be a part of Mandy's family for real because there was so much turbulence in her own home.

It really wasn't a stretch, Hanna thought. They were both athletic with chestnut hair and green eyes. People often mistook them for sisters. Mandy was a couple of inches taller than Hanna's five-foot-nine, and she wore her hair long while Hanna now kept her hair short. Mandy had chosen a black dress for the memorial, while Hanna had opted for a black business suit.

Edda was a local woman Hanna had known her whole life and someone she considered family. A beloved Sunday school teacher, Edda was a rock at the church Hanna attended.

"I knew both Buckley boys when they were in diapers." Edda shook her head. "So very sad to see this violent end to Scott."

"I always expected Chase would go first," Betty said.

"Why do you say that?" Hanna asked, the murder investigation still at the forefront of her thoughts. She'd not been able to get Everett or Chase to sit down for an interview yet.

"He was wild when he was younger. As wild as your father. Chase almost died at the cabin at Beecher's Mine." Betty was looking off toward the new section of the cemetery, where the markers for her daughter and son-in-law would be, Hanna guessed.

Pain marked her expression, and that did not surprise Hanna. Betty's daughter, Sophia, and her husband, Blake, were Joe Keyes's two murder victims. They were Amanda's parents. While the third victim, Chase, had lived, acid had been thrown on him. He lost his right eye immediately and, later, part of his left leg when those acid burns went septic.

It occurred to Hanna that while Blake and Sophia had markers in this cemetery, there were no bodies. Joe would never say where he buried them. Hanna knew that neither Mandy nor Betty bore her any ill will because of that historical fact, but it still jabbed when it was brought up.

"Have you had any luck figuring out who killed Scott?" Mandy asked.

"Not so far."

Edda took Hanna's arm. "I'm sure you'll find the person. You do a good job, Hanna. Your mother would be proud."

"Thanks for the vote of confidence." Hanna smiled. Edda was ever the encourager. Any mood brightened just being around her.

"How is your investigation going, Detective Sharp?" Edda asked. "I pray for you and your partner. My heart breaks for the young women who have died."

Nathan worked as a homicide investigator for the sheriff's department stationed in Sonora. Over the past two months, bodies of two women had been dumped along the highway. Fear in the community grew that there was a serial killer in the county.

He answered as they walked through the open cemetery gate along a stone path. "We're working leads, Edda. If this case has shown me anything, it's that women have to be careful who they open up to on the internet. It's possible that's where the killer found them."

"I have faith in you, Detective. Like Hanna, you are very good at your job."

They'd reached the outside patio area where the service would be held. A sea of folding chairs surrounded a gold-colored coffin on a platform. The white cloth skirt under the coffin flapped wildly in the wind. Valerie Fox, flanked by Everett and Chase, sat in the front row. Grover had already requested that Hanna wait to talk to Ms. Fox until after the service. He promised to bring the woman in himself.

"She fell apart when I gave her the news," Grover had told Hanna.

From several rows back, Hanna watched her now, sobbing on Everett's shoulder.

The front row also contained several Buckley cousins and uncles. Many of whom had called her, wanting to know if she had a lead on the killer.

"Not yet," she'd told them. "But I will find out who did this, I promise."

Here, in the somber setting of the funeral, Hanna meant that promise. She would get justice for Scott and relentlessly follow leads, wherever they took her.

❋

When the service ended, Hanna got a ride home from Mandy. Nathan had left immediately after the service to head to work. Mandy asked her to lunch, but Hanna declined, needing some alone time to decompress.

Too many unpleasant memories rambled around in her head. Death usually made people think, reflect. Her mom was dead center in her thoughts. Paula Keyes had been a bitter, difficult woman, consumed with anger at Joe for what he'd done.

"He ruined my life. I hate him for that," Hanna had heard more times than she could count.

The Beecher's Mine murders took place the day Hanna was born. She was four months old when her father was sentenced to two consecutive life terms. He had confessed to avoid the death penalty. Apparently, her mother had taken her to see the man once, but Hanna had no memory of that.

She'd grown up under the shadow of the brutal affair. Bullied and teased as the spawn of Satan when she was a kid, Hanna saw joining law enforcement as the only way to erase the stain of being related to a brutal killer.

Mandy's, Edda's, and Jared's friendships had rescued Hanna from bullies when she was a child and from bitterness as she grew up. She remembered the day she had realized that Mandy was an orphan because of what Joe Keyes had done. Paula had just broken up with Marcus Marshall. They'd dated all through the year Hanna was in first grade. The breakup was messy and loud, and Paula sent Hanna to spend the weekend with Amanda. It wasn't a problem for Hanna; she loved spending the night at Mandy's house. It was always calm and quiet there. Not chaotic like her own. Memories enfolded Hanna like a warm quilt.

Saturday morning, she and Mandy got up early. The house was quiet. Betty and Chuck were still in bed.

"I like being here," Hanna said.

"I like you being here too. You're my little sister."

Hanna laughed. "You're a nice sister."

They were in the den on the floor, playing a game of Monopoly.

"Can I ask you a question, Mandy?"

"I'm not going to let you win."

"Ha, I beat you last time. No, I wondered, do you know why my mom was so mad at Marcus? She threw his clothes out on the ground."

"It's the book," Mandy said. "Marcus wrote a bad book about bad things."

"Bad things?" Hanna pondered that for a moment. Then something clicked. "About Joe Keyes?"

Mandy nodded. "I heard Grandma Betty say the book opened old wounds. Your mom has lots of wounds that won't heal."

Hanna considered that. "Wounds? I've never seen any."

"They are the inside kind of wounds. You remember when those boys teased you?"

Hanna nodded.

"They hurt you inside. They wounded you, but it's not like a scratch or a bruise. Grandma Betty says that's why your mom's mad all the time."

Hanna understood that. When the boys had teased her, it not only hurt, it made her very angry. A light bulb went on, and she knew why her mother was angry. "Joe gave her inside wounds."

"Yeah. You don't know what he did, do you?"

Hanna frowned. All her life she'd been told Joe was evil, that he murdered people, but she didn't know who he killed or why. "He's a bad, bad man. He killed people and he'll never get out of jail."

"He murdered my mommy and daddy."

Hanna's mouth went slack. She stared at Mandy. "You're lying."

"I don't lie, Hanna. He murdered my mommy and daddy. That's why I live with Grandma Betty and Grandpa Chuck."

Hanna couldn't believe it. The worst person in the world was Joe Keyes, and he had done this horrible thing to her best friend. Hanna dropped the dice, covered her face, and sobbed. It never really hit home until this moment, when she understood exactly what Joe was responsible for.

Mandy set a hand on her shoulder. "Don't cry. I'm sorry I said anything. It's not your fault."

Hanna was inconsolable. Grandma Betty came into the room. "Here, what's happened? Hanna, why are you crying?"

Betty knelt next to her, and Hanna let the woman gather her into her arms. Mandy told her why Hanna was crying.

"Oh, baby, none of this is your fault. You're carrying such a burden. We've forgiven Joe in this house, and we pray for his redemption."

Hanna stopped crying, breathing in shuddering breaths. She stayed snuggled next to Betty for several minutes before she felt she could talk. "What's redemption?"

"It's salvation, honey. It's making someone's soul right. We pray that Joe will find Jesus and ask for forgiveness for what he did."

"Could Jesus forgive such a thing?"

"If Joe asks, Jesus will forgive."

"Did Joe ask you? Is that why you forgave him?"

"No, I forgave him because Jesus forgave me. Forgiveness is something we all need, whether we know it or not."

Hanna would never forget that weekend when she was six or the kindness of Mandy and her family. A Bible verse came to mind. *"Let all bitterness and wrath and anger and clamor and slander be put away from you, along with all malice . . ."* It was Betty's favorite, and it had become Hanna's. Paula's bitterness had ended her life early—she dropped dead of a heart attack two years ago. To Hanna, her mother was Joe Keyes's last victim. Hanna had to repeat the verse often to remind herself that she didn't want to end up like her mom: another victim.

CHAPTER 6

THE BALLED-UP PIECE of paper hit Jared square in the forehead.

"Hodges! I was talking to you," Bryce Fallow said.

"What?" He hadn't been listening to the firehouse banter. He knew Scott Buckley's fiancée was the topic, but that was it.

"What's your vote? Is she the prettiest or the second prettiest?" Bryce was Jared's training partner and ten years younger than Jared. At thirty-five, Jared was the oldest rookie at the station. After junior college, he'd wandered the country for ten years before coming home and settling down to a career.

"Uh." Jared's mind was on Hanna, not Valerie Fox. Hanna was pretty; she looked like her mother. Paula Keyes had been beautiful in a Las Vegas showgirl way, but there had been a hardness in her. Hanna had the beauty without the hardness. Compared to Hanna any other woman was the second prettiest. "I didn't get that good a look at her."

"Ah, you're no help." Bryce waved his hand dismissively and went back to talking to the other guys. They weren't being salacious. The dangerous weather conditions put everyone on edge, and they were just passing the time.

California was in the throes of a wicked drought, for years now with no end in sight. The land around Dry Oaks fit the name: it was all tinder dry. One spark in this heat with the wind as strong as it was right now would start a conflagration. Something none of them wanted to see.

"You're a thousand miles away, Hodges." Paul Stokes pulled up a chair, swung it around backward and straddled it, facing Jared. "Did you know Scott Buckley?"

Jared shook his head. "Not personally, but I grew up here and the Buckleys are a fixture in Dry Oaks."

"That's true. They sure seem to attract tragedy."

"Are you thinking about the murders?"

"Yeah, I just bought this." Stokes held up a book Jared recognized immediately. *Murders at Beecher's Mine Cabin* by Marcus Marshall. "I've been assigned to Dry Oaks for two years. It was time I read the book."

"I can't believe you bought that." Jared rolled his eyes. He'd heard that Marcus had set books out to sell at the memorial service.

"I've heard so many stories about what happened back then. This isn't a good source?"

"I'm sure it's an exaggeration." Jared didn't want to go into how much pain the book had caused for Hanna and her mother. Marshall had self-published the tome about eight years after the incident. Hanna hated that book.

"I don't know," Stokes said. "Maybe the facts don't need exaggeration. I mean, a guy kills two people, cuts them up in small pieces so they'll never be found, and throws acid on a third man, maiming him for life. Sounds like something Hollywood would dream up. You grew up here and never read the book?"

"I read bits of it. It's not very well written. Hanna thinks it's all rubbish."

"Chief Keyes?" Stokes chuckled. "See what I mean? Her dad is the killer, in prison for life, and she grows up to be the police chief. Remarkable. Hollywood stuff." He got up, put the chair back, and walked into the other room with the book.

Remarkable. Yeah, that was Hanna. Jared thought back to the first time he had the courage to approach her in junior high, but he'd known her his whole life. She was so different from other girls their age. She'd had to be. She was always being teased about her father. One afternoon he'd caught Jude Carver and his friends tormenting her.

"Jail baby, jail baby."

"Daddy's a murderer. Are you a daddy's girl?"

"Spawn of Satan!"

Jude Carver was two years older and the local bully. He led the pack. Jared came up behind them as Hanna turned on them.

"Shut up! I've never even seen him in person."

"Ooh, got you mad," Carver taunted.

"Why don't you idiots find something else to do?"

The boys howled. "We like what we're doing."

"I don't like it." Jared stepped up.

The three boys turned and faced him.

"Who asked you, Hodges? Wittle Hanna need a bodyguard?" Carver sneered. Jude had a few pounds on Jared, but Jared was tall for his age and had a couple inches on Carver. Carver was the key. Take out the lead bully and the rest would flee, so Jared concentrated on him.

"I think she can take care of herself. I also think you guys need to find another hobby."

"I don't care what you think." Carver dropped his book bag and started to get chicken chested. Hands balled into fists, he scowled and stepped toward Jared.

Jared didn't hesitate. He brought his right fist around and hit Jude in the nose.

The bully went down, and his friends stepped back. "Hodges, that was uncalled for."

"You guys are bullies, plain and simple. Knock it off."

Carver got to his feet slowly, blood flowing from his nose. "I'll tell your dad."

"So will I. He tells me to stand up to bullies. What you are doing to Hanna is uncalled for. Tease her, tease me."

That was the day Hanna's and Jared's friendship started.

Warm memories flooded his mind. He went to her softball games; she came to his track meets. Every free minute they were together. They learned to drive, to rock climb, and took junior college classes together.

It was perfect until Jared had ruined it. Now that he was back for good, he prayed that he'd find a way to fix it.

CHAPTER 7

WITH THE FUNERAL OVER, the media presence in Dry Oaks dwindled to nothing. For the most part, Hanna had her small town back again. It still wasn't quiet and uneventful. The day after the service, a huge fire broke out east of Dry Oaks. Fierce winds had blown a tree over into some power lines, and overnight the blaze had scorched thousands of acres. If the wind shifted, the Crest Fire would be a serious threat to Dry Oaks.

All Hanna could do was monitor the situation. It was mostly being fought by county and state personnel. Some of her reserve officers volunteered to support the firefighting effort. Terry Holmes had traveled to San Francisco to follow up on some information about Scott's business issues. As a result, her office was short-staffed.

Grover said he'd bring in Valerie Fox for an interview today, Friday. Hanna was eager to talk to Fox. She still hadn't been able to interview Chase or Everett.

Hanna had tried multiple times to arrange an interview and had been stonewalled every time. First the excuse was the memorial for Scott. Now it was the Crest Fire. Hanna had cut Everett some slack because the size of the conflagration and its possible path had everyone in town on edge.

Strangely, Everett didn't seem at all concerned about the status of the investigation. He and Chase were not the last people to see Scott alive—that would be the people at the airfield—but they were the closest to him.

Grover arrived around eleven.

"Good morning, Chief. True to my word, here's Valerie to see you. She's only in town for a few hours, but she'll answer your questions." He stepped aside and Scott's fiancée stepped in.

"Ms. Fox, how are you doing?" Hanna motioned to a chair in front of her desk so the woman could take a seat.

When Valerie entered her office, a few things were obvious. In spite of the grieving, she was drop-dead gorgeous. Hanna expected she could grace the cover of any fashion magazine and do it justice. Valerie was a lot younger than Scott, and she carried herself like a woman with a lot of money. Hanna doubted the woman planned to marry Scott for the Buckley money.

Fox looked back at Grover first. He nodded, stepped out of the office, and closed the door.

"I'm still standing, but it's not easy." She sat. "I know you wanted to talk to me. Thank you for being patient."

"I need to speak to everyone close to Scott." Hanna sat in her chair.

"Have you made any headway in the investigation?"

"I'm afraid that I can't tell you yes. Right now, we have no suspects."

"You're sure it was poison that killed him?" Her tone was laced with resignation and defeat.

"Cyanide in his coffee. We never located Scott's travel mug." Hanna held her hands up, palms out. "Do you have any idea who would have wanted to hurt him?"

"Ever since I heard the word *poison*, I've wracked my brain.

Hurt?" Ms. Fox gave a shake of her head. "Scott was a beautiful man. My soulmate. I sometimes don't know how to go on." Her voice broke and she paused. "I do know that he was preoccupied about something."

"Any idea what?"

"I think it had to do with that blogger guy." She frowned as if trying to remember a name. "Marshall, that's it."

"What was the problem?"

Fox nodded. "Scott was afraid he was writing a book about the family and their history. He was at the house a lot."

"Scott didn't want that?"

"No. He used to say that the nickname Muckraker fit. I don't think Scott cared for Marshall."

"Did they argue?"

"Sometimes. Scott didn't like it when Marshall was around. He didn't care for bloggers in general. People and their phones, ready to film tragedy and make a buck. Scott thought it was awful." Her voice broke again. It took a minute for her to compose herself. "Marshall filmed the crash, didn't he? How much money did he make at Scott's expense?"

"I'm sorry about that."

"It's not your fault. It's the world today. So obsessed with the latest juicy bit of news."

Hanna gave her a minute.

"We had so many plans. Please, Chief, you have to find out who did this. Scott bought a house in Corte Madera for us. Braden even has his own room there." Tears trailed down her cheeks, and she dabbed her face with a handkerchief.

"Braden was going to live with you?" That news surprised Hanna. Braden was Chase's grandson, not Scott's.

"We talked about it. Scott has been like a father to the boy, and since Braden's flaky mother left, he's floundered. Scott and I thought it would be good to let him grow up in new surroundings. We were ready for a fresh start." She dabbed her eyes and blew her nose.

"How did Chase feel about that?"

"He was fine with it. That's what Scott told me. Chase is moody and unpredictable. He never had time for the boy. Everett spent more time with him than Chase."

Braden's father, Devon, Chase's son, had died of cancer a few years ago. Braden's mother, Kelly, was aptly described as flaky. She had left him in the care of his great-grandfather not long after Devon had passed. She took the life insurance check and went to Hollywood to be an actress. Hanna was not sure how things were going for her.

"Have you checked into the mechanic Scott fired? That was an unpleasant episode."

"He is in the clear."

"The only other point of friction was a business deal Scott was working on. He wanted to buy a building in San Francisco. He planned to demolish it and build something else. Some crazy activists protested the sale. Have you looked into that?"

"My investigator is in San Francisco now, checking on that very thing." Hanna knew about the environmental group protesting Scott's purchase. Terry had e-mailed that it was a dead end. None of the protestors had ever been in Dry Oaks.

"Losing Scott left a hole in my life that will never be filled. Someone needs to pay for snuffing out such a bright light." She left the office still dabbing her cheeks.

Hanna considered the comment about Marcus. Fox had confirmed that there had been an argument. Strange she thought it had to do with something that Marcus was writing. Marcus had not mentioned that. He was usually chatty about his writing projects. If he was writing about the Buckley family with the same kind of exaggeration that he'd written about Joe Keyes, Scott would have good reason to worry.

Hanna had firsthand knowledge about Marcus's literary talent. He was a shock jock. She had no idea how much he wrote about her father was true. She did know it had made life difficult for her and her mother.

But Scott saying no to a book idea did not sound like a motive for murder. Hanna could see him punching Marcus out; she couldn't see the reverse. Marcus liked to murder people in print. Usually, people who couldn't fight back. She would still investigate, she just wasn't hopeful.

She finished her coffee about the time she got a text from Terry: **I'm back and in my office.**

Hanna headed to his office and leaned against the doorframe. "Scott's fiancée was just here." Briefly, she filled him in on the interview with Fox. "She says Scott was mad at Marcus because he thought he was writing a book about the Buckleys."

"Really?" Terry frowned. "Funny Marcus wouldn't mention that."

"It is. Yet, if Scott was the one who was mad, I'd think Marcus would be the dead one."

"True. What about the bit concerning Braden?" Terry raised an eyebrow. "Someone taking your kid might be a motive for murder."

She nodded. "We need to have a conversation with Chase."

"I have a pretty good picture of Scott's life and movements in the weeks before he died," Terry said. "Honestly, I haven't found anyone with any kind of real motive to kill him. The activists were the graffiti, screaming, making-life-miserable types, but there's no way they upped their game to murder. They really don't have the resources."

"I've read your reports. The only thing missing are statements from those closest to Scott."

"And those closest to the victim are usually the guilty ones."

Hanna said nothing for a minute. Chase and Everett would have had the best opportunity to give Scott coffee laced with cyanide. Did they have motive? Hanna didn't want to believe that either one of them did.

Everett had been in her life for as long as she could remember, and she believed him to be a good man. In no way could she conceive that he would murder his own son. She laid this aspect of the investigation on Holmes, recusing herself because she was too close to it.

Now she second-guessed her decision. She was in charge, and it was her job.

"We'll get the interviews, Terry, even if it means dragging Everett and Chase to the station."

Back in her office, Hanna provided an investigation update to the mayor. "We've run down every lead."

"I hoped we'd have a resolution by now. It's been nearly a month since the crash." Mayor Milton's tone was not angry or accusatory, but Hanna felt the heat from the spotlight.

"I feel the same." Hanna switched the phone from one ear to the other, trying not to let her frustration bleed into her tone. "We will keep at it. I won't let this go cold."

"I know you all work hard. Thank you for the update, Chief. Everett has been through so much. He deserves to know who killed his son."

"We all deserve to know who killed Scott."

Hanna certainly didn't want the case to go cold—though sadly, right now it was on that road.

CHAPTER 8

AFTER UPDATING THE MAYOR, Hanna opened her e-mail. Amid the work-related senders, a note from Edda caught her eye. That was odd. Edda had Hanna's personal address; she didn't need to contact her at work.

> *Hanna, I have something important I need to discuss with you. Well, more of a legal question. I don't want to throw out unsubstantiated accusations, but something has come to my attention, and I want to bring it to yours. When would be a good time for me to come by?*

Hanna looked at her calendar and was about to respond when there was a knock at her door. "Yes?"

The door opened and in stepped Tom Nelson, followed by another man Hanna didn't know. Nelson had been a bad boy whose life was turned around when he became a Christian. He now ran a nonprofit prison ministry she supported.

"Hello, Chief. Sorry to drop in unannounced. I know the last couple of weeks have been busy for you."

"That's okay, Tom. I try to have an open-door policy. What's up?"

Nelson jabbed his thumb toward the second man. "This is Gordon Giles."

Hanna stood and shook their hands. "What can I do for you?" The two men sat in front of her desk, and she took her chair.

"You know I spend most of my time in prison," Nelson said.

Hanna nodded, suddenly feeling uneasy but not knowing why. She had no problem with Tom Nelson.

"Gordon here works for the state Department of Corrections."

Giles smiled. "I've come to talk to you about your father, Joe Keyes."

Hanna blinked. "What about him? Did he die?"

"No, not yet. But he is near death. He has lung cancer and he's in hospice." Giles reached across her desk and handed Hanna a manila envelope.

"Paperwork in here details a program the department instituted a few years ago. It's a compassionate-release program that allows terminally ill inmates to be released into a home environment to die with dignity—"

"You want to release Joe Keyes?" Hanna held the envelope in two hands that went numb.

"For the remainder of his life, which could be less than a month."

Nelson spoke up. "He's a sick old man, Hanna. He's been a model prisoner. Corrections is trying to do the compassionate, human, even Christian thing here."

"I can't believe what I'm hearing." Hanna forced the words out, feeling as if she were paralyzed.

"It's happening more and more," Giles said. "With prison overcrowding a statewide issue, some dying inmates deserve a compassionate release. We're asking if you'd be able to take your dad home for his last days."

"I've never met the man, and I certainly don't consider him my father." A burning sensation ran up her neck to her face as anger percolated.

"Of course, I understand," Giles said in a way that told Hanna he did not understand. How could he understand the black cloud hanging over her whole life that had been Joe Keyes?

"Hanna, I grew up here, too," Nelson said. "I know the legacy Joe left and that this is not an easy request. But I submitted Joe's name. Maybe I was out of line to do so, but I think it would be a good thing for him. Think about it before you say no." His calm and conciliatory tone did nothing to ease the shock or growing anger the request generated. What was there to think about?

Giles and Nelson stood to leave.

Hanna had no words. Before she could find the right sentence, another knock sounded at the door. Nathan's knock. She remembered they were going to have lunch before he went to court.

He poked his head in. "Oh, sorry, I didn't realize you were busy."

"We were just leaving," Giles said to Nathan. Turning back to Hanna, he said, "I know this is a shock, and I know it's a lot to think about. I could have simply sent you a form letter, but I felt the request was important enough to deliver in person. Review the paperwork. It will explain more. Then call me at your earliest convenience. There really isn't a lot of time."

Giles and Nelson left.

"What on earth? You look as if someone died." Nathan shut the door behind the two men. "Was that about the lawsuit . . . ?" He held her gaze for a moment.

She shook her head. Hanna and the PD had been notified a few days ago that Jude Carver, a police officer she'd terminated for cause a few months ago, had filed a lawsuit for wrongful termination.

That had upset Hanna yesterday, but Nelson and Giles's visit made the aggravation of the lawsuit pale by comparison.

Finding her voice, Hanna told him what Giles had suggested.

"Wow," Nathan said when she finished.

"I'd probably pick a different word." She picked up the phone.

"What are you going to do?" Nathan asked.

"What do you think? I'm going to call Giles right now before he gets out of Dry Oaks, tell him *no way*. This would never work."

Nathan reached over and punched the button to disconnect her call.

"What are you doing? You don't think I should do this, do you?"

He held a hand up. "Maybe you should think about it a little longer than twenty seconds before you make a decision."

"What is there to think about?" Hanna crossed her arms and glared at Nathan, even as sharp pain pinched through her, telling her he was right.

"That request is huge. I'm sure they went through a lot of deliberations before they made it. It deserves some consideration."

She blew out a breath, tossed the packet of papers Giles had given her on the desk, then sat in her chair. "I can't believe this is happening. There's a huge fire threatening the town to worry about, I've got a lawsuit to deal with, and I have an unsolved open homicide, not to mention all my job duties, and this pops up?" She pointed both hands down at the documents.

"Holmes is competent to handle Scott's investigation, so no worries there."

"Hmph." Hanna clenched her jaw.

Nathan walked around the desk, leaned his hip onto the corner, and held her gaze. "You were elected in a landslide, Hanna Marie Keyes. Your first year is almost over, and the reviews are in:

you're doing a great job. The fire will be contained. Jude Carver is a knucklehead. This request won't derail anything."

Hanna leaned back in her chair, feeling some of the tension leave her body. She and Nathan had worked together for a couple of years, and Hanna liked him. They were good friends. She wasn't certain where their romantic relationship was going, but she enjoyed his company. One thing she really appreciated was that Nathan had a knack for often saying the right thing and keeping her grounded.

Hanna rubbed her forehead. "This just blindsided me. I really try not to give him any thought. What do you think I should do?"

"I can't answer that. He's your father—"

"He's not my father. He's a sperm donor. They tell me I saw him when I was a baby." She shrugged. "I have no memory of that."

"Fair enough. But you bear his name. At one time he and your mother were married."

"They were. But this request is insane."

"It's surprising for sure. Compassionate, though. The state's only asking that he be given the opportunity to die at home. I'm not surprised that the California Department of Corrections would make such a request."

"There you go again."

"What?"

"You think I should do it."

"Honestly, I'm only thinking out loud. The situation needs prayer. I'm not telling you anything you don't know. Maybe even talk to Pastor Rick. I can tell you what the Bible says, but this situation is between you and God. I'm not getting in the way of that."

Hanna looked away. Nathan was right, but she couldn't go there now. She considered what her mother would say, were she alive. Paula Keyes never forgave Joe. He was arrested for murder the day she went into labor with Hanna. The memory of her mother's voice reverberated in her thoughts. *"He can rot in a dark, hot hole for all I care."*

Everyone who knew her mother knew that she had been an angry, bitter woman. Did Hanna want that said of her as well?

"You still want to go to lunch?" Nathan's voice redirected her thoughts.

"Of course—" Her door being pushed open cut her off.

Sergeant Asa Parker burst in. "Chief, we got a situation. Braden Buckley fell into a gulch up off the Buttonwillow Trail."

Nathan stood. "He okay?"

Asa shrugged. "Cassidy was babysitting, she called 911, said he's not moving."

Hanna looked at Nathan. "County Search and Rescue?"

"Sorry, they are all up at the Crest Fire. I might be able to scare up some volunteers."

"Take too long. I'll take Big Red up there. It has climbing equipment and other emergency gear." She nodded to Asa. "Bring it around?"

"You got it." He left the room and Hanna went to the coat tree, where her gun belt hung when she worked at her desk.

Nathan grabbed her arm. "You be careful. No unnecessary risks, okay?"

Jared came to mind: *"Risks are a part of life"* was his philosophy. And Hanna agreed. She hadn't run for chief of police to play it safe. But Nathan meant well.

"Don't be a worrywart." She squeezed his hand, and he released her arm.

His pale-blue eyes were warm, supportive, and for a second, Hanna wished the letter were a cruel joke and she could erase it from her memory.

"I'd go with you if I could, but I have to be in court."

"I'll text you as soon as I can."

Hanna left the office, told Terry he would be the only cop in the station for a while, and rushed to Big Red. Once a search-and-rescue vehicle, the ancient Chevy dually had been with the PD for a decade. They got the hand-me-downs when the fire department upgraded. The beast was hard on gas, but it went anywhere and everywhere. The Dry Oaks PD ran on a shoestring budget, but it ran smoothly, and Hanna loved being a part of the organization.

Asa sat in the driver's seat. Hanna jumped in the passenger side, and he accelerated before she'd closed her door. Even though she was glad the situation with Braden had taken the stupid letter off her mind, she prayed the boy was okay and they were overreacting, even as she doubted that could be the case. Hadn't the Buckleys been dealt enough grief for one lifetime?

CHAPTER 9

Nathan Sharp watched the red dually speed away. He'd driven to Dry Oaks for lunch with Hanna, and he still needed to eat. He grabbed a coffee and a bagel across the street from the station and climbed into his car to drive back to Sonora for court. Once there, he checked in with the prosecutor, then joined his partner, Manny Pacheco, on a bench outside the courtroom. Nathan had been the arresting officer on this case, not the primary investigator, so he could not be inside the courtroom until it was time for his testimony. Manny leaned his head back, resting his eyes.

As Nathan waited, he thought about Hanna's predicament. Even though Nathan had not been raised in Dry Oaks, one couldn't be in the town for any length of time without learning about Joseph Keyes, even all these years after his arrest and conviction, thanks to Marcus Marshall. Everyone in local law enforcement knew Marshall. He was an "I know my rights" and "I pay your salary" kind of guy.

Murders at Beecher's Mine Cabin might not have been a national bestseller, but it sure had sold locally. The story of Joe Keyes was the "blackest black eye a small town could get," according to Marshall. He'd also self-published two other true crime tomes, one on the Zodiac Killer and one on the Green River Killer. As far as Nathan knew, neither of those sold as well as the story of the murders right here in Dry Oaks.

Marshall still laid out copies for purchase every week at the local farmer's market. Nathan had never purchased a book, but he had leafed through one. Joe Keyes was clearly the villain in the book.

Dry Oaks now had a police department because of the murders. Sonora had been the only incorporated city in the county. Every other city relied on the county sheriff, including Dry Oaks. But after the murders, Everett Buckley and his father, Al, made it their mission for the small burg to develop and pay for its own PD. The residents went for a bond measure and DOPD was born about thirty-three years ago. It started with one chief and three sworn officers. The pay was not extravagant. Being a cop in Dry Oaks was really a labor of love.

And Hanna loved Dry Oaks.

She was the third elected chief. Now she had six officers, including one who doubled as an investigator, as well as one sergeant and three volunteers. They all did a great job, and Dry Oaks was a safe and quiet place to live.

He supposed every town had a bogeyman. Joe Keyes was certainly that for Dry Oaks. He'd confessed to his crimes and was put away a long time ago, and Nathan felt that justice had been served. He didn't think the request for compassionate parole was out of line.

Of course, mysteries still surrounded the case, and Nathan wondered if Joe could, or would, try to clear those up. There was the matter of missing DEA Agent Brett Gilly. He'd been investigating Joe at the time. A few weeks before the murders at Beecher's Mine cabin, a meth lab had exploded in the forest. Gilly's last report indicated that he believed Joe was responsible for the meth lab and its destruction. If Joe was responsible, it had never been proven. After the murders, Gilly himself disappeared.

The agent had not been heard from in thirty-five years. Also, while no concrete evidence existed to connect his disappearance to the murders, they were forever connected in time by Marshall's book because Marshall talked a lot about Gilly and the meth lab destruction. The Feds investigated for many months after the murders and never found a trace of the DEA man. The issue still drove law enforcement crazy. Gilly's case was cold, and every so often an agent would come into the county and ask around, trying to find a rock that had not been turned over.

The Carsons' bodies were never found either. Beecher's Mine cabin burned down after Joe threw acid at Chase and the other caustic chemicals in the cabin caught fire. There was no indication that the bodies burned in the fire. Marshall put forth a theory in his book that Joe "hacked their bodies into little pieces" to destroy evidence. Nathan had heard others speculate that Blake and Sophia ended up at the bottom of an abandoned mine shaft. There was no shortage of those in the area.

Why Chase was spared was a question that was never answered. Marshall wrote that after dousing Chase with acid, Joe probably thought that he was dead. And he fled without making sure.

And now corrections wanted to let Joe out. Nathan figured corrections was not that concerned about a sixty-year-old man with terminal cancer.

Nathan had heard about Hanna before he met her. In a profession that could sometimes be chauvinistic when it came to women, she garnered a lot of respect. Even old-school cops in Sonora talked about her in positive terms.

He got to know her personally because, as an investigator with the county sheriff's department, Nathan had worked with Dry

Oaks PD often. When Hanna was the PD's only detective, they'd collaborated on a couple of cases together.

From what Nathan had seen, Hanna was nothing like her bitter mother. She didn't hold grudges, and surprisingly for a cop, she always looked for the good in people. Even when, after all the years, a lot of Joe's negative past had been thrown at Hanna when she ran to be chief. Nathan remembered the ads. *"Don't be deceived, the apple doesn't fall far from the tree . . ."* Hanna took it all in stride.

It had been like that her whole life, Nathan guessed. Living under the shadow of a double murderer was what made Hanna want to be a cop. And now she was the youngest chief to ever serve Dry Oaks PD.

He tried to shift his thoughts and review the case file in front of him. Shortly, he'd be testifying. He'd recorded some spontaneous statements that were incriminating. He'd need his thoughts centered on this case, not on Joe Keyes from years ago. And not on Hanna, who he hoped to be spending a lot more time with. She was the real deal as far as Nathan was concerned, the one he knew he could spend the rest of his life with.

This was one of the more straightforward cases he'd handled as a homicide detective. Boyfriend shot his girlfriend, there were witnesses, and they had the murder weapon and a lot of forensic evidence that assured victory.

His phone buzzed. The prosecution wanted him in court.

"You up?" Manny asked, his eyes open now.

Nathan nodded and stood. "Yep, here we go." File under his arm, Nathan opened the courtroom door, prepared to testify.

CHAPTER 10

HANNA HAD HIKED UP a long steep incline of Buttonwillow Trail. She wiped sweat from her brow, pushing damp hair off her forehead. Even Big Red couldn't make it up the narrow trail to this spot. The parched, dry air felt suffocating even as hot wind swirled around them.

Peering over the cliff, she could see the motionless ten-year-old boy lying perhaps thirty feet below. Braden had fallen into a gulch and landed on an outcropping. If he would've missed that, the next stop was two hundred feet down to the bottom.

The boy's small dog paced back and forth next to his master. A good sign? If the dog escaped the fall unscathed, perhaps the boy's injuries would be minor. Hanna hoped so. She refused to consider this mission simply a recovery.

Braden Buckley had to be alive.

"Is he dead?" Cassidy, Braden's sixteen-year-old babysitter, stood watching Hanna. She'd been chewing on a thumbnail, crying and pacing the entire time Hanna had been there.

"No," Hanna said, "I don't think so."

"I'm so sorry. I should have been closer to him. I—"

"You called us right away. That's a good thing."

Cassidy sniffled and went silent.

"You ready, boss?"

Hanna turned to Asa. He was her only sergeant and twenty years her senior. The volunteer EMTs looked like high school kids. They'd been waiting at the trailhead when she got here. Like most of the county's first responders, the regular day-shift patrol unit who served the community of Dry Oaks was currently providing mutual aid for the Crest Fire, which raged close enough that she could see a plume of smoke in the distance.

And it was a deadly fire. Two California Department of Forestry personnel were killed when their vehicle overturned as they were trying to escape fast-moving flames.

This rescue was up to Hanna and Asa. Hanna was okay with that because she knew her strengths and limits and she trusted those she worked with and around. They were well trained and conscientious.

Now, if she could just get the request about Joe off her mind. It was Jared Hodges who barged in on her train of thought once again. He and Hanna had done a lot of climbing as teens, some as young adults, and he was a stickler for concentration.

"A lapse in concentration means a fall, and neither one of us will bounce."

She took a deep breath, shook away Jared's face, and recalled something the chief she'd replaced had taught her.

"Keep your world small."

Retired military, Chief Barnes had served in combat, and while he never talked about specifics, he gave her plenty of tips on how to not just survive but thrive in stressful situations. Keeping your world small was one tip. It meant concentrating on the square you're in, not puzzling about any squares down the road.

It was not unlike something she'd heard often in church: *"Don't use today's strength worrying about tomorrow's troubles."* She'd appreciated all the tips.

"I'm ready." She'd quickly donned a climbing harness and was set to rappel to Braden.

The outcropping was large enough for her to reach the boy. She double-checked the anchor, set up her backup, and then put on her climbing helmet.

As she backed up to the ledge, Dave and Paulo, the EMTs, along with Asa moved forward to monitor her progress. None of them had ever done any climbing. So she prepared for the descent. A situation like this was why she went through extra training.

She unclipped her anchor and stepped off the ledge. Balancing with her legs, Hanna controlled her descent, gripping the rope in her strong hands. She touched the cliffside two times and then landed easily on the ledge a short distance from the boy's feet. She willed herself not to look at what was below the ledge. If Braden was seriously hurt, she didn't want to be distracted.

"Braden!" she called out. No response. She could see the rise and fall of his chest and her fear dissipated.

The little dog barked, expected for a Chihuahua mix. Hanna struggled to remember his name. Pancho? Giving herself some slack but staying in harness, she moved toward the boy. He lay face down, one arm bent unnaturally under him. There was some blood around his head, as well as some scrapes on his arms and legs.

Hanna took off her backpack to access her medical supplies. As she got closer to Braden, the dog's frantic barking increased.

"Pancho, it's okay, I'm here to help."

The dog continued to bark as she knelt next to Braden, but Pancho backed away and didn't threaten her.

Hanna carefully began her assessment, checking the boy's feet and legs, then moved up his back. Everything felt normal.

Cognizant that there might be a neck injury, she gently touched his shoulder. "Braden, it's Chief Keyes, are you okay, buddy?"

The boy stirred; his face scrunched in pain. "Ahhh, ow, ow."

His eye opened and he moved his feet. "It hurts." He tried to press up with his good arm and Hanna stopped him.

"I know, honey, but I've got to get you out of here, and I don't want you to move too much." The boy whimpered but stayed still. Hanna grabbed her radio.

"He's a little busted up but alive. I'll be ready for the stretcher in a few minutes."

"10-4, Chief," came Asa's response.

She pulled the neck immobilizer from her pack. "I've got to put this on you and roll you over slowly to see how badly you're hurt." She gently placed the immobilizer around his neck and fastened it. He moaned.

Carefully, bracing him with her body, Hanna rolled him over in one smooth motion, ensuring that his neck and back were in line, exposing his cut-up face. He screamed once when the movement disturbed his badly broken arm, and Hanna winced. His pulse was fast but not overly so. His breathing was not labored.

Blood ran from a deep cut on his forehead down his face. He would probably need stitches. She opened a gauze pad and put pressure on the cut and then grabbed some tape.

"Ow, ow, it hurts." Tears squeezed from his eyes.

"I want to stop the bleeding, Braden. Please, I know it hurts. Try to stay still. It might not hurt as much."

"Where's Pancho?" he asked, his voice wavering.

"He's here." Hanna looked for the dog. He had stopped barking and sat a few feet away, watching. "I've got to splint your arm to get you out of here. I'm sorry it hurts, bud, but it has to be done."

Hanna needed to make the splint a bit smaller. She pulled her folding knife from her pocket and cut off what she didn't need. The knife brought a smile to her face. It had been a gift from Jared so many years ago. The outline of Half Dome was etched in the handle.

A memory flashed—they'd spent a week in Yosemite at a rock-climbing school. Jared had been the most capable student in the class; he was a natural. He found the folding knife in a park gift store. He said, *"Everyone should have one of these. You never know when you'll need it."*

He'd been right. She had used it a lot over the years. Maybe one of these days she'd tell him how useful the gift had been.

Steeling herself against the boy's cries and tears, Hanna splinted the arm and readied Braden for the rescue basket. He stopped crying once his arm was splinted, and Hanna bet it felt much better. He also seemed more alert. Hanna checked his eyes—both normal and reactive. She had him move his legs and his good arm, then squeeze her fingers with his good hand.

"How does everything else feel?"

"Okay."

"Try to stay still. I'm going to get the basket that will take you up to the top. Got it?"

"Yeah."

Hanna left the boy's side and asked Asa to lower the rescue basket. Once down, she set it next to Braden and prepared it for him.

He quietly watched her arranging the straps. "Can you put Pancho in there with me?" Braden asked once she moved toward him.

"Afraid not, bud. I'll bring him up after."

"Promise? He's my best friend." The tears started again.

"I promise." Hanna lifted him as carefully as she could into the basket. He grimaced once or twice but didn't cry. Once she secured him in the basket, Asa and Paulo carefully pulled him back to the top. Dave and Paulo would have to carry the boy in the litter about a half mile to their ambulance.

For a few seconds she stood, looking up at where the boy had disappeared, sweat dripping off her face. Dry, hot summers in the Northern California foothills could be brutal. This was one of those summers.

She looked over at the dog and remembered her promise. Her radio crackled.

"You coming back up?" Asa asked.

"I have to get the dog." She turned her attention to Pancho. The little dog eyed her warily.

Hanna knelt. "Here, Pancho, come here." She moved toward him and he moved away. In her best baby-talk voice, Hanna tried to draw the dog to her. He was having none of it.

Her radio crackled. "Didn't you bring the bacon strips?" Asa asked.

"Ha, ha. I may ask you to run and get some."

"I might disobey. With you down there, aren't I in command?"

"I might stay down here just long enough to be certain you've done all the paperwork." Hanna backed up a step and turned, hoping that by ignoring the dog he'd settle down. She put her backpack back on and stepped toward the cliff wall. The dog was near; she could sense it. She bent and turned, grabbing for Pancho.

He squealed and bit her hand, but her gloves protected her. Still, the surprise made her stumble and fall backward.

Suddenly, there was nothing under her feet and she was falling.

CHAPTER 11

JARED SHED HIS AIR TANK, unzipped his turnout coat, and wiped sweat and grime from his face. *Smoke eater* was the perfect nickname for firefighters because today he certainly felt as if he'd been eating smoke all morning. The Crest Fire was a monster. He surveyed the fire line and prayed they'd get a handle on this soon. Jared had only been a sworn firefighter for four months. Working on this hellfire made him feel as if he'd been at it for years.

"Hodges, you ready for some chow?"

Jared turned. Paul Stokes walked toward him. Two days ago, his coworkers had stopped calling him "the grandpa rookie." He'd been the oldest recruit in his academy class and was reminded of it every day. Until now. The punishing work on the conflagration was a telling equalizer. He'd learned a lifetime's worth of lessons on this fire, and it was gratifying that his coworkers agreed.

"Thanks, I'll be right in."

Stokes came and stood next to him. "You're good at this job, Hodges. You held your own with Bryce today, and he's much younger than you. Why didn't you come on the job years ago?"

Jared sipped some water before answering. "I was born and

raised here. When I was a kid, all I wanted to be was out. The smallness was suffocating."

"I was raised in Sonora. I always thought that was small. Dry Oaks is minuscule in comparison. But it's a nice place to live."

"I guess it took my leaving to realize that."

Stokes slapped him on the back. "Whatever. Glad to have you on the team." Stokes strode off for the mess tent.

Jared took one last look at the fire line before he turned for the chow tent. It was good to be on the team. And it was good to be back where Hanna was. Jared could admit, only to himself, that she rarely left his mind.

They'd spent so much time together when they were growing up, he thought she'd go with him.

He was wrong.

"Dry Oaks is my home." Hanna twisted a lock of hair between her thumb and forefinger, an endearing habit Jared loved. Hanna had long beautiful, shiny brown hair, soft to the touch. It made her emerald-green eyes stand out.

"It's also been torture for you. No one here will ever forget what your dad did."

"I know." She held his gaze, her expression thoughtful. *"But I love it here. I know the smallness boxes you in, but to me it's comforting."*

He looked away and kicked a rock. This discussion was not going the way he'd hoped. "What about climbing? What about adventure?"

"I'm just not ready to leave. I've almost got my degree in criminal justice; you know I've always wanted to be a cop. It's not just that, Jared. My church home is here."

"It always comes back to that church, doesn't it?" Jared spoke sharper than he'd intended.

"The way you say that—" She shook her head. "Church is my family."

"I'm sorry. You know I struggle with what you believe. All that 'God is good' talk. I hate to see you be deceived. If he was good, why did my mom have to die when I was just a kid?"

"I don't have an answer that will satisfy you. This will always be a barrier in our relationship. It comes back to God—I believe, and you don't."

Jared felt like screaming. She was right—this was the only issue that came between them in all the years they'd been together. He couldn't fathom why it was such a big deal to her.

"Yeah, I'm sorry, it does. I don't want to be a jerk."

"I don't want you to leave, Jared. But I won't stop you, if it's what you really want."

He could admit now how much it had hurt when Hanna said no, and how angry he'd been. He'd initially told her he wanted to leave to see the world, and that was mostly true. But when she said no to traveling with him, he tried to run away from her and the memory of how happy he'd been when they were together.

Jared thought that eventually he could forget Hanna and build a life somewhere new, someplace with a few more layers. He'd spent years bouncing from state to state, confident the exciting life he sought was out there. He'd climbed mountains and skied in Colorado, then changed things up and found his way to New Mexico to build houses in the desert sun. After that there was Florida, New York, Canada, and many other places in between.

When Jared had left home, he wasn't exactly sure what he was looking for. What he did know for sure was that Dry Oaks was too tedious, too limiting. He wanted to be alive, not just live, and somehow the small town restricted him. Everyone knew him, and he knew everyone. He was certain that by leaving he'd find something different, something better.

"What do you expect to find?" his father had asked.

"I'll know it when I see it."

Jared never saw it. Some places he liked better than others, and he stayed there longer. But always, over time, the same restlessness enveloped him, and he had to move on. He began to dread moving on as much as he dreaded staying. It was an odd conundrum that had twisted him in knots.

Then the day nine months ago stopped him cold.

He'd been working on a friend's roof just outside of Coeur d'Alene, Idaho. Wherever Jared landed he'd find work. He was good with his hands and a trained welder. When he finished stapling in the last remaining roof tile, he stood and looked around. In the distance the snowcapped Sawtooth Mountains stood majestic. He'd been helping his friends build this house for six months. Now his part was finished, and he could move on.

He sighed, trying to put a name to what he was feeling, but he couldn't. He knew what he *wasn't* feeling. There was no joy in him, no sense of accomplishment, no excitement to move on. There was no sense that he should stay here in Idaho either. He felt simply bland. His emotions as dull as a midnight radio talk show.

A vehicle in the distance approached the house. Ken was back from town, and it would be time for lunch. Jared grabbed his tool bag and headed for the ladder. By the time he got down and threw his tools in his truck, Ken climbed out of his car.

"Got something for you, Jared."

"Yeah?"

Ken walked over to him, holding out what looked like a battered letter. "Kind of a miracle this found you. It's a few months old."

Jared took the letter and turned it over in his hands. When he'd first started traveling, he'd been good about calling and corresponding to let his father know where to send his mail. General delivery, usually. But in the past few years, he'd lived off the grid and been sporadic in his correspondence, and consequently, any mail he got was spotty. *"You have to write letters to get letters,"* an old man had told him once.

Because a sort of depression had been building inside him for months, Jared had not been good about keeping in touch with his father lately.

But this letter was not from his dad. It was from his uncle Gary. It had been mailed to the last place Jared had stayed for any length of time: Colorado. Jared agreed, it was a miracle it had found him here in Idaho, six months later.

He leaned against his truck and opened the battered, stained letter.

Dear Jared,

I hope this letter finds you well. I'm mailing it to the last address your father had for you. Maybe before it gets to you, you'll call and this will be unnecessary. But I have to give you some bad news. Your father passed away yesterday . . .

Jared reread the sentence twice, and his knees gave way. He slid down the truck, landing on his butt with his back to the rear tire. It was hard to breathe as he reread the same sentence over and over, the realization hitting him like a kick from a mule.

He continued to read through blurry, watery eyes.

He was working in the yard, and he had a massive stroke. The doctor says he was gone before he hit the ground. We're holding off making arrangements until we hear from you. But please know, we can't wait too long.

Uncle Gary

He'd also left a phone number, but Jared barely saw it. His dad had never told him not to leave but had said, *"Your dad and your room will always be here for you, when you decide to come home."*

Not anymore. Dad was gone.

Tears blinded his vision and he let them fall freely.

After a minute, Ken knelt next to him. "Hey, man, what is it?"

Jared told him, composing himself and wiping away tears.

"What a son I am. Dad's been dead for six months, and I had no clue."

"Don't beat yourself up. I doubt Ben would want that."

Jared pushed himself to his feet. With the pain he felt, he might as well have fallen off the roof.

"Come in and have some lunch or something."

Jared bent over, hands on his knees, and shook his head. "Thanks. I, uh, I've got to go."

He straightened, climbed into his truck, and started the engine. Tears began again as he drove down the long driveway. How on earth had his big adventure turned into such a disaster?

He left his dad, he left Hanna, and after all this time, what did he have to show for it? When the truck reached the road, Jared stopped, rested his head on the steering wheel, and wept.

When he finished, he went to find a phone in downtown Coeur d'Alene. Uncle Gary didn't condemn him.

"You couldn't know; none of us knew. I'm just glad my brother didn't suffer. You'll come home now?" Gary asked. "Haven't you wandered enough?"

Jared didn't give him an answer.

After he talked to Uncle Gary, Jared went for a walk through the downtown. The night air was frigid. Jared barely felt it. His mind kept churning over what a colossal waste his life had been. He thought of Hanna, not that she'd ever really left his thoughts.

She'd really made something of her life, achieved all that she'd dreamed of all those years ago. Gary had told him that she'd just been elected chief of police. All he had to show for his last ten years was a beat-up truck and a great set of tools.

He'd accomplished nothing. His life to this point was meaningless. His pride wouldn't let him run home with his tail between his legs now.

Hanna was the only person he wanted to call. She understood purpose and meaning; she'd tried to tell him about that often enough.

Even after all the years apart, he remembered the many conversations he'd had with her. She'd shared her faith with him often, when he'd listen. He'd always felt that church, like Dry Oaks, was a prison.

He was wrong about so much. Was he wrong about that as well?

Hanna and her pastor both had talked to him about sin and salvation and saving love. He'd thought it was so nebulous and unbelievable at the time.

"The church is my family," she'd said. *"It gives me purpose and direction."*

Jared stopped in front of a church. He needed purpose and direction.

Pain and loss forced him to open the door and walk inside.

"Can I help you, young man?" A white-haired gentleman arranging folding chairs greeted him with a smile. "You look lost."

Something in the man's soft tone, his earnest gaze touched Jared. He felt as if he'd missed a handhold on a rock face and was in free fall. For the first time in his life, he fell apart. He bared his soul to the old man. The guy just listened.

"I've wasted my life," Jared said when he finished. Exhaustion hit, making him feel as though his body were made of lead. Shoulders sagging, head down, he doubted the man could help him. He doubted anyone could help him.

"You're carrying such a burden. If pain brought you here, it's not a waste." He prayed, "Lord, I ask you to touch this man. You know what he needs, the burden he's bowed under. Help him, heal him."

Jared listened, remembering the prayers his father had prayed for his mother while she lay sick with cancer when Jared was ten. Dad's faith and prayers had not saved her.

"I've never believed that God really had much to offer me. I've heard about him my whole life, from my parents, from my friends . . ."

"What do you want God to offer you?"

"I wanted my mom to live. No matter what my dad prayed, she died."

"I'm sorry, I don't know why that happened. When I'm faced with things I don't know, I stick to things that I do know. Jared, I do know that God loves you. I also know that he has answers for you if you ask."

"I'm asking."

"That's a start. Next, let go of the burden you carry about the past." He handed Jared a Bible. "This is yours to keep. Sounds as if you know a little already. Read the Gospel of John and join the fellowship here, if you plan to stay."

Jared took the book and held it in both hands for a moment. He looked up at the old pastor. "Is it really possible for me to get right with God when I've spent most of my life running away from him?"

"It is. You're at the end of yourself, Jared. Turn the rest of your life over to Jesus. Ask him to forgive you and help you. He will. It sounds simple because it is."

Jared did just that. He felt as if he opened his hands and dumped the mess his life had become in God's lap.

When he walked out of the church, he felt like he was a thousand pounds lighter. Accepting the free gift the old man told him about had changed his entire perspective.

It was time to go home.

If nothing else, he needed to pay his respects to his father. Jared felt new and different, ready to stop wasting time and do something with his life. He bought a phone and asked Gary to send him job listings from Dry Oaks and Tuolumne County.

The wandering bug had run its course. He found what he was looking for when he found faith. When he got home, Jared hoped to reconnect with Hanna. After all, the one hurdle that had kept them apart all those years ago was gone.

But Hanna had moved on. She had an important job and a steady guy. It surprised Jared how much it hurt to realize he was still stuck in a world where he and Hanna were a couple, and for her that was ancient history. Now, every spot in Dry Oaks was a place they had shared, and his memories of that time had not dimmed.

Still, he was glad he'd come back, found a job, and got settled. Jared was where he should be. Now, if he could just win Hanna back.

CHAPTER 12

PANIC DIDN'T HAVE TIME TO SET IN. Hanna's anchor line held, jerking her body to a stop, then snapping her into the face of the cliff. The hard stop yanked her left shoulder, but it wasn't unbearable. The dog squealed and bit Hanna's thumb, though the heavy glove she wore protected her. She realized she was holding him too tight.

"You okay?" Asa hollered down.

"Good. Get me back on the ledge. I think I'll let you pull the dog up first."

Juggling the dog, she pulled some extra rope from her pack and fashioned a harness for Pancho. He'd calmed down quite a bit, and she had no trouble hooking him up. He didn't squirm while Asa pulled him up.

Once free of the dog, Hanna climbed back up to where Asa waited.

"Whoa." Hanna rested on her back until her breathing returned to normal. Drenched in sweat, she yearned for a nice, cool shower.

"Still with us, Chief?" Asa asked.

"Yeah, yeah. I am completely wilted."

"We're out here in the heat of the day. Let's head into Big Red for some AC."

"Good idea."

Together, they gathered up their gear and started the walk back to the truck. In the distance, the smoke from the Crest Fire still billowed.

"Is it my imagination, or is there more smoke over there?" Hanna gestured toward the Crest Fire.

"Could be," Asa answered. "But it's still blowing away from us. We'll be fine unless the wind shifts."

"I pray that the wind doesn't shift," Hanna said. As they finished the hike in silence, her thoughts fell unavoidably back on Joe.

❦

Though sweaty and gritty, Hanna wanted to follow up on Braden. Dry Oaks had an urgent care but no trauma center. Since his injuries were not life-threatening, Braden was transported to the Dry Oaks facility, not to Sonora. Hanna arrived at the medical center at the same time Everett Buckley pulled up in his large SUV.

When he climbed out, Hanna couldn't help but notice that the eighty-year-old multimillionaire was surprisingly spry. Scott's death had also forced him out of retirement. He did have Chase and his nephews to help with the Buckley empire, but from what Hanna had heard and read, Everett was the big boss.

Before the crash, Hanna would have said that Everett didn't look a day over sixty-five. Not so today. His craggy, worry-lined face revealed his age. No surprise considering his life of tragedy.

Seeing Everett always brought her mother to mind.

"Such a good man, Everett Buckley, the last of a good generation, and he raised Scott right," Paula used to say, always lamenting that Everett was too old for her and Scott was too much of a martyr to

be a good boyfriend. She never had anything good to say about Chase, or Devon for that matter, who was two years older than Hanna.

Scott never had children. All of Hanna's life she heard from her mother about how Scott had sacrificed his own personal life to take care of Chase and Devon. Devon's mother, Ellen, and Chase never married.

Born the day Chase was injured, Hanna knew little about him. He'd never been much of a father to Devon before being maimed, and being maimed didn't help matters. For a time after the murders, he stayed in San Francisco while his burns healed, and he went through physical therapy for his injuries.

Ellen was a drug addict, and she was never very stable. Around the time Marcus Marshall published his book about the Beecher's Mine murders, Ellen had disappeared. Scott and Everett had raised Devon. Everett groomed him to take over a part of his vast business holdings.

But it was not to be. Devon had been racing his motorcycle on a rainy night. He missed a curve, hit a tree, and died instantly. Braden's mother, Kelly, was another flighty woman. Paula used to go on and on about the Buckley inclination to hook up with flighty women. Three years ago, Kelly left Braden with Everett and moved to Hollywood, wanting to be a movie star. Hanna didn't think that was going too well. Gossip in town said that Kelly did Zoom calls with Braden from time to time, but that was it.

Hattie, Everett's wife and the mother of the boys, had died. Rumor had it that Dry Oaks's mayor, Evelyn Milton, had the hots for him.

Now, his face screwed up with concern, and maybe fear, as he approached Hanna at a brisk jog.

"I got here as fast as I could," he explained, breathless. Tall and thin, with a full head of white hair, Everett reminded Hanna of old-time movie actor Andy Griffith. He just didn't talk with a southern drawl. "I was out at the fire line. How is Braden?"

"From what I saw, his arm is broken, and he's scraped up a bit, but other than that, I think he's fine."

Relief eased his worry wrinkles some. "Do you know what happened?"

"Pancho chased a squirrel and Braden chased him. My guess is that he and Pancho got too close to the ledge and fell."

Hands on his hips, Everett sighed. "I'm too old for this."

"Boys will be boys. Aren't broken arms to be expected?"

He frowned. "I expected Cassidy to be a better babysitter."

"Don't be too hard on her. She called for help right away. By the way, Asa has Pancho in the car. What do you want me to do with him?"

"Hang on to him for a bit. I'll have Grover swing by and pick him up. I think we dodged a bullet as far as the Crest Fire goes. The wind shifted, eased a bit. They're getting a handle on it. The next forty-eight hours will be crucial."

"I thought the smell of smoke had eased."

"We've got the manpower now to work the blaze. I'm optimistic."

"Good news about the fire. Let's get you to your boy."

CHAPTER 13

TOGETHER HANNA AND EVERETT WALKED into urgent care. The admit nurse met them immediately and asked them to wait a few minutes before she could take Everett back.

Standing with Everett, two things ran through Hanna's mind: Scott's murder investigation and the pressing need to get Everett and Chase in for interviews, and the request from state parole. She didn't know why Everett kept brushing off interview requests, but it was time to step up and be chief. It was difficult for Hanna where Everett was concerned—she'd been too close to him her whole life, first through her mom, then later as he helped her with her career aspirations. His support had helped get her elected, and he'd never asked for special treatment— yet his delay in sitting down to speak with her about Scott gave her the feeling that special treatment was exactly what he expected.

She had to press him about the interview. Then she would bring up the letter. It would likely blindside him like it had her. Was now the time?

"Everett, I had a couple things to let you know. If Braden hadn't fallen, I would have been up to see you."

"Hmmm, I know you want to talk about Scott. I can't. I'm not there yet. It is so very raw."

"We need to get it over with. Don't you want to know who poisoned Scott?"

Everett grunted and jerked away. Before he did, pain blossomed on his face. When he turned back, he was composed. "You don't understand."

"Help me understand. I want to close this case and catch the killer."

He scrubbed his face with his hands. "I don't like thinking about that plane crash."

Hanna took a deep breath. "Tell me about that morning."

Everett closed his eyes. "I didn't even say goodbye." He opened his eyes, now a little watery. His voice stayed steady.

"I was tied up with Braden. Chase had brought three horses up from the valley. We were picking a horse for Braden, talking with the riding instructor. At some point, Scott left to do his property survey. I didn't see him leave."

"Where was Chase?"

"That I don't know."

"Was Marcus writing a book about your family?"

"What?" Everett was genuinely shocked by the question. "Who told you that?"

"It's something I've heard from folks."

"I know of no such thing. I would not be happy if I heard that he was. Marcus deserves the Muckraker nickname."

Hanna nodded. "Okay, thanks." She'd pushed as hard as she dared.

He cleared his throat. "Did you have something else?"

"I got an odd request today."

Now, a quizzical expression crossed his face. "It has something to do with me?"

"In a way." Hanna explained the request.

Everett's face darkened before she finished. He brought a hand to his mouth, then dropped it. "Have you given them an answer?"

"Not yet. It's a big request."

Now his expression went so dark it chilled Hanna. "Thank you for telling me. Of course, it's your decision. You do what you think is best." The way he ended the sentence suggested that he wasn't finished.

"Was there something else?"

He gave a shake of his head. "I'm in shock. A life sentence isn't a life sentence anymore, I guess. Joe Keyes tore this town apart, shattered our innocence, really. Consider that before you make your decision."

The admit nurse opened the double doors before Hanna could respond. "Mr. Buckley, you can go back now."

"Just let me know when you decide, okay?" Everett held her gaze before moving toward the nurse.

"I will."

Hanna watched Everett go through the double doors to where Braden would be. His dark expression stayed with her. But then what did she expect? Joe had ruined his son's life. Both sons' really. Scott's sacrificing his own personal life to take care of Chase always struck her as odd, even when her mother praised Scott for it. The Buckleys had plenty of money to hire the best care. Did it even apply now? Scott had planned to get married, so Chase must be able to take care of himself.

She decided to hang out in the waiting room until the boy was released or Everett gave her an update on his condition. She let dispatch know where she was and monitored the radio, which was quiet. A TV played at low volume in the waiting room. From time to time, Hanna would look up at the program when the dialogue hit a chord. It was about a boy whose father was in prison. He ran away from home to go visit his father because he didn't think his mother took him to visit often enough. After several minutes, it became annoying. She got up and turned the sound off.

In the silence, Jared Hodges intruded on her thoughts again. She knew he was working on the Crest Fire, probably in the thick of it, knowing Jared. And she did know Jared. At one time in her life, she thought that he was her one true love.

Hanna pinched the bridge of her nose. Before that day when they'd met at Scott's crash, he'd shown up at her front door one Saturday morning. He didn't understand why she was shocked.

"You never wrote or called me in ten years. I figured you just forgot me." She'd been through so many emotions since he'd left, Hanna believed that she was finally to the "don't care anymore" stage.

"I could never forget you, Hanna." He shoved his hands in his pockets, a sheepish expression on his face, followed by the same crooked half smile she'd loved when they were in high school. "I guess I just had a lot of growing up to do."

Hanna felt a twinge of old feelings bubbling up, and she pushed them down. "What did you do for ten years?"

"A lot of different stuff. Built houses, climbed mountains."

"Did you find what you were looking for?"

"Not in doing any of that stuff. I found it after I heard about my dad's death."

"Sorry about your dad."

"Thanks."

So much awkwardness between them now.

"I found what I wasn't looking for. I found faith."

She stared at him. He'd changed physically, that was sure—he'd filled out and gotten ten years older, just like Hanna. Had he truly found the faith Hanna had prayed he would all those years ago?

"What do you mean?"

"I mean I believe now, Hanna. That's why I came home. You were right. I wish I'd listened better to you, and to my dad. I wouldn't have left."

Hanna fidgeted, remembering how much she'd prayed for Jared to share her faith. How much different would life be now if he'd found faith all those years ago? She couldn't go there.

"I'm happy for you Jared, really, I am. But I've moved on. Did you really expect me to wait? I'm dating someone."

His smile was sad now. "I have no expectations. I just wanted you to know. I'm home for good. I've been hired by the fire department, and I've got a place out on the edge of my uncle's land. I hope we're still friends."

"We'll always be friends, Jared."

After his visit, all Hanna could do was shake her head. Of all the times to come home, why did Jared pick now? She finally felt settled. Her relationship with Nathan was new and promising, and she'd landed her dream job. Hanna still had not processed all of her feelings for Jared.

"What is there to process?" her friend Mandy had asked. "He left. He deserted you. Why should you care that he's back after all this time?"

Why indeed.

Hanna understood her friend's argument. She shouldn't care one whit that Jared was back. He'd forgotten her for ten years. So why, oh why, did it matter to her so much that he'd returned?

Hanna grudgingly admitted to herself that it mattered because she still did care for Jared.

CHAPTER 14

THE WAITING ROOM STAYED QUIET AND EMPTY. Hanna forced Jared from her mind and strove to concentrate on her job. She loved her hometown. Dry Oaks was safe, comfortable, and charming, and she loved being chief. Because she was bullied as a child and she'd been rescued by friends, people who were stronger than she was, she'd grown up with the desire to be the rescuer. That's what police officers did: they rescued people, kept them safe. Being elected as chief was her lifelong dream, and she vowed to do it to the best of her ability. Hanna wanted her force to be the best. Crime here was the lowest in the county, and she credited her proactive people with that statistic.

While she waited for Everett, her thoughts stuck on the letter and her "father's" predicament. It reminded her how hard Everett tried to be a good father, to Scott and Chase, to Devon, and now to Braden.

Chase came to town occasionally. She couldn't say that she knew him. The few times she'd been around him, he hadn't said much. He was a tragic figure, really—half of one leg gone, one eye gone, permanently disfigured. All she really knew about him was what she'd heard from her mother. That Chase was the black sheep of the family, a scary man, violent and unpredictable.

Was Joe Keyes also violent and unpredictable? There was a time when she'd wondered about him, a lot, but her attitude toward him had evolved over the years.

In the quiet, her thoughts wandered back to the first time she remembered seeing a photo of Joe. Paula had no photos in the house.

Hanna had been around nine and on a field trip to the library. Back then she read anything and everything. A lot of the books were way above her age level, but she slogged through them.

She made her way to the adult section of books—where she saw the book Marcus Marshall wrote. It was a bit scary. Her mother would not want Hanna to see this book, so she hid it under her arm and found a quiet, uncrowded area of the library to look through it.

A clump of pictures were in the middle. The book opened naturally to the first picture, and there stood Mom with Joe Keyes. She froze, almost in a kind of shock as she looked at him. He didn't look like Satan; there were no horns. In fact, he was a handsome man, with a square jaw, brown hair with a bit of a wave in it, a pleasant half smile on his face.

It was their wedding picture. Mom and Dad had eloped to Las Vegas. Hanna almost didn't recognize Mom because she was smiling and looked so happy. Dad was taller than Mom. His hair was long. It touched his collar, and he had a bushy mustache.

She remembered she had even smelled the page and thought, *What did my father smell like?* All the picture smelled of was book. She looked at the photos over and over. She even tore one out and took it home with her.

Remembering that day so many years ago still made Hanna blush. She'd held on to that photo for years. By high school, the taunts and jeers she'd endured about her father had destroyed any romantic fantasies about him. She came across the photo one day as she cleaned her room, and in an uncharacteristic fit of rage, she tore it into pieces.

What did Joe look like now?

Hard as she tried, she could not bring herself to think of Joe as her father. None of the men her mother dated ever fit the bill either. Most especially not Marcus Marshall.

In retrospect, Hanna thought perhaps her intuition started early. Marshall was a user. He called himself a professional writer, but he was no Stephen King. He'd told her mother that his book *Murders at Beecher's Mine Cabin* would be a national bestseller and he'd make millions. It hadn't worked out that way.

Was he working on a book about the Buckleys? Marcus usually crowed about his work, yet he'd said nothing. Scott and Marcus were arguing about something.

The double doors whooshed open, stopping Hanna's woolgathering, and out stepped a relieved-looking Everett Buckley and a tired, bandaged-up little boy. The only expression on Everett's face now was calm.

"He's gonna be okay," Everett said. "He's got the Buckley hard head, that's for sure."

"Glad to hear it." She knelt to look into Braden's eyes. "You be more careful when you're hiking, you hear?"

"Yeah, thanks for coming down to get me. Where's Pancho?"

"At home waiting for you," Everett said before Hanna could answer. "I called Grover and asked him to get the dog from Asa."

Standing, she shook Everett's hand. "You two have a good night, a restful night."

Everett cocked his head and sighed. "We sure will try, Chief. Remember, keep me informed."

They parted ways in the parking lot. It was dark now, and when Hanna relaxed and tried to unwind, she realized she was starving. She'd never gotten lunch and wasn't sure where Nathan was at this time of day. Court ended a couple of hours ago. She sat in her car, intending to text him, when she saw that her personal phone was completely dead. The department-issued phone was still charged, but Hanna never liked to use that for personal matters. She started the car, deciding she'd call Nathan from home, and made her way there.

To her surprise, Nathan's car was in her driveway and Hanna smiled, thanking the Lord for such a thoughtful man. A bag of takeout sat on the hood of his car. Of course, they'd missed lunch. She'd forgotten, but it was so like Nathan to remember and remedy the situation.

He leaned against the front fender. She got out of her car and hurried toward him, smelling the delicious food as she got closer. "Oh my goodness. You went to Faye's."

He picked the bag up. "I did. We missed lunch, and I wanted dinner to make up for that. I just got here. I tried to call you . . ."

"My phone died."

Holding the bag in one hand, he gave Hanna a side hug and a peck on the cheek. "I heard the boy was banged up but fine. I spoke to Asa."

"Yeah, a broken arm was the worst of it." She smiled and pulled out her house key. He followed her up the front steps to the door. "He'd been unconscious for so long, I feared he would have a head injury, but he didn't."

She turned back toward him as she pushed the door open. "How'd court go?"

"Jury has it now. You know how that goes."

"Hmm." She flipped on the light. "I'll grab some plates and drinks." They both walked to the dining table. "What would you like?"

"Sparkling water is fine."

"You got it. I'm starved."

"Let's eat, my dear." He set the bag on the table and took out the containers. When Hanna returned with plates and drinks, it only took a minute to dish out wonderful comfort food. Faye's was a local institution in Dry Oaks. People came from all over the county to dine there. Old-fashioned comfort food. Hanna's favorite was the pot roast, which Nathan had gotten her. He preferred meat loaf.

Over dinner they talked about their days: Nathan in court and Hanna rescuing Braden. And they discussed the Jude Carver lawsuit.

"I'm amazed he had the gall to sue. He was worthless. How many times did you find him sleeping on the job?"

She held up four fingers. "And he had four warnings. I honestly don't believe he thinks he'll get his job back. He just has an axe to grind with me. He was cordial when we were peers, even professional. As soon as I was sworn in as chief, everything changed."

He'd grown up in Dry Oaks, left after high school, and was a cop in San Francisco for a time. He came back to Dry Oaks and was hired on by Chief Barnes about three years ago. She guessed Carver's change in behavior happened because they had history. He'd been the leader of the boys who had teased her when she was a kid and didn't care for her being his boss.

It wasn't until dessert that Joe came up. With a large piece of lemon meringue pie between them, Hanna said, "I told Everett about the request from the state."

"What did he say?"

"That it was my decision, but it obviously upset him."

"I'm sure. With Scott gone, he's only got Chase, a vivid reminder of what happened."

"True. I guess in a way I'm lucky. Joe's never been in my life, so it's easy to shut him out of my mind. Everett can't do that with Chase. He'll always see Joe's handiwork."

"Have you met Chase?"

Her mouth full, Hanna held up her index finger in a "just a moment" signal. She thought about the time she and Jared had hiked up to Beecher's Mine cabin. An old memory but strong, of Chase sobbing and cursing the wind. She would not tell that story to Nathan. He'd been very tight-lipped when she explained to him about Jared.

"He's out and about every so often. When I was still in uniform, I handled a call where he was present. Traffic accident. His brother was driving and got rear-ended by another car. I'd always heard that Chase was generally confined to a wheelchair, but that night he was on crutches, and he got around pretty good. The scars make him look a little scary."

"Scary?"

"Yeah, the scars on his face. It almost looks as if he were made up for a horror movie. But he didn't say anything off. Just shook his head when I asked if he'd been hurt in the collision." She remembered that day and added, "Hmmm. I don't know how it would work, having Joe here. I can't imagine it would make Chase happy."

Nathan had just put a big bite of pie in his mouth, and she watched as he chewed.

He swallowed. "Okay, how about I list all the 'yes, it cans,' and you list all the—"

His phone buzzed. She knew that he was on call. He answered a couple of questions, then said, "I'll be there in twenty," then he hung up.

"A body?" Hanna asked, already knowing the answer.

Nathan nodded. "It looks like another one."

CHAPTER 15

SETTLING INTO HIS VEHICLE, Nathan paused before he started the engine. He hated leaving Hanna to tramp around a scene of death. That was doubled considering that he knew what kind of scene he'd be tramping in.

Another dead woman.

He and his partner dubbed the guy the "Lonely Heart Killer," and so far it was the toughest case he'd ever handled. The only thing they knew for sure was that the killer had found his first two victims online through a dating site. This would be the third in a little over three months. Actually, as he thought about the date, Nathan realized that it had only been three weeks since the last body had been dumped. Was the guy breaking form?

He started the car and pulled away, going over the details of the case in his mind. The first woman, Jane Haskell, had been a resident of Twain Harte, a small mountain town not far from Dry Oaks. Her purse, her phone, and her car were all missing. She lived alone and had no family and no great circle of friends. It was only when a rent payment was missed that a landlord stepped forward and filed a missing person report.

To Nathan it was tragic that Jane had lain in the morgue for two weeks before anyone missed her. It was also a hindrance to the investigation because it wasn't until they'd located her residence and her computer that they had any kind of theory about who'd taken her life. They did a deep dive into her computer and phone records and uncovered an online liaison.

About the time they'd discovered the online connection with the first victim, the second body was found: Barb Grant. Again, there was no purse, no phone, and no car. Barb had a unique tattoo of a VW Bug on her shoulder. Nathan and his partner sent a picture of the tattoo to local media, and they got an ID on the woman a little faster, but it still took a couple of days.

Barb Grant hailed from Sonora. Immediately similarities were noticed. Both women were middle-aged and single. There were no husbands or boyfriends to investigate. Both women had lived alone and didn't socialize much. Their computers and phone records both shared the same story of women in online relationships. The kicker was the profiles they'd been interacting with were both fake. The profile pictures had been stolen from legitimate people, two men Nathan and his partner reached out to, who were unaware that an online predator was using their photos to facilitate a fraud.

Tech crimes had the victims' computers and dissected them as best they could, but the trail went cold.

It was clear that both women had been trapped by catfishing scams. From the messages recovered, the suspect strung the women along, pledging love and devotion and asking for money. While they were dealing with two different fake profiles, Nathan and his partner were certain it was the same guy. With Haskell he called himself Franco, and with Grant, he was Gerard. He had used a lot of the same phrases, played on each woman's loneliness the same way.

"You're a beautiful, vibrant woman. I love the way you fix your hair."

"I love reading your posts—you are precious and insightful."

"Baby, you're beautiful. Actresses and models have nothing on you."

"If I was there, I'd never leave your side. I'd cherish you. Our time chatting is the highlight of my day."

"You are my lifeline."

He used the same excuses for needing money.

"My check is a little late. Your gift cards keep me occupied and online, so we can keep talking."

The first two victims parted with a lot of money. Haskell sent off about five thousand dollars, while Grant parted with twenty thousand dollars. Neither victim was sexually assaulted.

What didn't track was why the women were killed. They were giving the guy what he wanted: money. By killing them he cut off the money stream.

When Haskell was discovered, Nathan remembered thinking at the time that it would not be the first. Everything looked too methodical, almost careful. Grant was the same. Both women had been dead a couple of days, and both had been bound, shot, and dumped along Highway 108. No, *dumped* was not the right word. They were almost gently placed.

Nathan and his partner, Manny, voiced the fear after the second woman that it could get bad, and it appeared, from what Manny had told him on the phone, they'd been right. The fact that it was relatively early, not yet 9:00 p.m., also said something. Sooner and bolder, it was almost as if he wanted to be seen.

Unfortunately, the news media also got a whiff of the investigation and descended on the second scene. Nathan and Manny had a good relationship with most of the local network reporters. They were respectful and easy to work with. Marcus Marshall, while normally a laid-back guy, could be like a pit bull on scenes. He was always pushing boundaries, trying to get around the tape. The day after the second woman was found, Marcus wrote his usual hyperbolic headline, *Sadistic Serial Killer Stalks the County*, and inflamed citizens. Nathan guessed that it got him what he wanted: an interview on *Good Morning America*.

Marcus liked the attention, but Nathan and Manny did not. He made things difficult because he often reported on details he observed that they did not want made public.

Nathan soon saw the emergency lights of the sheriff's vehicle on the side of the highway, and he pulled in behind. Unfortunately, there were also lights from a local news van. He could not see who it was. Manny saw to it that they stayed back from the scene, but this could be a problem for the investigation. He got out of his car. Traffic crept by the bright lights, the distraction attracting people like a light attracted moths.

Manny walked back to meet him. "It's bad, bro." He shook his head. "This guy is getting more violent. But we might have gotten a break on this one."

Nathan jerked toward his partner. "A break?"

Manny nodded. "Take a look, and I'll fill you in." He glanced at the news crew. "They got here right after I did. They got some pictures of the scene. Sometimes I wish we could take their scanners away."

"Me too. Show me what you got."

He followed Manny around the cars, down into the culvert on the side of the roadway. The coroner's investigator was already down below, photographing the still form in the dirt. Nathan said a prayer for the woman, thankful that it would be impossible for any motorists above to view this tragic scene. He did worry about the footage the news crew shot. They weren't usually so callous as to air graphic stuff. Still, he felt as if the victim was further violated by their intrusion.

"Who found her?" Nathan pulled on his crime scene gloves.

"That's our break. A hitchhiker."

"In the dark?"

"Yeah, kid named Cully. He'd been hitching with no luck since before dark." Manny pointed down the road. "Cully slid down into the culvert to take a bathroom break. He was just finishing up when he realized an SUV ahead had pulled over"—Manny gestured—"right here. He climbed back up onto the road and ran, thinking he had a ride, but the SUV pulled away." Hands on hips, Manny turned his attention to the body. "He saw the woman and freaked. Came down to see if she was okay and lost his lunch over there."

"That's what I smell," Nathan muttered.

"He called 911 right away. The newsies probably picked up on the 929 DB call. He's in the back of one of the cruisers."

929 DB was the radio code for *dead body*. Reporters knew all the codes.

"You're sure he's not our guy?"

"Reasonably. You talk to him and tell me what you think. I believe we finally got lucky. She'd just been dumped. I'm guessing that she was just killed. The first two victims were not found until a couple of days after their deaths. No advanced decay here, so we'll get more evidence."

"You know that I don't believe in luck." Nathan knelt next to the body. Tied up like the other one, though this woman looked a bit older than the first two. Nathan frowned as he studied what he could of the woman's features. His stomach turned and twisted. Something was familiar here. He couldn't move her, the coroner would do that, but he moved to the other side to get a better look at her face and shone his light there.

His breath caught in his throat.

"What is it?" Manny asked.

Nathan sat back on his heels. "I know, oh my, I know her."

He turned off his light and stood. "It's Edda. Edwina Fairchild. She works for Mandy, Hanna's friend, you know, at the clinic." He wiped his mouth with the back of his hand as bile rose in his throat.

"You okay?"

Nathan nodded. "It's just the shock. This lady is like a kindly grandma."

"How well do you know her?"

Nathan looked away, out into the darkness. "I just saw her at Scott's funeral. Before that I'd spoken to her once or twice. Single, widowed, her son died from a fentanyl overdose about four months ago. We found him down by the train tracks. That was right before you and I became partners."

Manny's eyes widened. "I remember reading the press release. She's a receptionist at the pro-life clinic, right?"

"Yeah."

"Not exactly the profile of the other two. They were both pretty reclusive and looking for love in all the wrong places. Is she likely to be involved in an online relationship?"

Nathan stared at Manny. "I didn't know Edda that well. She was single but not what I'd call a recluse. She was active in church, I know that. And I can't picture her writing up a profile for a dating site."

"Are you thinking this is a different guy?"

Nathan brought a hand to his chin and considered this. "I hope not. One monster is bad enough. Everything else looks the same, from the way she was dumped to the rope used. But here, she's not placed. He dumped her. She rolled down into the ditch."

"You're right. Everything is similar, but not as precise. Even the knot on the rope, same kind but not tied as tight. We'll have to wait for the coroner to give us a time of death."

Nathan nodded, thinking about the funeral. Edda had asked him about the Lonely Heart case. She'd had faith that he'd catch the guy. The reality was like a kick to the gut.

I let you down, Edda, big time, and I'm sorry.

He shifted back to detached investigator mode. Her arms were restrained behind her like the others; a gunshot wound to the head. Everything looked fresh. Manny was right. This was a big break. The haste and timing of this dump could mean he was getting careless and would leave evidence.

After a few minutes, Nathan turned to Manny. "Let me talk to this witness."

He followed his partner to the patrol car. Manny opened the back door, and Nathan leaned down to look inside. "What?" He frowned and jerked up. "What did he tell you his name is?"

"Cully, why?"

Nathan shook his head. "That's Colby Ellis. He's wanted all over the county for everything from theft to malicious mischief. Come out of there, Colby, and tell me why you're lying."

CHAPTER 16

HANNA NEEDED TO WASH AWAY the specter of death. It haunted her when she thought of Joe Keyes and, sadly, Nathan. Old death, and now new death.

Fatigue and a heaviness in her soul descended on Hanna when she had the house to herself. It took all her energy to get up, clear the table, and head to the bathroom to run a bath. Sprinkling eucalyptus-scented Epsom salts into the water, she breathed deeply and worked to relax. Once the tub was full, she stepped in, carefully, because the water was hot, as hot as she could stand it. Steam rose from the liquid and Hanna sighed as she settled in for a soak. "Oh, Lord, I pray for peace and clarity."

Her body relaxed but her mind would not quiet. She'd read the paperwork Giles had given her and kept thinking about Joseph Keyes dying of cancer. All these years, knowing that he was in prison, he'd lived in a safe, locked-up compartment in her mind. Someone she'd never meet. He was a two-dimensional figment of her imagination.

But now he wasn't. He'd jumped off the page of that letter. In her mind's eye she pictured the mustached, smiling man from the photo she'd seen so many years ago.

". . . terminal cancer . . . receiving a compassionate parole . . . requesting release into your custody . . ."

My custody.

The father I've never met wants to die in my custody.

Hanna draped her arm on the edge of the tub and rested her head there, closing her eyes. She didn't know what to feel. The anger and shock were gone. Nathan had told her to talk to Pastor Rick, get sound Christian counsel before making any decision. Maybe she would, but she knew what he would say. *"Honor thy father and mother . . . Forgive as you have been forgiven."* She knew these truths, and she wrestled with them. Her thoughts were twisted in slippery knots as if they were mud wrestling.

In truth, the shadow of her father and what he had done had been a cloud over her whole life—a dark cloud, complete with thunderstorms, where her mother was concerned. Sometimes Hanna still wept for her mother. Her heart attack had been sudden and massive. There was no time for goodbyes, discussions about faith, or forgiveness.

I can't give him my mother's forgiveness. I'm not even sure I can give him mine.

It all came down to a very simple truth: she knew exactly what she should do, and she did not want to do it. He was a killer, he destroyed her mother's life and Amanda Carson's life. She had been two when her parents were murdered. Not to mention what Joe did to Everett Buckley's family and life.

I don't want to do him any favors. I don't want a killer in my home. Everyone should understand that, most of all God.

That was the decision she stuck with as she climbed into bed and went to sleep.

✻

Sleep was a phantom for Hanna for most of the night. She dozed here and there between tossing and turning. For the first time that she could remember, she was relieved when the alarm went off. Rubbing her eyes, she threw off the sheet and sat up. Stretching mightily, "Ow, ow, ow" squeaked out when the side she'd bruised yesterday protested painfully.

After the stiffness and discomfort eased, in a few minutes, she felt ready to get up and face the day. On Saturday mornings, she'd meet with her best friend, Amanda, for a brisk walk. Mandy lived a block over and would walk to pick up Hanna.

She strode into the bathroom, yawning, then rinsed off her face and pulled on her workout gear. The doorbell rang; Mandy was always on time. Hanna grabbed her phone, shoes, and socks and trotted to the front door.

"Sorry I'm a tad late," Hanna said as she pulled the door open. "I didn't sleep very well."

Mandy stretched. "That's okay, I'm moving slow this morning myself."

Hanna closed the door and sat on the porch bench to put on her shoes.

"Why are you moving slow today? Missing Brody?" Mandy's husband was a cycling coach, currently riding in Europe with his team.

"Yeah, that. But we had a good Zoom call yesterday. What kept me awake is I'm worried about Edda. Losing sleep over it."

Hanna looked up from her laces. "Edda? Why? She's the most stable, reliable person I know."

"Maybe. But she met some guy online, and I think she's being bamboozled."

"Online?" Hanna almost laughed, the thought of Edda being caught up in Tinder or Match.com being so absurd. Mandy's face made the laugh die in her throat. "That doesn't sound like Edda." Hanna tied her laces, grabbed her phone, and stood.

Mandy leaned against one of the porch pillars, tension stiffening her shoulders. "It doesn't. Apparently, it's been going on awhile. I thought she was a little distracted lately. I wished I had pressed her on it awhile ago. But . . ."

"You didn't want to meddle?"

"I'm more than her boss. I'm her friend. I should have meddled."

"So, how'd you find out?"

"I caught her on the laptop in a chat room. It was like pulling teeth to get her to tell me what was going on. She said the person contacted her on the memorial website she set up for Bobby."

"What were they chatting about?"

"At first she thought the guy was struggling with addiction, like Bobby. Now she's not sure. All she would say was that she thought someone was pretending, and she wanted to find out who it was."

"Pretending?" Hanna slapped her forehead. "Edda sent me an e-mail, said she wanted to talk."

"About what?"

"Legal help, I think. I never responded. Right after I read the e-mail, I was interrupted. I forgot all about it."

"Well, talk to her. Her son's death really hurt. She's not over it, and if someone got ahold of her online and is trying to take advantage, they need to be stopped. What if she thinks she found Bobby's dealer?"

"Why would you say that?"

"No specific reason. I'm just worried. I should have paid more attention."

Hanna took a step and stood next to Mandy. "Agreed. I should have answered her e-mail." She couldn't remember the exact wording of the e-mail now. Could Edda have been trying to find the man responsible for Bobby's death, or was it something more dangerous?

"Yeah, I'm hoping you'll talk to her and maybe look into this guy she's been conversing with."

"Consider it done. I'll drop by for a visit after church tomorrow. Ready?"

Mandy nodded and together they hopped off the porch. She changed the subject. "I know you had quite a day yesterday. Braden is a handful for any babysitter."

News always traveled fast in Dry Oaks. It was no surprise that Mandy knew about the incident.

"Yeah, the boy has endless energy. I hope that accidently falling from a cliff is the extent of his mischievousness."

Falling into step with Amanda, they headed for the local high school to walk the track.

Saturday was a light day for both of them. Amanda was an avid cyclist. Hanna's exercise of choice was running, and a normal run for her was around six miles. To mix it up, on Tuesdays and Thursdays she swam in the local pool.

While vigorous exercise always helped clear her head, Saturday was a welcome break. The pleasant easy walk and chat with Mandy helped center Hanna, especially when the workweek had been tough. She was certain she did the same for Mandy. Her friend ran a local crisis pregnancy center, and often Hanna could feel the hurt and sadness radiating from Mandy. Too many young women saw abortion as the only option, and it weighed on Mandy and, to a certain extent, Hanna as well. Saving and protecting the innocent was a central reason she went into law enforcement.

This morning, the most pressing thing on Hanna's mind was Joe. Mandy was more than Hanna's friend. She and her grandparents were family to Hanna. Joe murdered Mandy's parents.

How could his probable release not affect her? Hanna wasn't certain how to broach the subject.

"Braden only suffered a broken arm?" Mandy asked.

"Yeah, besides that, just bumps and bruises. He got lucky."

"Did he say how he ended up on the ledge?"

"Chasing the dog, who was chasing a squirrel. Cassidy couldn't keep up."

"Hmph."

For a few minutes, they walked in companionable silence. Hanna had the sense that something was on Mandy's mind. Was it still Edda?

"Sounds like there is more to follow," Hanna said.

"Yeah, but it doesn't make sense. It's certainly not a Christian thought. It's the Buckleys. Well, it seems sometimes as if they are cursed."

"Cursed?"

Mandy waved her hand. "I know, I know, we don't believe in curses. But so much tragedy for that family. First Chase, then Chase's son, then Braden's mother, then Scott . . ."

"As a law enforcement officer, I could say there is nothing cursed about it. Just a lot of bad life decisions and unfortunate situations. Chase hung with the wrong crowd, his son was an unfortunate victim of a motorcycle accident, and Braden's mother never had both feet on the ground—"

"Okay, okay, I hate it when you get all official and pragmatic on me. Whatever the reason, it's sad. And I hope this tumble is the worst thing that happens to Braden for a good long time."

They started their first lap around the track. Hanna could never do this boring type of workout without Mandy.

"Speaking of bad things and curses," Hanna began, "I got a strange visit yesterday."

"Visit? From whom?"

"The Department of Corrections."

"What?" Mandy stopped, and so did Hanna, a couple of feet ahead of her. She turned back.

"Did he die?"

Mouth half open, Hanna looked at her friend. Was there hope in that question or sorrow? She shook her head. "Not yet. But he is dying. Cancer. They want to grant him compassionate parole."

Mandy frowned. "Huh? What is that, how would it work?"

Hanna shrugged and started walking again, and Mandy hurried to catch up. "They want to send him to me. On hospice."

"You're kidding."

"I wish I was. My answer is no. I'm too busy. Running a PD means I'm at work most of the time, for heaven's sake. I don't even have time for a dog. Besides, he's really nothing to me."

Mandy grabbed her arm and they stopped again. "Don't tell them no, Hanna. Don't."

"What? Why not?"

"Because. He's at the end. Maybe he'll finally do the right thing and tell me where my parents are."

Hanna saw desperate hope in her friend's eyes. Surprise hit like a blow. "Wow."

"What?"

"I never looked at it that way, from your perspective. I—" The sound of a car pulling into the school parking lot stopped her. It was a county car. Nathan. That he was here, now, meant not-good news.

Mandy jerked around and followed her gaze. "I sincerely hope he just misses you."

Nathan got out and walked toward them. He looked tired. His clothes were rumpled, and the shadow of a beard darkened his jawline. Hanna bet he'd not been to sleep yet.

"Good morning. I thought I'd find you two here," he said as he approached.

"What gives? You look like you're the bearer of bad news." Hanna tried to keep her tone light even as her stomach turned.

He nodded, expression grim. "Afraid I am." He looked away from Hanna, and his voice softened. "Mandy, we found a body last night. Another woman." Nathan took a deep breath. "There is no easy way to say this. It was Edda."

"Huh?" Hanna felt as if all breath left her body. *Auntie Edda?* The pain she felt was real and ragged, but she held on to her emotions and watched the color drain from Mandy's face. Reflexively, she reached out and gripped her friend's elbow.

"You're sure?" Mandy asked, voice soft, unsteady.

"As sure as I can be. I talked to her enough. I know her son is gone. Is there any other family I need to notify? News agencies were all over the scene. I don't want any of her family to find out from a news broadcast."

Mandy shook her head. "Her husband passed a while ago. She spoke of a niece in another state, but how close they were, I'm not certain." Her voice broke, and Hanna felt for her friend. Then Mandy seemed to brace herself and swallow the tears.

"I know who did it." She folded her arms, anger rapidly replacing grief. "I tried to warn her. It's a guy she met online. Someone named Diego."

CHAPTER 17

HANNA STARED AT MANDY IN SHOCK at this revelation, but it was Nathan who spoke up.

"Diego? Someone she met online—like a date?" Nathan asked.

Mandy gave a sharp shake of her head. "Someone she felt sorry for at first. He claimed to have substance abuse issues and that Edda's connection with him was saving him from suicide." Mandy told Nathan what she knew.

The frown on Nathan's face deepened.

"What is it?" Hanna asked.

"The other two victims, they were both involved with online relationships. But they were dating relationships. Obviously, catfishing scams, at least on the surface." He stopped and looked at Mandy. "What do you mean *at first?*"

"She didn't tell me everything. She just said she thought he was pretending."

"Pretending about what?"

Mandy shrugged. "I just told Hanna I was afraid she was looking for Bobby's dealer. Maybe he gave her a fake name. I don't know."

"Edda sent me an e-mail, asking about something with legal

ramifications, I think," Hanna said. "She wanted to talk to me, and I didn't get back to her. I just got busy."

Hanna looked at Mandy. She'd shed some tears and wiped them away. But mama bear was emerging now.

"Have you been to her house yet?" Mandy asked.

"Next stop is to meet my partner there."

"Edda had a dog, Gizmo, her baby. He'll need someone to take care of him now. You won't take him to animal control, will you?"

Nathan hesitated.

"He's not dead too, is he?" Hanna loved dogs, longed to have one, but her life was too crazy.

"I honestly don't know. Until I get to Edda's house, I won't know."

"Can I take him?" Mandy asked.

"If she doesn't have some kind of will giving him to someone, I don't have a problem with that."

"I'll join you at her house," Hanna said to Nathan. "If the dog is there, I'll get him for Mandy."

Mandy hugged her arms to her chest. "I can't believe this is happening. No one in the world was sweeter than Edda. Catch the monster who did this."

"I plan to," Nathan said.

Hanna and Mandy hurried home. They parted at Hanna's house with a hug.

"I'm so sorry, Mandy. I wish I—"

"Don't, Hanna, don't blame yourself. I won't take any blame either. The only person to blame is the animal who did this."

Hanna hurried to shower and change, chilled to the bone by a murder hitting so close to home. Murder overshadowed the tragic accidental overdose of Edda's son, Bobby. He'd struggled so many years with chemical dependency, his death was inevitable. Edda's murder was shockingly unexpected.

Hanna called dispatch and put herself on duty. Once in the car, she paused to pray. *Oh, Lord, this hurts. This is so hard to understand. Please help us catch the man, please. No more life lost in this fashion. Amen.*

In short order she was on her way to meet Nathan at Edda's house. He'd said he'd wait for her unless there was some indication that he needed to make entry to the house right away.

Edda's small home was at the edge of town. It backed up to forest. When she got there, Nathan was not alone. And she recognized the SUV behind his county car.

He was in a heated discussion with Marcus Marshall.

"The people need to know there's a dangerous killer roaming free. Why won't you admit that three women were killed by the same person?"

"We're in the middle of an investigation. I can't say that definitively. I won't jump the gun and compromise the investigation. Making people panic won't help us find this guy."

"You're not helping either, Marcus."

Marcus swung around to face her. "Well, this is serious if you're here. Keeping tabs on these detectives, are you?"

"That's not what I'm doing. They're very good at their jobs, which right now you are keeping them from. The sheriff's department issues clear press releases. Why don't you wait for that?"

"I don't need a press release to tell me that we have a serial killer in the county. Three dead women in as many months. You need to tell folks what the common denominators are if there are any, so they can be more careful. The Green River Killer kept killing because information wasn't shared and broadcast."

"Let us do our jobs." Nathan was at the end of his patience, Hanna could tell.

"Are you going to leave, Marcus, or do I have to waste more resources and have someone remove you?"

He threw his hands up. "I think the sheriff's department is in over its head. They should ask for help. This is going up on my podcast. I care about public safety." Marcus stalked down the driveway and got into his car.

"Who tipped him off?" Hanna asked as she and Nathan watched him drive away.

"There was a news crew at the scene last night. And Marcus has his own scanner. Do you ever listen to his podcast?"

"No."

"I don't regularly, but when I have listened, I've heard him give people tips on personal safety. Last month he warned people about connecting with strangers online." He shrugged. "He's got an active imagination, that's for sure. It always goes to the worst possible outcome. He's convinced that our body count could reach the Green River Killer status."

"What does he think you're withholding?"

"Connections between the three victims. He wants to broadcast that we have a serial killer. I can't help but think he's hoping for a book opportunity that will launch him into stardom."

"Scott's fiancée thought that he was writing a book about the Buckleys."

"Really? I bet Scott was not happy about that. Marshall's style is early American. Well, he earned his nickname Muckraker."

"I can testify to that."

Nathan turned and gave her a warm half smile. "You sure can. Let's get inside the house." He turned and Hanna followed.

"Wait, where is Edda's car?" She remembered reading in the

reports that the cars of the first two victims had also been missing when the bodies were found.

"We haven't found it. DMV records told us that she has a red VW Bug."

"Yeah, it's a cute car. It fit Edda. Did you find the first two victims' cars? I don't remember the updates."

"Not right away. The first victim's car was found in a ditch near Oakdale, and the second victim's car was found in a park-and-ride lot outside of San Francisco. So we expect Edda's car will turn up sooner or later. There is a BOLO in the system."

Hanna knew that none of the victims had any personal effects on them when they were found. No phones, purses, watches. All the info they had on the probable suspect came from computers and phone records.

They were able to get into Edda's house because she kept a key under the back doormat. Her pup, Gizmo, a little Jack Russell terrier mix, was happy to see them. He needed to go out, so Hanna kept an eye on him while Nathan went in.

Gizmo ran around the yard for a few minutes, did his business, and then looked at Hanna expectantly. She took him back into the house, sticking just her head inside the door first.

"Clear to come in?" she called out to Nathan.

"Yes. Place is neat as a pin. There's no crime scene here. She met the guy somewhere else."

Hanna entered and went in search of dog food. She found the dog bowl and not much farther away was the food. She filled the bowl and watched the little dog attack it with gusto.

She looked around the little house. It was old and small; she'd grown up in a similar-type house. Two small bedrooms, one bath, small kitchen cut off from the rest of the house. While not many original structures from the gold rush period survived to the twenty-first century, the basic footprint of them had. This little house was designed like an old mining cabin. Edda rented from Everett Buckley, which was a normal situation in Dry Oaks.

Everything was neat and homey. Pictures of her son throughout his life were everywhere. So were crochet pieces. Over the back of the sofa hung a beautiful blue, green, and gray crocheted blanket. Edda was known for the blankets she crocheted. Hanna had one of different shades of pink that was her favorite bedspread. Edda also made small blankets for newborns. She'd slowed down a bit after her son died. Hanna had assumed it was grief and that Edda would eventually recover.

Not now.

"Lord, help us find the man responsible for this, please," Hanna prayed.

The dog finished eating and curled up on her foot. Chuckling, she bent down and picked him up. He snuggled into the crook of her arm.

"Looks like you found a friend." Nathan held an evidence bag with Edda's laptop in it under his arm.

"Yeah, I'd better be careful, or I'll be fighting Mandy for this dog."

"Maybe you should keep him."

"Aren't I always complaining about how busy my life is?"

He patted the dog's head. "Doesn't look like he'll take up too much time or space."

"Hmm." The little guy certainly wasn't very heavy. "Just the laptop?"

"Yeah, I'm looking for a journal. She has a whole row of journals in her room, dated, but the current month is missing."

"Hmm." For a few minutes, Hanna helped him search the small room. No journal to be found.

"Maybe it's in her car or purse."

Nathan nodded. "Possible. I've done all I can here. I need to get this laptop to the techies. I'll wait outside for Manny."

Together they walked out the front door.

"Have you thought any more about Joe?" he asked.

"I talked to Mandy about him."

"What did she say?"

"She wants me to say yes, she wants to talk to Joe, see if he'll finally come clean about where her parents are."

"It's not just her parents," Nathan said. "People will want to know about Gilly as well."

"He was never rigidly tied to that case."

"While that may be true, Gilly was investigating Joe and targeting meth labs. Joe might still have helpful information. He has nothing to lose now. It's time to come completely clean about what happened back then."

Manny arrived with a lab tech.

"I'll let you get back to work," Hanna said. "We'll catch up Monday morning. Doesn't look like you'll make it to church tomorrow."

"Probably not. I'll update you as soon as I can."

Hanna left with Gizmo. She took his bowl and food, and he curled up in a cute ball on the front seat. How on earth was she going to give him to Mandy?

CHAPTER 18

JARED WAS READY FOR RELIEF from the fire when it came. By Saturday afternoon, the winds had shifted, pushing the conflagration away from populated areas and into dense forest, where it was impossible to fight on the ground. Air tankers and helicopters with water drops were the only weapons that would be of any use now.

When they broke for lunch, Jared and his team were cut loose for thirty-six hours off the line. Cal Fire could handle things for a bit. He was glad for the break and eager for his own shower and his own bed. He was certain he could sleep straight through the entire thirty-six.

Hopping into his pickup, he pulled away from the command post and headed home, yawning as he drove. The strong, bitter cup of coffee he'd grabbed from the mess hall was half empty. He traveled back roads to Dry Oaks. Some were dirt, some partially paved. When he'd returned to the little hamlet after so many years away, he'd been happy that while there was growth, development had not destroyed all that he remembered. His path skirted private property and took him past the trailhead that led up to where Beecher's Mine cabin had stood. You couldn't see it from the road, but a rough trail wound up the hillside to the site.

Growing up in Dry Oaks, kids in town told obligatory ghost

stories about the place. The Carsons were said to wander through the trees, weary for rest. As a teen, Jared had acted on a dare and spent the night up there. Or most of the night. Buckley had security watching the site, and they chased him off the mountain at around three in the morning. He and Hanna had hiked up there one time as well. He thought of that odd night, when they hid behind a tree trunk, and a drunken Chase broke bottles and cursed the moon. No security ran them off that night.

Was it still a draw for kids in the area? And did Buckley still pay security to patrol? Jared let his eyes wander, peering into the trees as his truck rumbled and jerked over the bumpy road. For a second, he thought he saw movement in the tree line and he slowed.

No, just his imagination. He shook his head and accelerated. Thinking of the murders brought Hanna to mind. Would interest in the grisly murders ever wane? He hoped so for her sake. Though she'd obviously overcome the stigma; the town had elected her to be chief. For some reason that made Jared immensely proud.

One of the fondest memories he had of the time before he left was when Hanna won an award as a police explorer. She'd just finished her shift and was on her way home from Sonora when she passed a house that looked as if it was on fire. She stopped, got out, and saved a family of four and their pets. Hanna was fearless. It was something that distinguished her from all other women Jared had known.

And something that made it difficult for him to get over her.

Shifting from back roads to paved highway, Jared made it home in no time. Saturdays were laid-back sleepy days in the town. Most of the traffic would be downtown for the farmer's market. His cousin Clay had a booth there. Jared's father had willed his property to Clay, and Jared was fine with that. Clay loved farming, and since organic and cage-free were much more popular now, Clay and the farm were thriving.

As a result, Jared rented a small house on his uncle Gary's property. A tiny two-bedroom with a full bath, but comfortable, with a new kitchen. Jared traveled light, he wasn't home much, and he didn't need much room. The only problem was the structure was close to the next-door neighbor, Jude Carver.

Since the day in junior high when he punched Jude out for teasing Hanna, they had been adversaries. Jude hadn't changed a bit. Once a bully, always a bully. It made Jared laugh when he thought, in one of life's ironies, Hanna became the boss of the guy who'd been the boss of the bullies who had tormented her when she was a kid.

When Carver left Dry Oaks, he'd traveled to San Francisco to be a police officer. He laterally transferred to Dry Oaks a few years ago. From what Jared heard, he had to learn to be a small-town officer and had a hard time with it. Stokes had told him that Chief Barnes was a nice guy, but the closer he got to retirement, the less he was engaged. He never confronted Jude about the complaints directed his way.

Hanna inherited the Carver problem. And Carver didn't like Hanna, which immediately bothered Jared. She dealt with the problem head-on and fired the guy. Hanna was on top of things. Now, unemployed, Carver had a habit of staying up late, drinking and playing loud music.

Carver must have come home drunk this morning. He'd run his SUV into the mailbox. The box was under the front tire and the front fender was smashed. Jared maneuvered his pickup around the listing vehicle. At least the guy would be quiet this morning.

He was wrong. He parked his truck and climbed out. Carver was on his porch with a bottle in his hand. He glared at Jared.

"Good morning," Jared said amiably.

Carver responded with a rude hand gesture.

Yes, Jared thought as he unlocked his door. Firing was what this guy deserved.

CHAPTER 19

THE REST OF SATURDAY WAS somber and filled with shock. Hanna took Gizmo with her to the crisis pregnancy clinic to relinquish him to Mandy.

"I'm sorry, I'm not sure I can take him, at least not now." She stroked the little dog's head. "I'll be planning Edda's celebration of life and notifying people. Besides, I've got Grandma Betty with me. She's still recuperating from hip surgery."

Hanna remembered that Betty had had surgery right before Scott's funeral. "Oh, I remember, how is she doing?"

"Good. She should be home on her own in a couple of days. I'm not sure it would be safe to have little Gizmo running around while she's still using a walker."

"I'll have to stop by and say hi." Hanna looked around the normally happy and welcoming clinic. It was open, but there was no joy. Everyone there was crying or wiping away tears. Hanna felt like crying herself. Edda was everyone's sweet aunt.

"It's hard to be here without Edda. I mean, she was always here for me, for us." Tears started and Mandy grabbed a Kleenex. Hanna sat next to her friend, set Gizmo on the floor, and put an arm over her shoulder. It had hit her hard too. Mandy was right; Edda was family.

Hanna groaned.

"What, what is it?" Mandy asked, sniffling.

"I just thought about how horrible it will be at church tomorrow."

Mandy started crying harder, and Hanna couldn't stop her own tears.

❧

"Sunday was hard for me," Hanna said when she met Nathan Monday morning for coffee. "But it looks as if the whole weekend was hard for you."

Dry Oaks Beanery was across the street from the PD. It was their go-to coffee spot. They both sat with steaming cups of coffee to share a few minutes together before they had to start their workdays. Nathan looked as if he'd never ended his from Saturday. Hanna knew how that was. A case like he had, well, you wanted to solve it. You wanted to get the bad people off the streets as soon as possible.

"You have no idea." He yawned. "Maybe you do. I think I got four hours of sleep the whole weekend. Was everyone at church torn up about Edda?"

"Understatement. Everyone was in shock. Who could hurt the sweetest person in the world? You are chasing a monster."

"I am, believe me. I consider that every minute."

She reached over and put her hand over his. "You still need to take care of Nathan. Working yourself into the ground won't help the investigation."

He flashed a tired smile. "Yeah, Chief, I know. I'll work on getting some rest."

"Good."

He sipped his coffee, and she gave him a minute before asking for an update.

"Where are you guys at right now?"

He shook his head. "The only edge we have is that he killed her shortly before he dumped her. That's way earlier than with the others. If he was rushed, we might find evidence. The techies unlocked her computer, and they're going over the contents."

"You're frowning. What's wrong?"

"Edda's case is different. Hers was not a romance scam. From what I've read so far, she truly wanted to help the guy calling himself Diego, at first. Mandy was right. Then something changed, and Edda began to doubt. She feared that he was pretending. Her last messages were almost threatening."

"What do you mean?"

"She told him she didn't believe his name was Diego. That she was certain he was local and not in a faraway place. Her last message to him was, 'I think I know who you are.'"

Hanna stared, digesting this information.

"Out of three victims, it looks as if only Edda gave the guy good reason to get rid of her. He'd hooked her at first, but she was trying to wriggle off the line."

"Did she say who she thought he was?"

"No."

Hanna thought for a minute. "Scammers scam. They prey on people's weaknesses. Bobby was Edda's weakness. Scammers target pain, whether it's caused by loneliness or guilt."

"He played to her pain, but eventually she saw through it."

"You're not thinking there's two different killers, are you?" Hanna stared, her mind churning with the horrific ramifications of such a thought.

"No, no. It's too early in the investigation. You know me, I like the ducks to all line up. We've got a duck out of order here, and it bugs me. Could be he changed his MO because Edda found him out."

They sipped their coffee in silence for a moment. Could killers break form? Sure, it just wasn't terribly likely. She prayed that there were not two killers and switched back to Edda being vulnerable online.

"Bobby's death really knocked Edda sideways." Hanna broke the silence. "The thought that someone played with that information, scammed her, and then killed her because she figured it out is excruciating. My mom went on a date once with someone she'd met online. I'm thankful nothing came of it, and the only thing that guy lied about was his weight and his hairline."

"Yes, social media can make it so much easier for illegal and dangerous activity. And now it's probable we have a serial killer. I don't even want to look at Marcus's headline this morning."

"I saw it; it's sensational for sure."

"He's been dogging us since Victim Two."

"It's almost as if he's salivating for more victims." As soon as Hanna said the words, she regretted it. "Aw, it's probably not fair of me to assign motives to Marcus, is it?"

Nathan let out a rueful chuckle. "I would never assume he wants to see someone murdered, but that man cares little for anyone but himself, and sensational headlines get clicks. I'm tired of thinking about Marshall."

"If you had to give your investigation a progress report, where would you be?"

"Moving forward, but slowly. At least the online angle is clear in all three cases. Though catfish are usually all about money, not murder. I am worried that he's escalating. Right now, it looks as if he just got sloppy yesterday, leaving a witness, albeit not a great one. Good for us but dangerous for any potential victims."

"I have faith in you and Manny. You'll catch the guy."

"Thanks. By the way, where did little Gizmo end up?"

Hanna smiled, perhaps a little sheepish. "When I left this morning, he was curled up on a towel in my kitchen."

"Hmph."

"I did take him to Mandy. She's busy. She's going to co-ordinate Edda's celebration of life. And she has Betty staying with her, recuperating from hip surgery."

"Okay. Personally, I think you should keep the dog."

"Really?"

"He took to you right away. I'd say you guys fit together."

"Well, thank you, Nathan. I think so too." She finished her coffee.

He sipped his coffee. "Have you decided about Joe? I mean, will you say yes for Mandy?"

"I don't know. Her request surprised me. I never considered that she would still be thinking about finding her parents' remains. She was only two when they died."

"Working homicide, I've noticed how important having a body to bury is to some people. And with Mandy, well, she's never known the true story of what happened to her mom and dad. Really, all most people know about that is what Marcus concocted. The truth might be very different."

"How different can it be? You're not going to say Joe could be innocent, are you?" The question came out sharper than she intended.

"No, of course not. But you know as well as I do that his confession was short on specifics. I'm not sure why that would make you angry."

Hanna bristled. "I'm not angry, I just—" She shook her head. "I'm irritated, okay? Irritated that this all has come up now. Why now? In addition to everything else, we have to bury a friend."

"Will you help Mandy with Edda's arrangements?"

Hanna sighed. "If she asks me, yes. It's taking all my self-control not to jump into your investigation and find the guy who killed Edda."

"Since I'm a deputy and you're not the sheriff or a micro-manager, I have no fear of that."

Hanna smiled, feeling some of the tension leave her body. "Thanks. Call or text if you get any good information."

"Will do." He checked his watch. "Now I've got to go. Jailhouse interview."

"You're sure he can't be Diego?"

"I am. I can't see that at all. He was on foot. No way he could have dumped the body. But he was lying to me. There must be a reason for the lie. He had a legitimate warrant in the system, so I have some leverage. With luck, I'll get him to tell me the truth."

"Nothing lucky about it. You'll get him to tell the truth because that's the awesome investigator you are."

"Aw, there you go with the flattery. Maybe we should go out on a date, Chief Keyes." He leaned forward and kissed her cheek.

For a second, he held her gaze, and Hanna saw how tired and troubled he looked. Three dead women weighed heavily on him.

"I'm praying you get headway on this case," she whispered.

He released a faint smile. "Thanks."

Hanna watched him walk toward his car, get in, and drive away.

She had to get to work as well but tarried. Procrastination was normally foreign to Hanna, but today she dragged her feet. There was still the matter of Scott's murder and talking with Chase. They had zero leads thus far. The puzzle of the alleged Buckley book needed to be solved as well.

The reason she was glad Nathan hadn't pressed her about what she was going to do about Joe was that she still didn't know herself. How could she say no to Mandy one minute, while the next minute the thought of Joe Keyes in her house repulsed her?

CHAPTER 20

NATHAN'S THOUGHTS TURNED to Colby Ellis as he drove toward Sonora and the city jail. The kid was a liar and a thief, but like he told Hanna, Nathan couldn't see him as a cold-blooded killer, and he trusted his instincts. He'd let Colby sit in jail over the weekend. Hopefully by now he'd be willing to tell the whole truth.

Manny was already at his desk when Nathan got in.

"I've got all the outstanding warrants on Ellis here. He'll be in custody for at least six months on those. You ready to talk to him?"

"Oh, yeah, more than ready." Nathan set his briefcase on his desk and locked his gun inside the desk drawer. Friday night all Ellis had done was insist that he was not lying. He didn't invoke his Miranda rights though, and that was a good thing.

Manny already had Ellis sitting in an interview room. Nathan turned on the observation camera and tape and unlocked the door.

Ellis looked bad. Nathan guessed he was coming down off something, God only knew what. His red hair was matted to one side on his head, his face full of red blotches, and his nose runny.

"Sure looks like you had a bad weekend," Nathan said amiably as he sat across from the kid. The body odor emanating from him was rancid, and Nathan tried to breathe through his mouth.

Ellis only grunted.

"Are you ready to tell the truth today?"

"Will it get me out of here?" he asked with a froggy voice.

"You have outstanding warrants, Colby. Nothing I can do about that. The thing is, do you want me to tack murder on to the charges?"

Ellis shook his head, his eyes bleary. "I didn't kill that woman and you know it."

"I don't. Because you're lying to me. You're lying at most about committing the murder or at least assisting with the murder. Come clean, and maybe I'll help get you into treatment."

Ellis rested his forehead on the table and groaned.

"You need some water or coffee?" Manny asked.

He got an assenting grunt in response.

Nodding to Nathan, Manny got up and left the room. Nathan decided to wait and said nothing. Manny returned and put the coffee in front of Colby, who lifted his head and grabbed the cup in both hands. Nathan let the kid take a couple of sips.

"Better?"

Ellis nodded, rubbed his hands all over his face, and then his fingers through his matted hair. "Okay, um, here it is, um, I didn't lie about everything."

Nathan leaned back in his chair. "Okay, what's true?"

"I was hitching. No one was s-s-stopping." He gulped some more coffee. "I had to pee. That's what I was doing when the guy pulled up."

"Did you think it was a ride?"

Ellis shook his head. "I thought it was a cop."

"What?"

Ellis, more awake now, nodded. "It was a big black SUV. Cops drive those. I started for it, then stopped and watched for a few minutes. I saw him open the side door and drag that woman out of the back seat."

"Why lie?"

"'Cause if it was a cop, I'd be dead. I'd have been left on the roadside with the woman. Now I'm here, and you can't kill me."

"You don't think it was a cop now?" Manny asked.

Ellis gave another head shake. "Things are clearer now. He had cowboy boots on. There was a normal license plate on the car, not a cop plate. And there was a bumper sticker."

"Do you remember the plate numbers or letters?"

"No, no, just that it was white."

"And the bumper sticker?"

"Yeah, I remember that. They're everywhere. It said, *Vote Keyes for Chief.*"

Nathan felt a jolt and struggled to keep his face blank. "Did you get a good look at the guy?"

Ellis leaned back and closed his eyes. "Oh man, he was tall; it was dark."

"Come on, Colby, no more lies."

He put his hands over his ears and moaned.

Nathan resisted the urge to reach over and shake the kid. Instead, he slid a legal pad and a pencil across the table. "Write down everything you remember. The truth, Colby. If you help us catch this guy, there may be a reward in it for you."

That brought a little more light into the kid's eyes. He reached for the pen, and Nathan waited while he wrote.

CHAPTER 21

NOTHING WAS MORE DRAINING than a tough homicide case. Hanna watched Nathan drive away knowing Edda's death weighed on him like Scott's weighed on her. The frustration of not knowing where to look for the next lead bit like the sting of a wasp.

Back in her office, Hanna went through the pile of messages on her desk. Most of them were media inquiries about the investigation into Scott's death and the discovery of Edda Fairchild. A couple of reporters wanted to do on-air interviews about both stories. Hanna could speak to Scott's case, but Nathan's case was not her jurisdiction. All the bodies had been found on county land, so she would have to refer that case to the sheriff's department.

"You saw that request from channel seven." Terry Holmes poked his head in the door.

"Yeah. I'm fine with your doing an interview if you wish. We're at a standstill. Everett didn't have anything helpful to say, and we still need to talk to Chase."

Terry held up a folder. "Everyone I've interviewed lines up with what Everett had to say. According to Grover, the morning Scott left to fly, Everett was busy with Braden and the riding instructor. Scott was in the house, doing his own thing until he left. Grover is not even sure what time he left to go to the airfield. Chase was nowhere around. He doesn't live in the main house."

"I think I've heard that before. After his injuries, Everett built him his own place on the property."

Terry nodded. "It was just a normal morning. The only other person in the house was the housekeeper. You already read her statement. I have not been able to confirm that he made the coffee at home."

"Yeah, she was busy making a grocery list and preparing to go shopping. If he didn't make the coffee at home, he made it at the airfield."

Terry nodded again. "At this point, I'm leaning toward the poison being put in the coffee by someone at the airfield. I'll look through more security video. We missed something."

"I know. I'll push Chase. It's a loose thread that needs to be tied up. Everything is crazy right now, but I don't want that to be an excuse."

"I understand. Everyone who grew up in Dry Oaks knew Aunt Edda. Hearing about her was quite a shock."

"Yes, but I'm used to having a lot on my plate. I shouldn't be so easily distracted. I'm also still troubled about this Marcus-Scott dustup."

"I reinterviewed the guys at the airfield. No one else saw it. Only Jeff Smith."

Hanna thought about that. "I can't see Smith making that up. His alibi is solid."

"Valerie Fox confirms tension between Marcus and Scott, about a supposed book."

"That's weird too. Everett had no idea about a book, and Marcus won't admit to it. Chase may be the only one to settle this mystery."

Terry nodded and went back to his office. She called Marcus and left another voicemail.

Hanna was left alone with her conflicted thoughts about Joe. He'd been a boogeyman in her life since birth. A true monster who murdered her best friend's parents. Things had been tough when she was a kid, but Mandy and Jared were the two people who helped her the most during those years, the ones who made sure she survived, even thrived. They knew what she'd gone through. She'd already talked to Mandy.

Would talking to Jared help in some way? What would his perspective be?

Hanna got up and paced her small office. Jared had given her his number. She hadn't put it in her phone yet. It was so odd to her. She knew he was here. He was a firefighter, and once or twice she'd run into him at traffic-accident scenes, yet she didn't know how to approach him and just talk.

Putting him on the back burner for a moment, she redirected her thoughts to Joe. She didn't want him in her house. But neither did she want to say no to Mandy. Mandy had lost the most because of Joe, yet she befriended Hanna when no one else would. And she had been a steadfast friend for years.

I owe it to her. She deserves to know where her parents are buried. Still, Hanna's hand hesitated on the phone. Joe was in prison for murder. What kind of danger might there be in bringing him to her house?

She'd have to ask Giles. Maybe this was an out. Hanna certainly didn't want to put her life or anyone else's in danger. Mandy would understand if that were the case.

Taking a deep breath, she punched in the number for the Department of Corrections. She'd get her questions answered before she committed to anything. Gordon Giles took her call.

"Thank you for getting back to us, Chief. I'm hoping you considered the request."

"I'm considering. However, though on paper Joe is my father, I don't know him. I've never lived with him. And he's a convicted murderer. I once arrested a man in a wheelchair for stabbing someone. Is it safe for him to be in my home?"

Giles gave a little chuckle. "I understand your concern. I can't predict the future, but I can say that Joe Keyes has been an exemplary inmate for almost his entire time served. Ten years ago, he saved the life of a corrections officer and stopped a riot, and he's never been out of line here. And physically, well, he's semimobile, with the help of a walker or a cane, and he's on oxygen twenty-four seven. Prison doc thinks he has less than a month left. Does that help you at all?"

Less than a month left.

Hanna bit her bottom lip. Despite Giles's obvious respect for Joe, she was unable to quell the uneasy feeling in the pit of her stomach. That Giles spoke glowingly of Joe did surprise her. And the time Joe had left—would he even last long enough to be brought to her house?

"It helps some . . ." She couldn't bring herself to say that she'd take him in.

"We have not come to this decision lightly. The vote of the parole board was unanimous," Giles said. "If there were any hint that your father would be a danger to you, or anyone, he'd never be considered for release."

Hanna sighed. If it weren't for Mandy, this decision would not have been so difficult.

"I do have questions," she said. "Okay, he walks with a walker, and he needs oxygen. What other kind of care and how do I manage it?"

"No fear; we have that taken care of. He's being released on hospice. There will be a team attending him. Before he's released, a member of the hospice team and I will visit your home and let you know what's needed. Right now, I'll start the paperwork. When would be a good time for our visit?"

Hanna ran her hands through her hair, stunned by how quickly things were moving along. Mouth dry, she swallowed before squeaking out, "Ah, what day did you have in mind?"

"The sooner the better. I can be there Wednesday morning. Around noon?"

She glanced at her calendar, barely seeing it. So soon?

"That would be fine, I guess."

They finalized the arrangement, and for a time, Hanna sat at her desk and prayed. She felt no peace, only confusion. What had she done?

She called Nathan, wondering if he'd be able to tip the scale one way or another. It went to voicemail, and he was most likely in an interview room. No help there. Then it occurred to Hanna that maybe she should notify her boss about the arrangement with Joe. It was conceivable that having Joe here might disrupt her schedule, and she should let the mayor know.

Next, she rang the mayor's aide and asked if Mayor Milton was available for a brief chat, and she got an affirmative answer. Hanna headed across the street to the courthouse. The mayor's office was on the third floor, the top.

The mayor's door stood open, and the aide waved Hanna in.

"What a sad day in Dry Oaks." Evelyn shook her head. "I'm having trouble processing the fact that Edda was murdered. We went to school together."

"A lot of people are having a hard time with it."

"Do we have any leads?"

"Nathan and Manny are working hard. I have faith in them."

Evelyn smiled. "Good. I was going to call you just before you called. Great minds think alike. Do you have an update on Scott?

I thought all the media inquiries had calmed down, but I've seen the news agencies who want on-air interviews."

Hanna sighed, not sure if the misdirection was a good thing. She updated the mayor on the investigation.

"Surely you don't think Chase had anything to do with Scott's death? Maybe whatever killed him was accidentally ingested?"

"It doesn't matter what I think. It's an investigation. That means talking to everyone who was close to Scott. Chase should understand that."

Milton considered this for a minute. "I'll talk to Everett. I'm sure he and Chase want to help as much as they can."

"Thank you."

"So what's on your mind, Chief? Great job on Friday with Braden, by the way. I had coffee with Everett this morning."

"Just doing what you pay me for." Hanna sat in the chair in front of the mayor's desk. "I wanted to give you a heads-up. I've taken on a responsibility and I'm not certain that it won't affect my job from time to time."

Evelyn frowned and leaned forward. "What kind of responsibility?"

"It's Joe; the Department of Corrections called me. He's dying. They are giving him compassionate parole and asking that I take him in, give him a place to spend his last days."

Shock crossed the mayor's face, and she sat back in her chair. "What? They're letting Joe Keyes out of prison?"

"Yeah, they contacted—"

"You're sure about this?"

Hanna swallowed, nonplussed by Evelyn's reaction. "It's a state thing. I can show you the letter. You know they must ease overcrowding. Every inmate they can release is being released. The parole board was unanimous—"

"Why is this the first I've heard? Shouldn't there have been public comment before they made such a decision? He caused this town so much pain. Why would you bring him here?"

"I felt an obligation—"

The mayor stood, her brows lowered. "This was not a wise decision."

Anger took her by surprise, and Hanna felt compelled to stand as well, and to defend Joe and the decision she hadn't really made yet. "He's dying, on hospice, so he won't be here long. I've made my decision."

"Huh, best keep this quiet then. A lot of people in this town have long memories. I wouldn't want anything bad to happen."

"What is that supposed to mean?"

"Just that everyone alive during that time will remember those days. They were dark days. It wasn't only the murder, it was the meth that poisoned the county. Joe was cooker. Not to mention the search for the FBI agent. For six months federal officers tore this town up looking for their man. Everyone was affected."

"There was never any evidence that Joe had anything to do with the agent's disappearance."

"It's the principle of the thing. Joe was a dark cloud in our horizon. Your father won't win any popularity contests in Dry Oaks. And with Marshall's book being in so many hands, who knows what some angry person may do."

Hanna knew that was true. It hadn't entered her mind before, but because of the book, everyone in town knew a certain story about what had happened thirty-five years ago.

How would that play in town now?

And if Joe came clean about Mandy's parents, would that help at all?

CHAPTER 22

LIKE A GOLF PUTT THAT CIRCLED THE CUP, going in before popping back out, Hanna's decision about Joe kept going in and out, yes and no. The mayor's anger set her back on her heels. This decision would not simply affect her, Mandy, and the Buckleys, but the whole town. Used to trying hard to look at the whole picture, Hanna wondered why she hadn't seen that issue when she first got the letter.

Back at her office, she dug Jared's phone number out of her desk drawer. After punching the numbers into her phone, she paused. It was almost noon. Was Jared home, or was he still at the fire? He'd have his phone with him either way, and if he didn't want to talk, or couldn't, he could just let it go to voicemail.

Taking a deep breath, Hanna pushed Call.

The phone rang four times. She was about to disconnect when Jared's sleepy voice came over the line. "'Lo."

"Jared? Did I wake you?"

"Hmm, yeah, but it's okay. I needed to get up. What's going on, Hanna?"

"I, ah, well, where are you, at the fire? Or home?"

"Home for a few more hours. Do you need something?"

"I just need to talk to you, run something by you . . ."

"You want to meet somewhere? You want to come here?"

"Ah." Hanna thought for a moment. Did she want to meet somewhere? This was a small town, Jared and her meeting someplace was bound to start tongues wagging.

"I can come by your place. Say when."

"Now, ah, well give me fifteen minutes to shower and get some coffee."

"How about I come by in about forty minutes?"

"Fine, that would be great. See you then."

As Hanna disconnected and sat in her chair, an odd feeling came over her. She shook it off. *I'm only going to talk to him about Joe. That's it.*

❋

Fully awake after Hanna's call, Jared checked the clock and jumped in the shower. Still a few hours left of his leave, so he had time to visit with Hanna. As hot water pounded down on his head, he puzzled about the visit. What on earth could she want? Maybe she wanted to know about the fire lines.

No, she'd get her info about that straight from the fire chief.

Could she want to know what Jude was up to?

No, he doubted she'd come to talk to him here if that were the case.

Lathering up with shampoo and soap, he tried to shut out the questions in his mind. She'd be here soon enough, and he'd find out. He shaved close and dressed in clean jeans and a tank top. Even after using all the soap and water, he could still smell smoke and knew it would be a while before he didn't. He hoped Hanna didn't smell it.

He checked the mirror one more time. Staring at his reflection, he started laughing. He felt as amped-up as a teen going on his first date.

His smile faded. This wasn't a date. Hanna was spoken for, at least for the time being. He paced a bit, still struggling to guess what she wanted to talk to him about.

He hoped she knew about Carver. Surely Hanna knew the disgruntled ex-cop lived next door. Jared peered out the window. The busted SUV was gone. Carver must've had someone come tow it. Jared was surprised he'd not heard, but then he'd fallen asleep as soon as his head hit the pillow. The house looked empty, and there was no audible music. Just then, Hanna's cruiser turned down the drive. Jared opened the door and stepped out onto the porch to greet her.

As Hanna drove up to Jared's house, she almost stopped before turning into his driveway. That's why the address was familiar—Jared was staying right next door to Jude Carver. She saw the smashed mailbox. What was up with that? Hanna was not in the mood to get into it with Carver.

Oh well. She continued down the drive and saw Jared step out his front door. Though she'd seen him many times since his return, today Hanna felt a jolt as if she'd just touched a live wire. Memories exploded in her thoughts like claps of thunder. Ten years had aged him in a good way. He'd been lanky when he left, even thin; his ropey-muscled physique had helped him to be a good rock climber. Jared had been a talented all-around athlete. He never played organized sports, always bristled at the rules and coaching. Structure was not his friend. Even belief in God was too structured for Jared back then.

A thought yanked Hanna like a full stop on an anchor line after a long fall. If things had been different, if Jared had embraced faith and asked Hanna to marry him, she would have run away with him in an instant. But he couldn't and she didn't.

Moving on.

Jared had filled out, shoulders and arms well muscled, his brown hair longer and a little wavy, and Hanna wondered how he liked being a firefighter. Talk about structure. Obviously, a lot had changed besides his build. She'd not been by to talk to him for a lot of reasons. The primary reason being that it made her feel disloyal to Nathan.

That was silly. She wasn't certain her relationship with Nathan would evolve into a serious one. True, she considered him her steady, and she loved being around him, but what she felt for him did not yet meet the intensity of the feelings she'd had for Jared at one time.

That thought jarred her for a minute. Were her feelings past tense?

They had to be. Jared was simply an old school friend; that was how Hanna knew she should see him. A comparison came, unbidden, to her mind: Nathan looked more like an academic, while Jared looked every bit a firefighter, a jock.

It took some mental gymnastics to get the comparison out of her mind. She kept her expression neutral and climbed out of her car. This conversation was to be about Joe, that's all.

"Hello, Jared."

"Hanna. Good to see you." He took a step off the porch. A lock of hair fell over his forehead when he did. He brushed it back with one hand. "I will admit it's been driving me a little crazy."

"What has?"

"Why you suddenly wanted to come see me. Sometimes I feel as if you're avoiding me like the plague."

Hanna stopped about four feet from Jared, holding his gaze, watching his hazel eyes dance.

"Not avoiding. Just staying busy with a lot of stuff."

"Is some of that stuff why you're here?"

She nodded.

"Do you want to come inside? Have something to drink?"

Hanna shook her head. "I won't keep you long. You said you had to go back to work. Can we sit on the porch for a moment?"

"Sure." He swept his arm to point to the two old rockers on the porch.

Hanna walked past him and took a seat, and Jared followed.

"I'll get right to it. It's about Joe."

"Joe?" He stopped halfway into his chair, eyes wide with surprise.

Hanna nodded and then let the words tumble out, telling him about the letter, Nathan, Mandy, and the mayor.

"Wow," he said when she finished. "You have been busy with stuff. And not just plane crashes."

Hanna sat back, exhausted by the recitation. Yeah, *busy* was correct.

Jared leaned forward, elbows on his knees, rubbing his hands together, a pensive expression on his face. "You're not asking me to tell you what you should do, are you?" He looked at her sideways.

"I don't know what I'm asking. You and Mandy are the only two people who understand how difficult it was to have Joe called my father. I know what Mandy thinks, and I'm inclined to say yes for her. But . . ."

"It's a big request, a big responsibility."

She nodded.

"I can understand Mandy wanting closure. She forgave Joe a long time ago. Where her parents' remains are is a loose end." He steepled his hands and tapped his chin with his fingertips. "What about you?"

"What about me?"

"Have you forgiven Joe?"

Hanna took a minute before answering. "Before I got this letter, I would have said yes. But now, I don't know. Joe Keyes has been a monster in name only my whole life." Hanna surprised herself with the answer. She doubted that she would have been as candid with Nathan.

Jared straightened and sat back in the rocker. "Don't look at Joe through your mother's eyes. Paula took everything so personal. What Joe did was horrible, but it was never about your mom. She never saw anything except how her life was affected. I doubt she ever even considered the real victims. I always loved the fact that you never let her bitterness affect you. Don't start letting it do that now."

"You think that's what I'm doing?" His analysis of her mother was spot-on. If Hanna had a nickel for every time her mother moaned about what Joe had done to *her*, she'd have a truckload of nickels.

"I don't know. What I do know is that you are a kind and compassionate woman. I imagine on some level it bothers you to think about Joe dying alone in prison. He's paid for his crimes here, and he'll face God eventually. Dying alone would be an empty death."

Hanna considered this. Joe's crimes should have merited the death sentence. His plea deal forestalled that. Though California had not executed anyone in years, and now had a moratorium against the death penalty, it was unlikely he'd have been put to death even if he'd received that sentence. He'd served thirty-five years in prison. Some killers nowadays got off with much lighter sentences. Looking at the situation as chief of police, could she agree that Joe had paid for his crime?

Am I holding something against him?

"Nothing in this world will bring back Mandy's parents or change what happened that night," Hanna said, looking past Jared to the roadway, thinking out loud. "I know that. Maybe the bottom line is, I just don't know what to say to him." She redirected her gaze to Jared. "Am I supposed to tell him I forgive him? Do I pretend that he didn't tear my mom up, destroy my childhood?"

"That's something else that can't be changed. What do you expect him to do about that now? You survived, came out stronger I bet. There is something to Romans 8:28."

"You think that I should say yes."

"Doesn't matter what I think or don't think." He held out both hands palms up. "Here"—he raised up his left—"is you saying no and never having the chance to talk to Joe about anything, and here"—he lowered his left and raised his right—"is you saying yes and making the mayor and maybe the whole town angry but opening the dialogue with the man who ruined your mother's life. Same weight, but what can you live with?"

Hanna folded her arms. Jared was right. It did all come down to what she could live with. She felt as if a weight slipped off her back and she could stand up straight. An issue that had seemed so clouded a few minutes ago was now crystal clear. Jared did that for her. He seemed to have a clearer vision when it came to difficult subjects.

When they were in high school, Marcus Marshall was interviewed about his book *Murders at Beecher's Mine Cabin*. It was an anniversary interview, she didn't remember which one, and it stirred the subject up again. It was Jared who helped her navigate the questions and the stares.

"It's history, it will always be history. Just make peace with it."

He had come to dinner and even helped calm her mother down.

"That's an even-keeled guy," her mother said, high praise coming from Paula for any man. Hanna wanted to give him a hug. She resisted.

"Thanks, Jared," she said now, then stood, and so did he. "You helped me put things in perspective."

"I wish all problems caused by stuff were so easy. Glad I could help." He shoved his hands in his pockets, and Hanna stepped past him.

She turned back when she reached the bottom step. "Why do you think it makes the mayor so angry?"

"I have thoughts." He leaned against a support post. "She is sweet on Everett; everyone at the station knows that. Maybe she's worried about how this will affect him. Then again, she grew up here too. What is she, ten or fifteen years older than us? Maybe it ruined her teen years in some way. But I would not give her attitude too much sway in your decision."

Hanna reached her cruiser and opened the door. "When do you have to go back to the fire line?"

"Couple hours. The wind dying down has helped a lot. Before you go, can I ask you a question?"

"Sure, what?"

He hopped down one step. "How about dinner one night? Prove you're not avoiding me. I've been back awhile and I'd really like to have time to catch up."

The question both surprised and excited Hanna. *Yes* was on the tip of her tongue. It took a beat for her to answer. She would like to sit down someplace quiet and get reacquainted with Jared. Better sense prevailed.

"Dinner? Ah, I'm seeing someone."

"We're friends, Hanna. Friends talk. Years ago, it was easy for us."

She had to look away from his piercing gaze. "Yeah, it was." Turning back, she said, "I'll think about it. Be careful."

"I will. And Hanna?"

"Yeah?"

"Don't be a stranger."

CHAPTER 23

AFTER LEAVING JARED, Hanna felt confident about her decision. It was the Christian thing to do, to bring Joe home. She would be honoring her father, though she never thought of him that way; more importantly, she'd be honoring God. Hanna still had no idea what she'd say to Joe, but she knew beyond a shadow of a doubt that she'd not be able to live with herself if she'd said no.

Parole would visit her house Wednesday. She texted Nathan and Mandy that information. Mandy responded to Hanna's text by asking to meet for lunch if she hadn't already eaten. Hanna realized she was starving. Her light breakfast had faded a while ago. They planned to eat at the sandwich shop across from the clinic. Hanna was checking to make certain she wasn't needed anywhere else and that things were rolling along smoothly in the field when her phone rang.

"Chief Keyes."

"Hanna, is it true they're letting Joe out?"

She recognized Marcus immediately. He wasn't a full-time reporter anymore, but he did write pieces for the local paper on occasion. Because he'd self-published three true crime books, he liked to call himself the roving crime reporter. The only way he could know this about Joe was if the mayor or Everett had called him, and it was doubtful Everett had made the call. That the mayor would call surprised Hanna. Then again, this was a small town, and there was no way to keep a secret about something like this for long.

"I'm talking with parole about the situation. And he's not being released into the community if that's what you think."

"No, but he was supposed to die in prison. I think that's what the families of his victims wanted."

"He is dying, Marcus. From what I've been told, he's not going to last long. All parole is asking is that he be able to die in a different setting."

"With you?"

"I'll know more after I meet with parole."

"When is that?"

"Frankly, I don't want to get into this with you right now. I consider it a personal matter."

"With how Joe Keyes affected this town? If he comes back, it affects all of us. Does Everett know? He just lost Scott, for heaven's sake. Why would you do this?"

"It's about Joe, not Everett, and yes, I told him of course."

"What did he have to say?"

"Only that it was my decision."

"Hmph."

"That's all I have for you, Marcus. I'm late for a meeting. Goodbye."

She hung up and immediately dialed Everett. He should know that this situation with the letter was going to be in the newspaper and that someone would be calling him. He should hear this from her and not from Marshall.

According to Grover, Everett was not available. All she could do was leave a message and ask him to call her as soon as he could. Then she left to meet Mandy.

The clinic was still a somber place. Edda's death affected everyone. Staffed by mostly volunteers, some were praying, others were crying, and still others were trying to keep on conducting business. Mandy picked at her sandwich. Hanna didn't have much of an appetite either.

"It was harder to come to work today than Saturday. Edda was the heart and soul of the clinic."

"I'm sorry, Mandy, truly I am. And it wouldn't do to close today, would it?"

"No, never. Above all, Edda would want us to save babies."

"I know that." She ate some chips, sipped her iced tea. "Is Brody coming home?"

"No. I told him, of course, but they are in the middle of a competition. I don't want him to cut his trip short. How's Gizmo?" Mandy asked.

"He's good. Seems happy at my house. Cute dog."

"He was Edda's baby. I know that you'll be good for each other."

Hanna smiled. "He is the sweetest little thing. Would it be fair for me to keep him?"

"You'll work it out, my friend." Mandy smiled and patted Hanna's hand. "Maybe you need the watchdog with an ex-con coming to live with you."

"Ha, funny. Thanks, friend." Hanna was happy to see Mandy perk up a little bit. It was good to see, considering the next news she wanted to share.

"I went out and saw Jared today."

Mandy's head jerked up. She was still mad that Jared left town and abandoned Hanna. It did break Hanna's heart.

"Why on earth would you do that?"

"Because I needed his perspective on Joe. You and Jared are my oldest friends. You both understand what I went through growing up. I had a weird meeting with the mayor about Joe, and I needed to run the whole thing by Jared."

"What happened with the mayor?"

Hanna told her.

"Maybe she's afraid there will be negative media attention. She obviously didn't make you change your mind."

"No. In fact, Jared helped me stay on track. Like I texted you, I'm meeting with parole tomorrow. They're coming over to make sure my house is an okay setup for Joe."

"When will he be here?"

"I'm not sure on the timing." Hanna took a bite of her sandwich.

"And you'll let me talk to him?"

"Of course." Hanna finished chewing. "Are you ever going to forgive Jared?"

Mandy huffed. "He didn't devastate me; he devastated my best friend."

"I'm over it. Yeah, it hurt at the time, but . . ." Hanna smiled as she remembered what Jared had said about Romans 8:28. "I've forgiven him. I can't forget how close Jared and I used to be."

"What's funny?"

"Sorry, just something Jared said about God working all things out for good. Jared needed to leave for his own faith journey. Now I'm glad to know that he's embraced faith. That's a good thing."

"Yeah. Leaving you is certainly his loss." Mandy gave her the side-eye.

"What?"

"Just make sure you're looking at Jared in the rearview mirror. Nathan's a nice guy."

"Please." Hanna frowned. "Just because I spent five minutes talking to Jared doesn't mean I've forgotten Nathan. He's a s— great guy." Hanna swallowed when she realized she'd almost said *safe* instead of *great*. Mandy didn't seem to notice.

"Okay, I can lighten up. What did he have to say about Joe?"

"He pointed out that I would have to live with my decision, whichever one I made. And I don't think I could live with saying no. Unless something comes up tomorrow that I can't handle."

"Then let's pray that doesn't happen."

"And that Joe finally comes clean."

Mandy nodded. "Amen."

They both bowed their heads and prayed. Hanna still felt anxious, but not about Joe. She'd made the right decision there, she was certain. But had she made the right choice where Jared and Nathan were concerned?

CHAPTER 24

NATHAN WENT OVER Colby Ellis's statement several times before sending him back to a holding cell. Ellis tried to get Nathan to forget about the warrants, but there was no way that would happen. Ellis had looked at pictures of large, late-model, black SUVs and told Nathan he was certain the car he'd seen was a Chevy Tahoe. That didn't narrow things down. In this part of the county, that was a very popular vehicle, for ownership and as a rental.

Seeing a *Vote Keyes for Chief* bumper sticker told Nathan that not only was the SUV not a rental or someone passing through, it was local. He wished they could narrow it down to only SUVs in the Dry Oaks area, but Hanna's campaign had been supported by people all over the county. Hanna made an impression on people. Even if they couldn't vote for her, a lot of people in the county supported her. They saw her as competent and trustworthy.

He took out all the paperwork related to all three cases and spread it out on a table in the conference room. He pored over everything while he drank strong coffee. Manny had left right after they'd talked to Ellis in order to attend Edda's autopsy. That it was happening so quickly was a good thing. Nathan had been going over the cases when Manny sent a text.

Same caliber bullet—9mm—but too fragmented to test for a match to the same gun.

Nathan was glad to hear that. It pushed the pendulum back to one killer. It had to be one killer. For some reason, he changed tactics with Edda, but it still had to be the same guy.

Manny got back to the office, bearing an expression of guarded optimism. "We got another break. Edda had skin under her fingernails. It looks as if she scratched her attacker. There was enough material that we should get a DNA match."

"Some good news. How long will DNA results take?"

"Don't know yet. Here's a little more good news, though. I stopped by tech crimes on my way here. They got something when they went back over the first two computers." He put a paper down in front of Nathan and pointed out some numbers. "It's interesting and a likely lead . . ."

"But?" Nathan raised an eyebrow.

"Comparing the computers, the first two victims were contacted at least once from the same local network. It's a coffee shop in Sonora. They were both on a dating site called Mix and Match."

"Did they get IP addresses for the computers used?"

"No, suspect used a VPN and/or a burner. All the techies can tell is that the victims were contacted once by someone who was using the coffee shop's network. They can't trace back any further than that."

"Just the first two?"

"Yeah, the third was different. The local address doesn't show up on Edda's device. And she was not on any dating sites. It looks like she connected with this Diego through her son's memorial page on Facebook."

Nathan considered this information. "Could anyone access the memorial page for Bobby?"

"She had it marked public."

"So anyone from anywhere could have engaged her on the site," Nathan said.

"True."

"Still, Edda thought he was pretending, thought she knew him. To me that says we're dealing with a local who did know her."

"Agreed," Manny said. "Even the way he asked for money was softer. He might have been experimenting, fishing, and Edda took the bait. He doesn't seem to need money; he's killing the women giving him money. Maybe it's the con that turns him on, and when he gets bored of the con, he kills."

"And Edda saw through the con, surprising him. He killed her for a different reason than the first two, maybe that upset his MO."

Manny nodded. "Makes sense. I put in the paperwork for the coffee shop warrants, cameras, receipts, everything. We can check the place out."

"Can we speed up the DNA?"

Manny glanced at his watch. "I'll call again tomorrow. Everything concerning the state is slow. Hanna still doesn't have the toxicology back on Scott Buckley from a month and a half ago."

"True. We'll just have to catch this guy without relying on the lab."

"Not a problem, partner. I think this lead at the coffee shop confirms for us that he's local. We will have to dig into every bit of evidence we have in our hands."

"That's what detectives do." Nathan felt energized. The two men shared a fist bump.

They had a local killer who pretended to be elsewhere. It was good to be on the hunt following even the faintest trail.

CHAPTER 25

JARED CHECKED THE CLOCK after Hanna left. He had time to get a good hot meal, and he was starved. Faye's was the ticket. Before he grabbed his keys to leave, he checked his e-mail, and then the local news site, and saw the story about Edda. Shock hit Jared like a punch. He sat down hard in his desk chair. "Not Edda," he whispered.

Bobby had started in with drugs after they graduated from high school, and he and Jared lost touch. Jared had gone to see Edda when he returned to town. They'd had a nice afternoon chat in her dining room over coffee and homemade cookies. She was so happy that Jared had come to faith, and she shared some good stories about his father.

And now she was dead. Tossed on the side of the highway like trash.

Anger kindled and he slammed the computer shut. He wished he'd seen this before he saw Hanna because he would have asked her about it. He'd head to the clinic. Someone there could probably tell him something. Maybe Amanda, if she'd speak to him.

He pulled up to the clinic and saw Hanna's cruiser. A quick survey of the area and he caught sight of her at a table at the sandwich shop, with Amanda. He jogged across the street.

Surprise shot across Hanna's face. "Jared? What are you doing here?"

Amanda turned to face him as well.

"Sorry to interrupt, but I just read about Edda. I can't believe it. What happened?"

Hanna stared at him while Amanda spoke up. "Have a seat. Misery loves company."

Jared sat across from Hanna and next to Amanda.

"You never went to church with me. I didn't know you and Edda were friends," Hanna said.

"I knew her, like everyone else. She and my dad were close. And I was friends with Bobby a long time ago in another life. He ran cross-country with me. Edda and I connected when I got home. Who could do this to someone as sweet as that woman?"

"I don't know much more than what was online. I need to check in. The sheriff's department is handling the case."

"It was someone she met on social media," Amanda said.

"Really? They know who did it already?" This struck Jared as odd. Edda didn't seem to be a computer-savvy person.

"No, that's conjecture." Hanna turned to Amanda. "You can't keep telling people that. You have to let the investigation play out. Jared, detectives are working every angle. I have faith they'll catch the guy."

He rubbed his face with his hands. "She was just, well, like a sweet grandmother. I can't believe anyone could do this. What a cold, soulless person."

"Agreed," Amanda said.

A phone rang, and Hanna glanced at the screen. "This is Everett; I need to take it. Thanks for lunch, Mandy." She put a hand on Jared's forearm. "I'm sorry, Jared. I didn't realize you knew her so well. I would have let you know."

He nodded and watched as Hanna hurried to her car.

"What made you say that it was someone she met online?" he asked Amanda.

"She was sending money to some guy calling himself Diego. He sold her some sob story about trying to overcome substance abuse. You know, like Bobby. He played her, but we think that Edda was on to him. Probably why he killed her."

"You're kidding." Jared tried to remember his long conversation with Edda, but it was months ago. He'd seen her once or twice since then. She attended his fire department graduation ceremony.

"I apologize."

He turned to Amanda, for a moment he'd forgotten she was there. "For what?"

"For thinking that you were a coldhearted jerk. You really did love Edda."

He nodded, throat thick. "I wasn't here when my dad died. I was three thousand miles away, and I missed his funeral. When I got back home, my uncle told me I should go talk to her and I did. It was a wonderful, healing conversation. Because of what she told me, I know my dad is in heaven with my mom. Edda was kind of sweet on the old man. Edwina was a special lady."

"She was. I should have realized how much Bobby's death affected her. I can't believe she was still hurting so much about him that she would let someone online take advantage of her. I was her friend. I should have seen something." Amanda looked so forlorn, Jared's heart broke for her.

"Don't blame yourself, Mandy. Edda never would have wanted that. If there is more to this, I'm sure Hanna will get to the bottom of it." His alarm buzzed. Fire line. "I gotta go. Don't beat yourself up."

Jared jogged to his car. He was heading back to a kind of hell on earth. The kind of environment the guy who killed Edda deserved.

CHAPTER 26

"I JUST GOT A CALL FROM MARCUS MARSHALL," Everett said when Hanna answered the phone.

"Sorry, Everett, I didn't tell him."

"It was only a matter of time before he dug it up. You do know that more inquires will come from this? What have you decided?"

"I'm going to say yes. Mandy wants the chance to talk to Joe, and well, I don't think I could live with myself if I said no. I have a meeting with parole on Wednesday."

The line went quiet.

"Are you still there?" Hanna asked.

"I am. I hope you know what you're doing. I remember vividly the turmoil this town went through over three decades ago. The stress of that time probably killed my father."

Hanna didn't remember exactly when Big Al passed away. She did remember her mother being sad about it.

I hope I know what I'm doing as well. "He's a sick, dying old man."

"Yeah. Do you have an arrival date?"

"Not yet. I'll let you know as soon as I do." She paused briefly and then took advantage of the fact that he was still on the line. "Everett, we still need to talk to Chase about Scott."

Everett said nothing, but she could hear him breathing.

"You can't think he had anything to do with that." It was a clipped, staccato sentence. He almost punctuated every word with a pause.

"It doesn't matter what I think, Everett. We need a formal statement."

"You searched my house and his room, took Scott's laptop and phone, and interviewed me. I doubt Chase can add anything else. I'm tired of all the intrusions."

"The sooner he talks to us, the sooner we'll be out of your hair."

"I'll talk to him and get back to you." The line went dead.

It was the first time Hanna could ever remember Everett being angry. In general, he was easygoing, pleasant. He was not a hard-charging type A personality. Scott was, but not Everett. Hanna chalked it up to grief and loss.

She tried to rub away the tension in her neck. Right now, the advice to keep your world small was perfect. Hanna concentrated on Joe and what it would look like to have him in her home.

Tuesday rolled by in a cloud of administrative duties. Hanna found it hard to concentrate on anything. By Wednesday morning, anticipation for the visit from parole had her imagination running in overdrive. Though she'd made her decision, worst-case scenarios flooded her thoughts. What if Joe was a disgusting old con, vicious and mean? What if he was unrepentant? What could she expect from a man nearing his sixties who'd spent more of his life in jail than he had free?

On top of everything, she was getting attached to Gizmo as well. Something about the dog calmed her, gave her peace. They walked in the warm, dry morning, just before the sun rose. Then she'd feed him, and he'd curl up somewhere. When she was on the couch, he'd curl up in her lap. There was something so settling in petting a sleeping dog. Hanna would have to find a way to make it work because there was no way she could give the dog to Mandy.

Nathan offered to try and take time off to be with her when parole got here, but she wanted to handle it on her own, and she didn't want to take him away from Edda's investigation. Besides that, she wasn't certain Nathan really understood the situation with Joe. At least not the way Jared or Mandy would.

She walked into her guest room with Gizmo on her heels. So far, the only people who had used it were a visiting missionary couple. The people Hanna bought the house from had been older, and the husband was confined to a wheelchair. The guest room had an en suite bath with a shower made to accommodate a wheelchair. With everything that had been happening in her life, Hanna hadn't really thought about the nuts and bolts of everything, but that was probably a perfect situation for Joe.

She leaned against the doorframe, considering the bedroom, and became more convinced that she was doing the right thing. God had provided her this house long before she ever knew she'd be hosting an invalid.

There was a knock on the front door. Parole was early.

Hanna went to the door only to discover that it wasn't parole; it was Marcus Marshall with a film crew.

"What do you want, Marcus?" Hanna asked, keeping the screen door closed.

"I want an interview. I want you to justify why you're bringing a monster back to our town."

"I don't have to justify anything to you. I'm agreeing to a request made by the California Department of Corrections. They've assured me that Joe is no longer a threat."

"He was sentenced to life without the possibility of parole. This flies in the face of that sentence."

"It's a compassionate release, Marcus. And I'm not going to argue with you. I've nothing more to say. I'll have to ask you all to leave."

"You're the chief; we elected you. I'll remind you that you got my vote. You owe us an explanation."

"Having Joe come here has nothing to do with my official duties. Technically, you all are trespassing. I'm asking nicely that you leave."

Hanna looked over Marcus's shoulder as two more cars pulled up in front of her house. One was a state vehicle; the other was a plain sedan. She tensed. Was Marcus going to make this a circus? She recognized Tom Nelson and PO Giles as they got out of the state vehicle.

"Is this the parole officer?" Marcus turned to follow her gaze. He didn't wait for an answer but strode away from Hanna's porch toward PO Giles. While he fielded their questions, Nelson dodged around the crowd and stepped up to her door.

"Hello, Hanna."

She thought about Tom's story. Before her time as an officer, Tom had been a problem for police. A member of a local motorcycle gang, Tom was tatted up and used to like to get drunk and start fights. One day he started a fight in a bar. Other bikers joined in the brawl, and a man was stabbed to death. Tom was not charged with the killing, but according to his testimony, it changed his life.

Feeling responsible, he went to the man's family and begged for forgiveness. He expected to be beat up, spit at, anything, but he was completely forgiven. The family was professing Christians, and they took Tom to their church. He came to faith and completely turned his life around.

Today he was the local prison chaplain. He lived in Sonora and went to a different church than Hanna did, but she'd met him in various places and even listened to a couple of messages he gave about ministering to those behind bars. He believed anyone could change. God could redeem any soul, no matter how heinous the crime. Hanna believed that as well. At least she thought she did—until it came to Joe.

"Hi, Tom. You're going to help Joe settle in?"

"Yes. I've often chatted with your father. I—"

"I don't consider him my father. You can call him Joe. You talk to him? How is this the first I've heard of it?"

"My conversations and my relationships with inmates are private and guarded. I only mention it now because I've asked him if it was okay to tell you and he said yes."

Hanna considered this. "You've been thinking about his release for a long time now."

"I have. People change. Joe made mistakes and he admits to them. He is not a bad man, not now. I think he deserves some grace."

"Hmmm." Hanna's attention shifted back to Marshall and Giles because Marshall's voice had risen. "Should I try to stop that?" she asked Tom.

He shook his head. "Giles can take care of himself."

He was correct. In another minute, Giles and the woman with him were headed their way and the TV crew was leaving.

"Hello again, Chief Keyes." Giles approached.

"Hello. You can call me Hanna."

"Call me Gordon." They shook hands. He nodded to the woman. "This is Grace, part of the hospice team."

Hanna shook Grace's hand. "Why don't you all come inside?"

Even as she stood aside so they could enter, turmoil gripped her. She arrested people like her father, glad to get them off the streets. Was Marcus right? Was she making a bad decision?

She cast one last glance at Marshall and the TV crew and then led the three people inside.

CHAPTER 27

By Wednesday Nathan felt stretched. He'd offered to be with Hanna today and felt relieved that she'd declined. He'd barely slept the last few days. Things were going agonizingly slow with the murder investigation. He hoped to hear from the state lab on how quickly they'd get a DNA profile. While the coffee shop in Sonora was a good lead, it didn't come without negatives. Their recordings were only kept thirty days, so there was no way to view any of the footage from months ago.

He'd showered, dressed, and come to the shop to scope out the clientele. He sat with a double-shot espresso, combing through his notes and looking up to people watch. Tech crimes had been working hard to trace the money the three women had sent, but it was virtually impossible. Catfish asked for gift cards precisely because they were difficult to trace. Diego/Franco/Gerard was slick and crafty. He used burner phones and VPNs for each victim because trying to trace the victim's last message to the receiver had proven to be impossible.

Nathan sipped his coffee and let his gaze wander. He had a seat in the back of the shop with a view of the front door and the service counter. It was a long shot to hope the perpetrator would be here now, scoping out another victim, but Nathan wanted to get a feel for the place and its customers. If the killer kept to his timeline, they likely had a month before he killed again. Nathan would not bet anyone's life on that. From what Edda's scene looked like, the guy was escalating.

The customers in the shop were a mix, a nice cross section of humanity. Old, young, and in between. In one corner four senior ladies sipped coffee and chatted. Along the back wall, three singles, each at their own table, were deeply involved in their laptops. Two of them had earbuds and they seemed to be scanning websites, from what Nathan could see. The third was typing fast sometimes and slowly at others.

At another table a man and woman sat, each with a cup of coffee and intently concentrating on their own phones. At another an older gentleman read the newspaper and munched on a bagel. In the front of the shop at an outside table, three young moms with small children were having an animated, happy conversation. There was an endless stream of customers purchasing coffee and food and then leaving. No one in the place looked like a loner trying to hook up online. Of course, a weekday morning might be the wrong time of day to be in the shop.

Nathan watched the door, hoping someone would come in and activate his cop sense. He wished Hanna were here. She had great intuition and was one of the best people readers he'd ever known. And she was good company. Nathan enjoyed every moment he'd spent with her.

Marcus Marshall came in with his laptop. He picked up a large coffee, took a look around the place as if he were searching for someone, and then saw Nathan. He walked over to his table.

"Detective, something happening here I should know about?"

"Just good coffee." Nathan held up his cup. "You come here to work?" He pointed at the laptop.

"Writing my story about Chief Keyes bringing that murderer back to our town. Just spoke with the parole officer." Marshall made a face. "What a bunch of hogwash about Joe not being a threat. How does that sit with the sheriff's department?"

"Pretty much that it's her decision. Hanna needs to do what's right for Hanna." Nathan hoped the visit from parole was positive for her.

"It sets a bad precedent, letting a killer out like this."

"The state needs to reduce the prison population. Seems the ones who are the least threatening should be the ones to be let go."

"It's still wrong. I have to write about this travesty. People care about the safety of their communities. The book will be a guaranteed bestseller." He saluted Nathan with his coffee cup and walked off to a table in the back.

A few minutes later, Nathan saw another familiar face. In through the door walked Jude Carver. Nathan's gaze hardened on the man. He'd been a thorn in Hanna's side and that made Nathan angry.

The guy still walked like a cop, as if he wore a gun belt and was looking for a suspect. He surveyed the shop, sweeping the room with his gaze. His eyes rested on Nathan, and surprise registered briefly before Carver caught himself and his features went blank. He ordered coffee, and after he paid and grabbed the cup, he strolled over to where Nathan sat.

"Waiting for your girlfriend there, Nate?" Carver sipped his coffee, the smirk on his face making him look like a three-year-old who just stole a cookie.

"I'm working, Jude. *I* have a job." He couldn't resist the juvenile taunt.

Carver's features darkened. "Yeah, about that. I'll win in court, my job and back pay. I don't need to litigate it here. Just that you need to watch that gal of yours. She's two-timing you for sure. Seems she prefers firefighters to cops now."

"What are you talking about?"

"Just that women are fickle. Any man in uniform is a catch. Especially when old friends are involved." Carver grinned and left the shop.

Nathan frowned. What was that jab about? Two-timing? Jude meant Jared Hodges. He knew Hanna still had feelings for Hodges, even though she wouldn't admit it. It bothered him more than he liked to admit. He had no idea how to broach the subject with her.

He sat back in his seat. Jude's jab had done what he had intended—and that made Nathan even angrier at the guy. Before he could let his mind run too far down that rabbit trail, Manny arrived. He saw Nathan right away.

"You look like week-old roadkill," Manny said when he sat at Nathan's table.

"I didn't get much sleep last night." Nathan finished his double-shot espresso and hoped the caffeine would jolt him awake. He put Jude Carver out of his mind. "I keep praying for a smoking gun, a surprise ID, something."

"That would be nice," Manny said. "I spoke to the lab supervisor about the fingernail scrapings. She's confident we have enough to get a full profile. Edda might have caught her own killer."

"How long do we have to wait?"

Manny gazed down at the ground. "Yeah, that's the bad part. It could take a couple of months. They're backlogged."

Nathan threw his hands up. "We could have two more victims by then."

"They know there's an urgency. The downside is just because we get a profile doesn't mean the guy is in the system."

"True. I'm hoping something will point to a guy we can start watching. With a profile already in hand, we'd just have to find a way to get a sample from the guy."

Manny looked around. "Anyone catch your eye here?"

Nathan immediately thought of Jude Carver. He didn't like the guy, but that didn't make him a killer.

"No. Just that it is a busy place. Someone could blend in here for just about any purpose."

CHAPTER 28

THE HOSPICE NURSE LIKED THE SPACE in Hanna's home. "All we need to do is have a hospital bed moved in. We can have that done later today. Other than that, this room, your house, looks perfect for a man on hospice," Grace said.

"I realized that this morning," Hanna agreed. "The room was designed for older, less mobile people. I'm hardly ever home. That's why I haven't had a dog until now. It wouldn't be fair."

Nervousness had Hanna wanting to talk. Gizmo seemed to sense her anxiety and pawed at her leg to be picked up. She did so, barely giving it a thought. So many questions were going through her mind. Ones she didn't know how to ask and ones she was afraid to ask.

"You probably have a lot of questions," Tom said, reading her mind.

"I don't know where to start."

Tom and Giles exchanged a glance.

"I'd better start with full disclosure." Tom reached into his pocket and pulled out a letter. "This is from your fa— Joe. He asked that you read it before we finalize anything." He held it out, and Hanna hesitated, awash in emotion. Something Joe had written. For her.

"What is it?"

Tom shrugged. "It's for you to read."

Haltingly, she reached out, and Tom put the letter in her hand.

In an instant, Hanna was a small child again, hiding in the library, looking through a book she wasn't supposed to have for a photo of a father she'd never met.

She set the dog on the couch, then held the number ten envelope in both hands. Her name was printed in neat block letters across the front. *Chief Hanna Keyes.*

Hanna swallowed, turned the envelope over, slid her finger through the top, and pulled out the letter. The same neat block printing covered about a quarter of the page.

Hanna,

You don't know me. I only saw you once, and you were just a button, so I expect it's hard for you to call me Dad. You probably haven't given me much thought over the years, and I don't blame you. Saying I'm sorry doesn't fix anything, but I'm sorry for missing out on your life. Some days you're all I think about. But this ain't about me. The state is making a request of you, a hard thing. I want you to know that if you say no, I don't hold nothing against you. Don't say yes because you think you have to honor a man who was never there for you. I'm a happy man knowing you've done so good for yourself in this life. I'm proud of you. No matter what, I'll die a blessed man.

Love, Joe Keyes, "Dad"

Throat thick, Hanna looked up from the letter to see Tom and Giles discreetly looking the other way. She slid the letter back in the envelope, wiped her eyes, and cleared her throat.

"I've already decided the answer is yes, Tom." She kept the letter in one hand and let her other hand drop to her side. "When would Joe be brought here?"

Giles answered. "We will process him out quickly. Hopefully, it will only take a couple of days. He is still somewhat ambulatory. Once we get him here, a person from the hospice team will be with him twenty-four seven. They will handle his oxygen and pain management. Right now, the only change is putting the hospital bed in your guest room. Joe can't sleep lying flat. His lung capacity is very poor, and the head of the bed needs to be raised."

"Is he in a lot of pain?"

"Occasionally," Tom said. "His lung cancer has metastasized to his spine and bones."

Hanna nodded. For the next few minutes, Giles and Tom explained to her the process of a compassionate release. He also highlighted the fact that Joe had a spotless record in prison. He followed the rules and did not cause problems. The prison doctor gave him one month at best. It was a no-brainer to offer the compassionate release to him.

Hanna listened and interjected at times. Still, her mind stuck on the words *I'm proud of you.* She could not understand why those words affected her so, but they burned like a fire in her mind—and heart.

CHAPTER 29

JOE EXPECTED THE VISITOR. Other than Chaplain Tom, an occasional reporter over the years, the Feds a few times asking about DEA Agent Gilly, and one brief visit from Paula, there had been no visitors in thirty-five years. But he knew his release would bring people out of the woodwork. People who'd been safe in the darkness for all these years. Those same people now smelled blood in the water where he was concerned, and someone would come. He wasn't disappointed.

"Keyes, you have a visitor. Are you up to it?"

Joe nodded and slowly got to his feet. It took him some time to walk to the visiting area, and his breath got short, but he made it there. His breathing labored, waiting for him to speak first, he sat and stared at the man on the other side of the glass.

"I hear you're getting out."

"Maybe. Not sure a final decision's been made." The eyes on the other side of the glass were hard, the glare meant to intimidate. Funny thing about knowing that you were dying, Joe thought. You didn't intimidate easily. As Joe held the man's glare, he thought he saw something else there, maybe fear.

"I think it has. You'd better tread lightly, Joe. You'd better be careful."

"I don't have anything to lose anymore."

"Not true. Police officers are killed every day in this country. It happens. I'd hate for anything to happen to your daughter."

Joe swallowed. This was his Achilles' heel, he knew it. But he also knew that he had to trust God for Hanna.

"You're afraid of the truth coming out. I won't spill it. I gave my word a long time ago. I keep my word. But the funny thing about truth, it wants to be heard. And it always has a way of bursting forth."

"You better hope it doesn't in this case." He shoved the chair back and left the room.

While Joe waited for the jailer to come for him, he prayed. For Hanna, for the man who'd just left, and for the truth.

❧

Hanna sat in her kitchen and reread the letter from Joe. The shock of how much it affected her had faded.

What did she expect? He'd be here, in this house. She'd have to talk to him. The reality of the situation sunk in like a heavy stone.

After all this time, what am I supposed to feel? Say? Do?

The doctor gave him less than a month. An eternity. If he was the man her mother described, Hanna would hate him.

She refused to think of the other alternative—her mother's view was skewed, and Joe was a good man. That couldn't be true— he brutally murdered two people.

She was hardly ever home. She'd rarely see him. And when he died, it would simply be the end of an unpleasant chapter. There was no comfort in that thought, and Hanna was happy when the shrill sound of an emergency call blared from her radio.

"All units, 999—officer needs assistance—all available units, respond to the Gold Dust Bar, all available units . . ." The dispatcher's voice was calm and clear, but it still set Hanna's heart pumping. She never wanted to hear a 999 code. One of her people was in a bad way and needed all the help he could get right away.

Hanna roared to the parking lot of the bar, code 3. All the units on duty this time of day were already on-scene, and a large crowd milled about, some people still spilling out of the bar. One of her officers had a bloody lip. She notified dispatch she was on-scene and got out to help. She strode to Asa, who was struggling with a large man he'd just handcuffed.

"Asa, what's going on?" Hanna grabbed the man to lend a hand. The pungent smell of alcohol radiated from the man's sweat.

"Bar fight that spilled out into the street. Jenna got clocked by this guy."

"It was an accident! She got in the way," the drunk man protested. "I don't hit girls. I was trying to hit someone else." Despite his protestations, Drunk Guy was securely handcuffed. Hanna helped put the man in the patrol car.

"Yeah," Asa said when he closed the door. "He was. Trying to hit Jude Carver, he's the one who started this mess." He then got on the radio and called code 4 on the situation. Everything was under control.

Hanna shook her head. Jude Carver was bad news from start to finish. She turned to Jenna, the officer with a bloody lip. She held her left hand protectively. "You okay?"

Jenna nodded. "Mostly. When he hit me, I went down, and there were several groups of people fighting. That's when Carver split." She held up her hand. "Someone stepped on my hand. I think it's broken. Everything was out of control, so I hit the emergency button."

"You needed backup, that was a good call. Carver is at the root of all this. You didn't see where he went?"

Jenna looked around. "No. And I don't see him now. At one point he was with Chase Buckley."

"Chase Buckley was here?"

That was a surprise. Chase was rarely seen around town, and when he was, he was low-key. Hanna did a quick crowd survey; she didn't see him. She saw her people interviewing witnesses and the crowd rapidly dispersing. Jock, the owner of the Gold Dust Bar, waved his arms around in an animated conversation with someone. It was probably about the damage to his establishment. She'd have to calm him down.

Hanna turned back to Jenna. "I'll take you to urgent care. Asa, are you going to book the assailant?"

"Yeah, he's in my car. I've got enough of an idea about what went on to book him."

"How did Carver start all this?"

Her officers exchanged glances.

"He was drunk and bad-mouthing the department. Just being obnoxious as usual. The crowd got riled, somebody threw beer on somebody, and things escalated," Jenna explained. "It's so hot and dry today, everyone is on edge, even cranky. Tempers are as volatile as the dry grass. Carver was just the match."

"Wait in my car. I'll go talk to Jock and then take you to urgent care."

Jenna nodded and opened the passenger door.

Hanna felt uneasy suddenly, creeped out. She got the distinct impression someone was watching her. Jerking around, she saw him.

Chase Buckley. He was in the doorway of the tavern.

What surprised Hanna was that he was standing; there were no crutches. He leaned on a cane, and he had a prosthetic leg. How long had he had that?

He didn't look happy, but then the few times she'd seen him, Chase never looked happy. The scarring on the right side of his face made certain he'd never smile. And he looked old. Chase was probably in his sixties. Maybe even the same age as Joe Keyes.

Had Everett told Chase about Joe? Probably. Forgetting Jock, she headed Chase's way. "Hello, Chase."

He nodded, dropped his cigarette on the ground, and crushed it with the end of his cane.

"I hear your daddy's getting sprung," he said, his raspy voice difficult to hear.

"Yes. He'll be on hospice."

He cursed. "A lot of people aren't happy that he's getting out."

"People like you?" Hanna kept her voice level.

"He should have gotten the chair."

"Well, he's got a death sentence now, one there is no parole from." Thinking of her mother's sad life, she added, "Will you hang on to your anger for the rest of your life, Chase?"

"Hmph." He straightened. "I know the guy better than you do. He crossed me more than once. Don't trust your daddy. That would be a mistake."

"We still need to sit down and talk about Scott, the morning he died."

He didn't meet her gaze. "I didn't kill my brother. I wouldn't mess with poison."

"Did you see or hear anything that morning?"

A jerk of his head she took for a no.

"Did anyone have a beef with Scott?"

Another jerk.

"I heard that Scott planned to take Braden to Corte Madera. Was that fine with you?"

Chase hiked a shoulder. "Planning and doing are two different things."

"You didn't like the idea?"

"He's my grandson. He'll stay with me." Chase's tone was flat, devoid of emotion. Not what she'd expect if he was passionate enough to fight for his son.

"How about Marcus Marshall? Did Scott have a bone to pick with him?"

That got a different reaction, as if Hanna hit a nerve. Chase glared at her. "Marcus?"

"I heard that he had a fight with Scott. Is Marcus writing a book about your family?"

He made a sound that Hanna thought was a chuckle. "You're way off track."

"Enlighten me."

"Marcus rubbed Scott the wrong way since high school. That's just Marcus. He's always been soft."

"If he didn't kill your brother, who do you think did?"

"Someone at the airfield, it has to be."

An SUV pulled up; Hanna saw Grover in the driver's seat.

"I got to go." Chase turned his back on her and made his way to the passenger side. Limping, using the cane, but navigating okay.

Hanna watched him. He'd lost his right eye and part of his left leg, but after his brother died, he'd still been cleared to drive. Rumor was that Everett had paid people off to get Chase his license back. Hanna never put much stock in rumors. In her lifetime, she could count on the fingers of one hand how many times she'd seen Chase out and about, so she figured he didn't drive much.

A thought occurred to Hanna. Chase and her father were the only two people who knew what exactly happened that night thirty-five years ago at Beecher's Mine cabin. Chase always claimed he had no idea what had happened to Mandy's parents. As the story went, he was doused with acid first and then woke up in intensive care.

"Chief, Chief."

Hanna turned, her train of thought derailed by Jock. He'd calmed down but was still visibly angry. She forgot Chase and listened to Jock's complaints and concerns. He was angry with Carver but didn't want to press charges.

"It would help us if you do press charges, Jock."

"Sorry, Chief, I can't. Yeah, he did start things with his big mouth, but others had the choice to walk away, and they didn't. I think I will ban him from the bar, though."

"Your choice."

Hanna returned to chief mode and shut out the daughter of Joe Keyes. Something she hoped she could still do when he was residing in her home.

CHAPTER 30

AFTER THE COFFEE SHOP, Nathan and Manny split up. Manny went back to the office to work on the list of Chevy Tahoes registered in the area. Nathan spent most of the day retracing their steps with Jane Haskell. He traveled to Twain Harte and reinterviewed everyone he could. He got lucky and reached the first victim's landlord, who had not been around when they did their first canvass.

"I was shocked to hear what happened to Jane," the woman said. "She'd been scammed before online, gave the scammer a lot of money. She was lonely, I tried to set her up with a friend, but she was a sucker for an interesting online profile, I guess."

"She told you about the prior scam?"

"Grudgingly. She was embarrassed. I thought she'd learned her lesson then," she said. "Poor gal thought she was being romanced by Orlando Bloom. She got behind two months on the rent. Had to take on a second job. You're saying she was mixed up with a scammer again?"

"It looks that way."

The landlord shook her head. "She never said a word to me about being involved with someone online again. Maybe she was afraid I'd remind her of what happened before."

Nathan nodded, thinking she could have felt a little ashamed, or maybe the scammer told her not to say anything. They had so little to go on, he was getting frustrated.

"This whole online dating thing is risky," he commented to Manny on the phone. He'd called to give him an update as Nathan was heading back to Sonora and the second victim's address.

"A person can say anything, pretend to be anything online. People should meet and date the old-fashioned way."

"Bars and pickup joints?" Manny asked.

"No, church, school, the community. In person at least."

"True. It's easier to hide behind the computer for some people. Especially whack jobs who want to victimize others."

"Yeah, and sad that people are so lonely they'll believe scammers and send money to perfect strangers."

✤

Busy at her desk, Hanna got the call late in the afternoon that Joe would be brought to her house the next day.

"That was fast," Mandy said when Hanna told her.

"Yeah, well, apparently the state got dinged by another inmate who was supposed to be released on hospice. They took so long approving the release that the guy died in prison. This after parole assured his family he'd be able to die at home. They sued. So the state moves a lot faster now."

"Are you ready?"

Hanna thought for a moment. "I don't know. As ready as I'll ever be, I guess. From what Giles, the parole officer, told me, Joe has been an exemplary prisoner. He . . ." Hanna stopped, wanting to pick the right words. While Hanna tended to always look for the best in people, she didn't believe in jailhouse conversions. It was easy to behave well in such a structured environment where consequences were quick and sure. It was only living out in life and freedom that someone could prove their heart.

"What were you going to say?"

"Just that Tom Nelson, you know, the prison chaplain, says Joe is a committed Christian now." Hanna shrugged. "Maybe he is, and maybe he isn't. I'll just wait and see."

"I only want to know about my parents. Joe can claim to be a Martian if he wants. One thing surprises me. Marcus Marshall is sure doing his best to stir up animosity toward your dad."

"I noticed. Did he call you?"

"Me and my grandma. He wanted us to be outraged that Joe is being released."

"What does your grandma say?"

"What you'd expect. He tried to dredge up all the horribleness of the crime. She just said that she'd forgiven him a long time ago and now prayed for his soul."

"Your grandma is special."

"She is. I love my nana. As Christians we're all called to forgive. I hope that is the response Marshall gets from everyone. I wonder if he's gone after Everett."

"I'm sure he has. Everett is none too happy, I can tell you. I doubt forgiveness is in his vocabulary."

"Granny prays for him too, and for Chase."

"I saw Chase yesterday. He was at Jock's place."

"I heard the ruckus on the scanner. What happened there?"

"Carver started a big fight."

"Carver needs to find a new place to call home. Was Chase involved? He never comes to town."

"I don't think he had anything to do with the fight. He was just there socializing, I guess, and he warned me about Joe."

"Warned?"

"He said I can't trust him. Told me not to be fooled."

"Hmm. Hanna, I think the best thing you can do is greet Joe with an open mind, asking God for discernment. Everyone deserves that, until they prove otherwise."

In principle, Hanna agreed with the sentiment. But in practice, she knew that people proving otherwise could do some awful things. What was Joe Keyes capable of?

CHAPTER 31

HANNA WAS UP EARLY ON WEDNESDAY, more nervous than she thought she'd be. She checked her computer for news, knowing that Marcus had plenty of contacts to leak the fact that Joe would be coming to her house today. It was the comments generated by his story about Joe's imminent release that surprised her the most.

"It was thirty-five years ago, for heaven's sake. The guy is dying. Give him a break."

"It's a good idea to save taxpayer money. Let the guy die in peace."

"If the people most affected by old crime don't mind, why should we?"

All his efforts to stir up animosity seemed to have failed. Would he show up here this morning? Surprisingly, even the mayor had lightened up. She'd called Hanna the night before and apologized for overreacting.

Hanna filled her cup with coffee and sat in the living room with her Bible, trying to do a devotion while she waited.

The hospice team arrived first. Grace was the nurse and Arthur was the aide. They explained that one person from the team would be at her house all the time, tending to Joe.

"He wants to be totally independent," Grace said. "But he can't be. He gets short of breath easily, which will only get worse, and he is a fall risk, even with his walker."

They were half of the four-person team. With them came medical supplies, a nebulizer, an oxygen tank, and a few other items. They took the items into the guest room and began to set up the area for Joe.

Hanna felt a little guilty at the relief she felt that there would be very little she would have to do for Joe. Other than provide the room for him.

Shortly after the hospice team arrived, Marcus showed up, film crew in tow. They set up on her front lawn. Just as she thought, someone spilled the beans. Hanna went out to talk to him. The last thing she wanted was a media circus. When she stepped outside, she saw her next-door neighbor out on the lawn watching. Her across-the-street neighbor was also watching from his porch.

"Marcus, why are you doing this? What do you hope to prove?"

"I'm not proving anything. I'm warning people. We have a serial killer running around the county slaughtering women, while you're letting a really bad criminal out."

"One thing has nothing to do with the other. Joe is not a threat to anyone."

"I'm a newsman. I'm giving people the news."

Hanna turned at the sound of a motor. The Department of Corrections van rolled slowly up the street. Her heart caught in her throat. This was the moment of truth. Marshall turned to his cameraman and directed him to set up and start filming. More neighbors came out of their houses to watch.

Hanna stood still, unable to do anything else. Giles got out of the passenger seat. She could hear the conversation.

"Please, guys," he said to Marshall and the cameraman, "let us get him out and into the house."

"I have questions for him," Marshall said. "Will he answer my questions?"

"Now is not the time," Giles said, hand on the van's sliding-door handle.

"There is no better time than the present." Marshall waved the cameraman closer.

Giles shook his head and opened the door.

Tom stepped out first. He reached back in the van and pulled out a wheelchair, set it on the sidewalk, and opened it up, then set the brake.

Hanna held her breath.

Tom leaned back inside, and he appeared to be having an argument with someone—Joe, she guessed. After a few minutes, Tom threw his hands up, then pulled a walker out of the van. Moving the wheelchair out of the way, he opened the walker on the sidewalk. A hand reached out of the van and Tom grasped it.

Hanna watched, transfixed, as an old man emerged from the van, slowly and very unsteadily. Joe was sixty and he looked eighty. She couldn't help but think of the contrast between Joe and Everett. Everett was nearly eighty but he looked sixty.

Joe had a full head of steel-gray hair, an oxygen nasal cannula, and a small O_2 tank on his shoulder. With Tom supporting him on one side and Giles standing by on the other, Joe stepped out of the van and grabbed the walker. Once both hands were on it, he looked up.

Marshall started in with questions, and Joe turned toward him.

"What did you do with the bodies, Joe?"

Hanna barely heard. Her heart pounded in her chest, the thumping drowning out all other sound. Joe was so much smaller than she'd expected. The only picture of him that stayed in her head was the one she'd seen years ago in the library book. He'd been so large, towering over her mother. Of course back then, Hanna had been a child. Everyone was bigger than she was. Though she'd seen his picture many times since that day, it was that first glimpse that had stayed with her.

The man gripping the walker was decrepit and unimposing. Certainly not fear inspiring.

"Come on, Joe, it's long past time. Tell us where the bodies are buried." Marcus would not give up.

Joe said nothing, but a smile played upon his lips. Giles spoke into his ear, and they started walking up the walk. Joe's gait was slow and steady. He paused every few steps. He walked better than Hanna would have thought. At one point, he looked up and saw her. He paused, stood up straight, and held her gaze.

Hanna's mouth went dry. Her heart had stopped its pounding, but she had no words. This man was a total stranger to her, but there was a connection. She felt it. Marshall stepped in between them, badgering Joe with more questions. To Hanna his tone grated.

"That's enough, Marcus." She strode forward. "He's got nothing to say right now. Giles, let's get him into the house."

"You can't protect him forever," Marcus protested.

"No, but I can protect him for as long as he's got left. Give it a rest, Marcus."

Grace hurried down the walk by then, and she and Giles got Joe moving toward the house.

Marcus backed off, but the camera kept filming. Hanna got ahead of Joe and entered the front door. She picked Gizmo up and braced herself for the man with the walker to come inside.

CHAPTER 32

JOE'S ARRIVAL WAS ANTICLIMACTIC. The activities of the day, the walk up to the house all served to wear him out.

"I tried to get him to use the wheelchair," Tom explained. "He wouldn't have it."

Grace had him settled into the hospital bed in the guest room. She raised the back of the bed so he was in a sitting position and busily arranged his oxygen tank.

"He needs to calm down and rest. Too much exertion makes it difficult for him to catch his breath."

Hanna stood in the doorway for a moment and saw him in the bed, chest heaving, Grace helping him with a nebulizer. Giles had carried in a small valise and set it on the chair next to the bed. He said it contained all of Joe's belongings. Next to the valise he set a large well-worn Bible.

How am I supposed to feel? The pit of her stomach had that funny feeling you get when you're on a roller coaster at the top of the ride, preparing to drop down at high speed.

After stepping out of the doorway, she went to the kitchen and filled her travel mug with coffee. She had to go to work. Her insides were a jumble. She wasn't certain adding caffeine to the mix was a good thing, but the smell and taste of coffee was a comfort.

"He'll be better after he rests a bit," Tom said.

"It looks as if Grace has things under control." Hanna screwed on the mug's lid.

"I agree. The entire hospice team are good at their jobs."

"How long will you be here?"

"I'll stick around for a bit. I know you have work to do. Things will be fine here if you're worried."

"I'm not worried." She paused. "I don't know what I am, to be honest. This is just strange."

"I can imagine. You're a cop; he's a crook. Look past that, Hanna. Try and look at him as a soul who will be facing his maker soon."

Hanna considered Tom's advice as she got in her car and headed to the station. It didn't help. Seeing Joe, having him in her house was *Twilight Zone* territory. She wanted to talk to Jared. Maybe Mandy. Hanna winced when she realized Nathan was last on the list. As great as he was, Nathan wouldn't understand her mixed feelings regarding Joe. The realization made her sad.

When Hanna pulled into the station, she recognized Everett's truck parked at the curb. She bet he wanted to talk to her about Joe. He waited in her office.

"Good morning, Everett."

"Chief."

"How can I help you?"

"Is Joe settled in?"

"Yes. The whole transfer here wore him out. He was out of it when I left."

Everett seemed to consider this. "That Marshall is certainly trying to stir things up."

"He is. I haven't noticed that he's been successful, as hard as he's trying."

"True. This is a good town, a compassionate town." He steepled his fingers. "Joe's presence does stir up a lot of pain for me."

"I'm sorry, Everett. I'm really hoping he'll tell Mandy what she wants to know. Then maybe this will be worth it."

He grunted. "When will she talk to him?"

"I guess when he's up to it."

"Let me know before Marcus finds out."

"I don't plan on telling Marcus anything."

"Hmph, he always seems to hear about everything. Don't let any of this distract you from your job."

"I won't. I'm on top of things."

"I've got to get back to the fire line."

"I heard things look good there."

Everett nodded. "The weather is in our favor right now. The wind has calmed, and what there is of it is blowing away from us. That fire will be burning for a while though, especially if we don't get any rain."

"It doesn't look like any rain is in the forecast." Was something else on Everett's mind? He didn't appear to be ready to leave, and she had work to do. She was about to ask when he spoke up.

"That was a dark time in this town, a horrible crime." Everett seemed to be staring right through her. "I know your mother filled you in on what specifics she knew. The thing is, no one really knows all the particulars except for Joe. Chase doesn't, that's for sure. It's as if he lost time after the acid burns. If Joe cares to share those details, please let me know."

"Count on it."

Nathan glanced at the clock. Joe was most likely settled into Hanna's house by now. He'd wanted to be there when Joe came home, but the case kept him away. He hated to admit it, but he wanted to talk to Joe. If he'd been running the investigation thirty-five years ago, there were a lot of questions he'd have asked Joe that had not been asked. Would he get the chance to talk to the guy?

As far as the investigation into the Lonely Heart Killer was going, Manny had compiled a list of black SUVs to check. The number of black Chevy Tahoes registered in the county was huge. It needed to be pared down.

Edda's red VW Bug had not been discovered yet, but Nathan was not anxious for that. The other two victims' cars had not yielded any evidence, and he doubted that Edda's would either. It would probably just turn up somewhere like the other victims' vehicles had.

It still bothered Nathan that Edda was not on a dating website. He wasn't leaning toward there being two killers anymore. What he feared now was that the killer was evolving. He'd gotten some type of thrill by killing women who thought he wanted to be their boyfriend. Maybe it wasn't enough of a kick, so he moved to a different platform.

If Nathan was correct, would the killer stay on Facebook, or would he move on from there? Heaven knew there was no shortage of lonely and/or naive people online. How could they stop him when there was an abundance of social media platforms for the killer to exploit? Nathan hated it when his job depended on something other than his own hard work. They were waiting on DNA. That could be the big break, but how long would they wait?

He was running on little sleep and knew he'd not get much more until this guy was caught. They needed to stop a killer.

CHAPTER 33

HANNA MET MANDY FOR LUNCH at The Beanery because they both wanted something light. When they had lunch there, they usually shared a ham-and-cheese sandwich, which was what they did today.

"What's he like?" Mandy asked, before Hanna had a chance to take her first bite.

She set her half sandwich down. "He's weak. The trek from the car to the house wore him out. When I left, he was breathing with the help of a nebulizer. So I really didn't talk to him."

"Do you think he'll be strong enough to talk to me later today?"

"I don't know. I think sooner than later would be best. He is very frail."

Mandy sat back and sipped her tea. "I'm nervous about it. Were you nervous when he got there? What did you feel?"

"Wow, where do I start? I really don't know what I feel. After all these years, seeing him in person is not what I expected. And, like I said, he's so frail. I was raised to respect the elderly and infirm, to help them, and I find myself even feeling a bit protective. And then I remember what he did. Where he's been for all these years. All the horrible things my mother used to say about him. I'm in knots."

"Knots? Have you forgiven Joe, Hanna?"

"Huh?" Hanna stared at Mandy. She'd just asked the question that had plagued Hanna since the day she received the letter from the Department of Corrections.

Have I forgiven him?

"I honestly don't know."

"I don't have to guess for myself. I have, but it was hard. My grandparents have always been about forgiveness. Holding bitterness, unforgiveness against someone is like drinking poison and expecting the other person to die. I've heard that warning my whole life. When I was a kid, the phrase gave me an oversized fear of drinking poison. I expected if I ever did, all my insides would leak out and I'd die in a puddle. I think because of that, I can say I've forgiven your dad completely. It's finding out where my folks are that has me in knots."

"I hope he'll tell you what you want to know. Come over after work. Ask him whatever you want."

They made their plans. After lunch Hanna went back to the station. It was a quiet day. She stopped at Terry's office. "You saw my note about the talk I had with Chase after the bar fight?"

"I did."

"What is your read?"

Terry shrugged. "I can't see Everett killing his son. Chase is an unknown to me."

"He didn't seem to like the idea of Scott taking Braden."

"That could be motive."

"I think so too. Although I can't see Chase using poison. He's more of a direct kind of guy. Any luck with the security cameras at the airfield?"

Terry rubbed his eyes. "Not so far. I decided to go back to the last time he flew the plane. No one used his coffee machine but him. Maybe someone tampered with the coffee awhile before the day he flew."

"Good idea."

"I've been everywhere I can go, talked to everyone I could. People liked Scott. Sure, some businessmen didn't, but that's just normal." He took a deep breath. "The only viable suspect is Chase."

"We know Chase is not a flight risk. Even if we talk to him and he is the killer, he'll deny it. We need more evidence. I wish we had that coffee container."

"Me too."

"Keep at it. And remember, if you need help, ask." Hanna went back to her office, listening to the chatter on the radio.

Like Everett had said, the fire was winding down. Her reserve officers who'd been helping were back in town, ready for their normal shifts. She had a note to call the city attorney about an upcoming hearing concerning the Jude Carver lawsuit. She also wanted to call Nathan and check on his progress with Edda's case. There was a BOLO out for Edda's car. Other than the ongoing drought and the fact that a man she hadn't seen in her whole life was in her guest room, everything was slowly returning to normal.

Would Joe tell Mandy what she wanted to know? Hanna prayed that he would. She had no way to force him to do the right thing. When it was time to go home, Hanna texted Mandy and told her she was leaving.

I'll be at your house in a few minutes was her answer.

Hanna still beat her there. She walked into the front door expecting Gizmo to wiggle in and out between her legs. There was no dog.

"Grace?" Hanna called out.

"Yes?" Grace stepped out of the guest room. Hanna could hear a television show coming from the room.

"Where's Gizmo?"

"In here with Joe. Is that okay?"

"Ah, yeah." Hanna stepped in the doorway. Joe was sitting up in bed, with Gizmo curled up at his feet. The dog looked up and thumped his tail but made no effort to move.

Joe gazed up at her, looking alert and awake. He smiled.

"Hello, Hanna." His voice was raspy and weak, as if it took every breath to form a word.

The photo from the book flashed in Hanna's thoughts. The hair was thinner, and the mustache was gone, but it was the same smile.

"Do you feel better?"

"I do. Thank you for letting me come here. You look so much like your mother." He paused. It seemed as if each word took a lot of effort. "You're prettier though."

Hanna didn't respond, not sure how she should.

"I can't take back those years," Joe continued haltingly. "But I want you to know ever since I saw the light, I've prayed for you and your mother. I'm sorry she's gone."

Hanna didn't know what to say. If her mother were still alive, Joe would not be here, that was for sure. She heard the front door open and felt relief that Mandy was here to focus the conversation in another direction.

"Joe, do you remember Amanda Carson?"

His brows scrunched together as if he was trying to remember. "Sophia's girl?"

"Yeah. She's my friend, and she wants to ask you something. Do you feel up to talking to her?"

An indefinable expression crossed his face. He brought a hand up to his chin and with his index finger scratched under the nasal cannula. "Sure."

Hanna felt Mandy's presence behind her. She turned and saw the hopeful expression on her friend's face.

"Joe, this is Mandy Carson."

Mandy stepped forward.

Joe looked at her, his eyes widened. "My goodness, the last time I saw you . . ." He leaned forward, his face lost all of its color, and he coughed. Gizmo jumped off the bed, and Grace got up from her seat on the bed to attend to him. Joe waved her away.

She picked up the nebulizer and stood to the right of the bed.

"You were in diapers," Joe continued. "You don't look at all like your mama. You take after your dad in a good way." He coughed some more, but the color slowly returned to his face.

Mandy pulled the chair that was next to the bed closer and sat. "Hi, Joe. I'm sorry you're so sick."

"Oh, honey, don't be sorry for me. I'm getting what I deserve. I'm sorry your parents are gone." He paused again, seemingly trying to catch his breath. "Your dad was a hothead, but your mama was sweet."

"I forgive you, Joe. I did a long time ago. And I have a favor to ask."

He gave a mirthless chuckle, punctuated by coughs. "I'm in no position to do any favors." His cheeks shone red from the exertion of talking. Hanna also had the feeling Joe did not have much more time on this earth.

"This is one you can grant. I'm sure of it. Please, Joe, will you tell me where my parents are? Where did you put their bodies?"

Joe's chest rose and fell, breathing labored. He put his gnarled, liver-spotted hand over Mandy's, but it was several minutes before he said anything. "I can't."

Hanna barely heard him.

"Joe, please, after all these years. I'd like to lay them to rest. I hold no grudge against you."

"Understand." Long pause. "I'm sorry, I can't."

Mandy stood, agitated. "You have nothing to lose now, Joe—"

He shook his head.

"Why can't you tell her?" Hanna asked. "It's the Christian thing to do."

"I can't tell you where they are because I don't know."

CHAPTER 34

WHEN THURSDAY MORNING ROLLED AROUND, all Dry Oaks fire personnel were released from the fire line. County and state firefighters continued the fight. Jared was glad to be back in town. Dry Oaks was no longer in danger, and without the wind, the fire was laying down.

The county had one large station in Dry Oaks on the west side, near the reservoir. His first morning back, he and a couple of other guys, Paul Stokes and Bryce Fallow, were on a fitness run that took them to the east trail around the shrinking body of water. He'd never seen Buckley Lake so low. California was often in and out of drought, but this one was the worst he could remember.

As they jogged along the trail, he noted that the launch ramp was all the way exposed. To launch a boat, a person had to travel some distance on mud. A couple of people were out on the lake in kayaks, and a few people were fishing from the shore, which was way, way down. It was early in the day, not too hot yet. Since their shifts were twenty-four hours, the best time to exercise was first thing, after they'd checked in to work.

They came to the turnaround point, and Jared saw a couple of guys out a ways, on rocks that in a normal year would be underwater. They both appeared to be struggling with something. A big fish? That was unlikely. There were plenty of fish in the lake but not many big ones. Jared and his coworkers stopped to stretch for the run back. They would most certainly sprint part of the way in impromptu races.

Jared stood with his hands on hips and watched the fishermen.

"What's got your attention, Hodges?" Stokes asked. He was the one with the radio in case they had to head back fast for a call.

"Those guys; they hooked something."

One of the men jumped off the rock into the water. It was about knee-deep. He appeared to be struggling mightily with a large object.

"Maybe a boat that sunk?" Paul guessed.

"I don't think so. Let's go help." Jared turned to Paul. He did not look as if he were curious at all.

"Go ahead. I'll give you five minutes."

Bryce joined Jared, and together they jogged toward the fishermen. The exposed bottom had hardened in the unrelenting sun so it was not a difficult path.

By the time Jared and Bryce reached the men, they were both in the water struggling with what looked like a large metal drum.

"You guys need some help?" Jared asked.

He got an affirmative answer, so he and Bryce waded in.

It was an oil drum, old and rusted. Water drained out of several holes as the men dragged it along, and it lightened a bit. As they got it out of the lake, more water drained out.

It smelled musty, moldy, and old.

"Let's open it," the first fisherman said.

"It's old and rotted," Bryce noted. "Shouldn't be difficult to open."

Jared felt the hair rise on the back of his neck. He wasn't certain he wanted to see what was inside the barrel. Before he could voice disagreement, the fisherman jerked the top rim and it gave way, splitting off the top with a metallic groan.

The pungent smell of death wafted from the barrel. Jared peered in, then stepped back, shocked. "I think it's a body."

"No, no, it's not," the fisherman protested. "It's just rocks—"

He was about to reach in but Jared stopped him. "That's a skull, not a rock. Look at the eye socket."

Bryce stepped forward and peered in.

Jared caught his gaze and knew his coworker saw the same thing. There was no question—it was a human skeleton.

"Oh, wow, you're right," the fisherman agreed. "What have we found?" He stepped back, a mystified expression on his face.

CHAPTER 35

"HE SAID THAT HE DIDN'T KNOW?"

"That's what he said." Hanna had managed to meet Nathan for breakfast. "Not 'I can't remember' but '*I don't know.*' How could he not know?"

"That is odd. Did he say any more?"

"No. He started coughing and the hospice aide said he'd talked enough for the day."

"Poor Mandy."

"She handled it well, but she was disappointed," Hanna said. "I'm going to ask him again tonight."

Nathan sipped his coffee, and Hanna had the distinct impression that something was on his mind. Was it just the investigation or something else?

"You seem distracted. Is something going wrong with the investigation?"

He tapped on the top of his coffee cup. "Not wrong, just something off. I ran into Jude Carver yesterday."

"Oh my goodness. What did he have to say?"

"He said that you were two-timing me with a firefighter."

Hanna burst out laughing but stopped when she saw Nathan's face. "You believed him?"

"Everyone in town knows that at one time you were tight with Jared Hodges. I've always felt that you're not very honest with yourself about how you feel about him. Now you're having lunch with him without saying anything to me?"

"Tight? Yeah, ten years ago. I thought we went through all this months ago when he first got back. He's a friend, an old friend." Anger kindled. Hanna didn't like having to defend herself where Jared was concerned.

"So you just had a friendly lunch?"

"I didn't have lunch with him. I had a short conversation with him. Carver must have been home. Honestly, I can't understand why this is even an issue. Why are you upset about this?"

"What on earth did you have to talk to him about?"

"I don't have to explain the conversations I have with other people to you. You still haven't told me why this is even an issue."

"I don't like hearing from a lowlife that my girlfriend is seeing other men."

"I can't believe . . ." Her angry response was interrupted by the tone on Hanna's radio as she was summoned to a call.

"*Chief Keyes, respond to the east trailhead at Buckley Lake. Contact fire department personnel from Fire Station 2. More information is sent to your MDT.*"

"10-4, I copy and I'm en route," she answered with clenched teeth. "Nathan, I'm not sure I like this vibe I'm getting from you."

"Vibe? Maybe I don't like being on the fence. Makes me rethink things. Are we a couple, or are you playing the field?"

"If you don't like hearing things from lowlifes, why is it so easy to believe them? Maybe I need to rethink things as well."

She left him at the table and stalked off to her vehicle. Casting a glance back at Nathan, she saw his head down as if he was deep in thought. Hanna hoped all this came simply from stress. Jealousy did not look attractive on anyone.

Once in the SUV, she started the engine and powered up the computer to read the additional information, working to calm down and concentrate on her job.

Reporting Party states that the lowering lake level revealed an old oil barrel. When the barrel was opened, the R/P discovered human remains.

That was why the information was not aired. Hanna could kiss Charlie, the daytime dispatcher. He always thought ahead. Because of that she doubted the scene would be crowded out by Marcus and his news crew.

Hanna was at the trailhead in five minutes. Asa was already there, and she saw five other men, one of whom was Jared. That gave Hanna pause. But she recovered when she realized that he was on duty. The fire station's pumper was parked in the trailhead parking lot.

"What is it, Asa?"

"Body in a barrel. It's been there for a long time."

"Have you notified the coroner?"

He nodded. "Charlie's on it. But it looks like there's a second barrel."

"Two?"

"Yeah, the second is stuck farther in the bottom. Bryce and Jared from Station 2 got in the water and checked it out. We could force it free, but it might break apart."

"You're thinking it might contain a body as well?"

"You never know."

Hanna followed Asa out to where the barrel stood. She recognized everyone gathered around the area, the advantages of being chief of police in a small town. Her eyes settled on Jared. "Everyone here found the barrel?"

"We saw these guys struggling with it and came down to help." Jared jerked his thumb toward the fishermen.

Hanna peered inside. A human skull was obvious, along with the bones of an arm as if it were flung over the head. From what Hanna could see, there was what looked like a bullet hole in the skull. At least that was her guess. All of it was not visible. The clothes were rotted, the flesh gone—this body had been in the barrel for years.

She straightened up and stepped back. The question was, how many years and who was it? She looked around at the waterline of the lake. This was certainly the lowest she had ever seen the water. These barrels would have been sunk at a time when the water was high, and this would have been roughly the middle of the lake. She immediately thought of Mandy's parents.

Slowing down her thought process, she remembered that the lake had been dragged several times back then by federal authorities when they were looking for DEA Agent Gilly. They found nothing. Was it possible they missed these barrels, or were the barrels dumped later?

Folding her arms, Hanna frowned. It couldn't be the Carsons, could it? To her knowledge, after Joe's crimes and the formation of Dry Oaks PD, there had been only one homicide in the city limits. It was a domestic violence situation, and the body was recovered. The three bodies Nathan was dealing with had been dumped on county property.

Sure, Dry Oaks had a handful of missing person reports but no homicides. Of course, Tuolumne was a big county. Was some out-of-towner using their lake as a dumping ground? If so, there could be more.

Hanna pulled out her phone and called the dispatcher. "Charlie, can you call county search and rescue, see if they can send us some divers? We need to search the entire lake."

�֍

"I've got to get back to work." Jared walked up to Hanna after she ended her phone call with Charlie. "Before I leave, I wanted to ask you how it went with Joe. We watched Marcus's podcast at the station. He included footage of Joe walking up to your front door. He looks old and sick. Did Mandy get a chance to talk to him?"

"He is old and sick. Mandy came by last night." Hanna wished they were someplace where she could talk to Jared. He might be able to help her untangle her feelings about the old man. He was just a friend. Nathan getting touchy about it bugged her.

"He told her he didn't know where her parents are. What an odd twist to get this call now." Briefly she told him about Mandy's visit.

He arched an eyebrow. "Really? I don't have to guess where your mind's going with the discovery of this body."

"Hodges, we got a call."

Jared leaned toward the pumper. "Sorry, got to go." He sprinted off to the truck, which had already started rolling. "Call me if you want to talk."

Hanna watched him go, dwelling on the mystery of the barrel. If it was the Carsons, what did that mean? How could Joe not know where he hid his victims?

✖

By the time it was dark, county divers had recovered the second barrel. It, too, contained a body. They also found something else.

They found a car. It was going to take specialized equipment to retrieve the vehicle from the muddy lake bottom. Calling out divers had ensured that what was happening at the lake could not be kept a secret. There was a circus-like atmosphere prevailing at the lake's edge. Marcus was at the scene, as were other news outlets, as well as half the town.

"It must be the Carsons," Marcus said.

Hanna heard him talking to one of the fishermen. Hal was a lifelong resident of Dry Oaks; he certainly remembered the murders. Yet, he wasn't convinced. "Why do you say that?"

"Those barrels are at least thirty years old. Who else could it be?"

"What about the car?"

"I think the car is unrelated to anything else," Marcus said. "Maybe a dumped stolen vehicle."

Hanna considered what she'd heard. She hated to agree with Marcus about anything, but her mind had gone down the same track. While she tried to derail it, it kept on the same track. Especially since the second body had been uncovered. Asa was already checking outstanding missing person reports from all over the county, not just Dry Oaks.

Hanna kept circling around to the great possibility that these two corpses could be Mandy's parents. It didn't make any sense. Joe could have told them the bodies were in the lake, yet he said he didn't know where they were. She hadn't been home all day. Her hope was that she wouldn't get home too late to talk to him.

The coroner had to make special arrangements to transport the drums back to the morgue. He didn't want to remove the remains from the drums until he was there. It took all of Hanna's personnel to secure the scene while the drums were transferred to the coroner's van. Marcus was being ghoulish and trying to get images of the remains.

Hanna followed the van back to the morgue, planning to be there to watch their removal.

✖

Hanna left the morgue knowing she'd have to wake Mandy and Betty up. The corpses were a male and a female. The man was tentatively identified as Blake Carson. He had a soggy wallet with ID in his pocket. They would still have to do a positive identification through DNA or dental records. They assumed the female was Sophia, but again, dental or DNA would need to confirm the identification. The car would be pulled up from the lake later in the day.

Still, for Hanna it was enough info to talk to Mandy about. She called and woke her friend up. When she stopped in front of their house, she saw the lights on. She was glad Betty was still recuperating, though Mandy said she'd be going home soon. Hanna preferred to tell them the news together. Hanna had them sit beside each other on the couch when she told them.

"I don't know what to say." Mandy reached over and grasped Betty's hand.

"We'll finally be able to lay them to rest." Betty wasn't upset; she was simply resigned.

"I've wanted to know for so long." Mandy's voice sounded far away. She gave a humorless chuckle and rubbed her forehead. "It's ironic that just last night I was trying to get Joe to tell me. It's like God decided to unearth my mom and dad because Joe wouldn't."

CHAPTER 36

WHEN HANNA GOT HOME, her intent was to shower, make some super-strong coffee, and go back to work. But the light was on in Joe's room. One of the caregivers told her that though Joe tired out quickly, he often had difficulty sleeping. She poked her head in. The caregiver sat in the corner reading a book. Joe was in bed reading the Bible. He looked up. His expression brightened. "Hanna."

"Joe. Do you feel up to answering some questions?"

"Will answering them help you?" Each word was slow and halting.

"Yes. If you tell me the truth."

"I'll tell you what I can."

"We found two bodies in Buckley Lake. They were in oil drums. They'd been there a long time. Thirty-five years, we think."

Joe blinked, then swallowed. Hanna saw his Adam's apple move. An odd expression rolled over his eyes; the look there became far away.

"So much excitement . . . when your mother told me . . . she was pregnant. Wanted to be a dad . . . was ready . . . and I was going to . . . straighten up and . . . fly right to provide for you." So many words seemed to take a toll on him. His chest heaved, the Bible closed, and he gripped the top sheet tightly, closing his eyes for a moment.

Hanna stood next to the bed. He was deflecting her. She needed to redirect him, but she also wanted to hear more. For as long as she could remember, she wondered if Joe ever wanted to be a father. If he was happy not to have any responsibility for her. If he thought of her, if he missed her. She was too tired to put up all the walls that kept her from melting into the little girl who wanted her daddy.

"Joe, we found Blake and Sophia. You put them in oil drums and dropped them in the lake."

His head slowly went side to side. "No."

Hanna squeezed the bridge of her nose, not sure where to go now.

"You believe, don't you?" He croaked out the question while tapping on the Bible.

"What?" At first, she was going to say no, she didn't believe, that she thought he was lying, but then she realized that wasn't what he meant.

"Yes, I believe. I'm a Christian. What does that have to do with your answering my questions?"

"Warms my heart."

"Joe, I want to talk to you about Blake and Sophia."

He put both hands on the Bible.

"Amanda was wrong. I do have . . . something to lose. Truth will come out . . . It always wants to come out. You're smart. You will find it."

He started to cough, a hacking cough where he couldn't catch his breath. The caregiver got up and began to prepare the nebulizer. "Probably enough for today."

Frustrated and exhausted, Hanna left the two of them and

went into the kitchen. Part of her felt that Joe was sandbagging, that he had more energy than he let on. But leaning on his weakness kept him from answering the important questions. She started coffee so it would be ready when she got out of the shower.

Hanna had never looked through Joe's arrest report and the accompanying crime report. He'd never been a part of her life, and she'd never wanted to dig that deep into his. Something was off here. She'd have to go get the file and look over everything.

After the shower, she ran her fingers through her hair, then untangled it with a comb. It was short enough to air-dry. It was getting light outside. The sun was beginning to rise on Friday morning. She filled her travel mug and headed out her front door and almost ran into Jared.

"What are you doing here?"

He had two cups of coffee in his hands. "I just got off work. I was hoping to have a cup of coffee with you and talk about that find yesterday. Have you gotten any sleep?"

Hanna shook her head. Though she'd been laser focused on getting to work, she was glad to see Jared. Maybe he could help her sort the myriad emotions running rampant inside.

"All afternoon into the early morning hours, I was with the coroner."

"Was it Blake and Sophia?"

She nodded. "That's preliminary. Do you mind sitting on the porch steps? I don't want to go into the house and wake Joe."

He grinned. "Not at all. My porch or yours, we can talk anywhere. You'll need to get yourself some chairs if we make it a habit."

Hanna chuckled, feeling as if the bit of humor brightened the dark morning. "I'll work on that."

They sat on the top step and Jared put the extra cup of coffee between them.

"I had a bad feeling when we helped pull that barrel out," Jared said. "But it does solve a mystery."

"Maybe. Unfortunately for me, finding the remains raises more questions than it answers." Hanna sighed.

"You mean because the story is wrong now?"

"Exactly. I have to dig back into the original investigation. The story most people know now is what Marcus wrote. Is it the truth? I don't know if he had official details."

"Where does Marcus say he got his information?"

Hanna gave a mirthless chuckle. "It was all a figment of his imagination, at least that's what my mom always used to say. Though I know he included some things she'd told him in confidence. I remember her complaining about that. I need the report the original cops wrote."

"I would have thought you'd have already read that by now."

"I didn't. All my life I've just wanted to move on from Joe, you know? It was a done deal. He confessed and went to prison, justice satisfied." She held Jared's gaze. "I made peace with the past."

He nodded. "Yeah. I remember. What's he like now? Repentant?"

She stared off across the lawn. "He claims he found faith, and he's apologized some. But he's weak, very weak. He won't answer direct questions. And when he does talk, he loses steam quickly. He's certainly not the big bad murderer Marcus or my mother always described."

"Thirty-five years in prison and stage-four lung cancer would change anyone. Are you sorry you let him come here?"

Hanna jerked around to face Jared. He watched her with a neutral expression and a warmth grew inside her. She knew he didn't ask the question with any judgment intended. He understood her and her struggle. For a second, they were fifteen again and he was encouraging her to ignore the bullies. She had to look away.

Turning back to look straight ahead, she sipped her coffee. "I don't know. What am I supposed to feel? What I know about Joe came from my mother. I've been a cop long enough to know that there are two sides to every story. I—" Hanna stopped. Emotion bubbled up and her throat thickened.

"What?"

She swallowed and sniffled. "I find myself wishing my mother hadn't kept us apart. Maybe I should have visited him over the years." Back in control, she told him about the TV program she'd seen when she waited for Braden.

"A few days ago, I was in the waiting room at the hospital. A show was playing on the television. I don't know what it was, but there was this kid whose dad was in prison. He didn't think that his mother took him to visit often enough; the prison was a couple of hours from home. So, one day the kid skips school and takes a bus to visit his dad. His mom doesn't find out until she goes to school to pick her son up. And then it's the corrections officer calling to tell her where her son is."

"Mom probably wasn't happy."

"No. The kid so wanted to see his dad. I don't know what the guy was in for, but this boy, ten or twelve years old, I guess, is allowed to visit and he gives his dad a hug and they catch up on life. Even though the dad was in prison, he was still Dad. It kind of hit me. What if my mother had allowed visits? What if I'd been allowed to get to know him? I know it's useless to ask such a question, but I might feel differently now."

He leaned close, his voice lowered.

"Your mom pounded it into your head that Joe was a monster. That must cloud your thoughts and emotions. Try and get her out of your mind and look at Joe without blinders on."

She met Jared's gaze and kept her voice steady, aware that the emotions swirling inside her right now were stronger than anything she felt when she was with Nathan. "Easier said than done, I'm afraid."

His crooked half smile shone back at her. "You'll figure it out. Why were you headed to work so early?"

"I'm going to Sonora, to the sheriff's department to dig up the old case file. I need to do it before the firestorm erupts over the bodies we found. And I want to be back in time to watch them pull that car up."

"You have a busy morning. I'll let you go then." He stood.

About the same time, a car pulled up, a county car. Nathan. Hanna tensed. Where would he go with Jared being here?

He parked and walked toward them. "Good morning. I was worried."

Hanna stood. "Worried? Why?"

He cast an appraising gaze toward Jared. "I've been trying to call, got no response."

"Oh." Hanna grabbed her phone. "I shut it off at the coroner's last night, uh, this morning. Sorry, forgot to turn it back on." She noticed the way he was looking at Jared.

"Nathan, this is Jared Hodges. Jared, Nathan Sharp."

"Nice to meet you, Nathan," Jared said amiably. "I just stopped by on my way home to ask about the barrels. I'll be on my way now."

Nathan nodded, his expression cold. "Likewise. Have a good day."

Jared walked off to his truck and Nathan watched him go, while Hanna watched Nathan. "What's that about?" Hanna asked.

"What do you mean?"

"You seem angry."

"Like I said, I was worried about you. I didn't expect to find Hodges here. I was coming to apologize, and I walk up on this."

"You didn't walk up on anything. He's a good friend. He was at the lake yesterday when we pulled up the barrels. His curiosity was understandable." Hanna struggled to stop from becoming furious.

He blew out a breath and scrubbed his face with his hands. Nathan looked at Hanna. "I'm sorry. I'm tired and frustrated." Stepping closer, he said, "I heard about the tentative ID. You've found Blake and Sophia after all."

Hanna relaxed; she was tired and frustrated as well. "I'm headed to Sonora. I want to look at the original crime and arrest report."

"That's right, you've never looked at it before." His brows scrunched together.

"What? It's still in storage, isn't it?"

"Oh yeah. It's, well, there is not much to it. Since Joe's here, why not ask him?"

"He weakens easily. And he's not been very forthcoming about anything. I take it you're not getting anywhere with Edda's case or the other murders."

"No. This online suspect is good at covering his tracks. Tech thinks he used multiple burner phones. Nothing we've found on the victims' computers provides any clue to his identity. I wish we had their phones."

"I'm sorry. I wish I could help."

"You have enough on your plate. Maybe we can carve out some time for lunch today. I'd like things to get back to normal for us."

"I'd like that too. But Nathan, Jared will always be my friend."

"I guess I'll have to live with that."

Nathan walked Hanna to her car, but a distance yawned between them.

Is that distance my fault or his?

CHAPTER 37

HANNA WAITED TWENTY MINUTES for the box of Joe's case files to be brought up from storage. It was simply one box. When she signed for it and took it to a cubicle, she studied it for a moment before she opened it. One box for two murders and a near murder. In this day and age, there would be a room full of boxes of evidence for such an investigation.

She opened the box and took all the items out: two thick file folders, one for the homicides and one thinner one for the arrest report. She started with the homicide folder. On top were photos of the cabin, Beecher's Mine cabin. It hadn't been completely destroyed. Obviously, fire had torn through the small building, but two walls still stood. By the time she'd gotten up there with Jared, the years had taken down those walls. There were remnants of meth-cooking hardware; some of the pictures were labeled. Bottles labeled *acid*, trash, and liquor bottles. There were pictures of blood spatter—a lot of blood. Some were labeled *Victim One* and some were labeled *Victim Two*.

There were no pictures of Chase.

Hanna rifled through everything and could find no photos of the one living victim. That was odd. He would have been part of the investigation. There should have been photos to document his injuries.

Things got odd with the report narrative. *Reporting officers were notified by an unnamed subject that there had been a shooting at Beecher's Mine cabin. He told officers that he heard gunshots and saw Joseph Keyes running away from the cabin. He also reported that he saw smoke coming from the cabin. Reporting officers arrived at Beecher's Mine cabin and found it almost completely engulfed in fire.*

She skimmed the whole report. The "unnamed subject" was never named, not even to be redacted. Observations that *someone* had been cooking meth followed once the fire was extinguished. There was nothing about Chase, or anyone else. Most of the pages were lab reports on the different substances removed from the scene. It was a meth lab.

Frowning, she turned her attention to the arrest report. Joe was arrested at the hospital in Sonora. He was pulled off the maternity floor. In 1991 officers did not have to file a probable-cause declaration. The simple arrest report declared that officers again followed the tip by the unnamed subject. He saw Joe Keyes running from the cabin.

They also noted that Joe had been suspected in the explosion that destroyed another meth lab a month prior. An older crime report was attached. It was more detailed than anything concerning the Beecher's Mine fire. Hanna had heard the story before, but this was the first official report she'd read that wasn't town gossip. The meth lab had exploded on county land. And the investigator mentioned DEA Agent Gilly, including the agent's theory about the cause. Gilly believed the lab had been booby-trapped; the cooker destroyed it when he was discovered.

Hanna paused for a moment. Chase Buckley and Blake and Amanda Carson were also mentioned in the report. Amanda

Carson was seriously burned but denied knowing about the lab. She and Blake claimed they were hiking and saw the fire and went over to investigate. Chase found them wandering in the forest and took them to the hospital. Blake was arrested at first but released.

Gilly left a note naming the known drug deals in the county. Joe Keyes was on the top of the list. At the time of filing, there was no evidence to say conclusively who was responsible for the meth lab explosion. She noted that there was only a brief sentence concerning Chase—he was not a suspect in any way. But the details about Joe and the Carsons were meticulous, even though no one was arrested for that incident. Hanna frowned, noting all the investigation and interviews connected to the older report. Why hadn't all that been done for the Beecher's Mine investigation?

Joe was arrested, and twelve hours later he confessed. All investigation stopped.

Hanna stood and began to pace. Running her fingers through her hair, she thought about all the information in Marcus's book, all the stories about the murders she'd heard her whole life. Where did all that come from? Certainly not from Joe. Her mother was right about Marcus's imagination.

The only other thing in the box was the transcript from Joe's confession. Hanna sat back down and began to read.

I, Joseph M. Keyes, confess to the murder of Blake and Sophia Carson. I was up at the old Beecher's Mine cabin to cook a batch of meth with them. While we were cooking, we fought. Blake wanted a bigger cut. I killed him and then Sophia when she got in the way. Chase came by. He was mad that we were cooking in his father's cabin. He saw Blake and Sophia. We got in an argument, and I threw acid. I

was high; I don't remember anything else. I thought I killed
Chase. I turned stuff over and started the fire, then I ran.

Less than half a page. No details. He should have had to give
details for the judge to accept his confession.

She looked over all the names involved in the arrest. Sheriff
Don Peterson. DA Geoff Robbins. Judge Walter Griggs. All three
men were now dead. The public defender was listed as Alister
Driscoll, and Hanna was not familiar with that name. She made
a note to do an internet search and check with the court. There
should be more names. In a double homicide of this magnitude,
she couldn't believe that only three people were involved in the
investigation.

The rest of the evidence was likewise weak. Shards of an acid
bottle with Joe's fingerprints on them. A cast from Joe's shoe print
found near the cabin. There was evidence of a fair amount of
blood in parts of the cabin that had not been destroyed by fire,
later determined to belong to Blake and Sophia. Nothing about
DEA Agent Gilly.

Hanna went through everything three times. There was nothing here that would have convicted Joe in court. He never even
made a statement about where the Carsons' bodies were or what
he'd killed them with. More than that, when would he have had
time to put their bodies in barrels and dump them in the lake?

She stood and paced. Something was so very off here. Her
phone rang. The county recovery team called to tell her that the
equipment was in place to remove the car. Frustrated, confused,
and a little angry, Hanna returned the evidence box to the custo-
dian of records and headed back to Dry Oaks. On the way, she
called and asked a court clerk to check on Driscoll for her. The
clerk said they would call her back.

Nathan paced his office, frustration spurring every step. Not only did this thing with Jared Hodges rub him the wrong way, but no matter which way they turned in the investigation, they hit a dead end. Edda's car still had not been found. The techies were all over social media, trying to trace the guy who hooked the first two victims. Subpoenas had been served for their phone records, but none of the information was getting them any closer to finding the killer. He wished he could light a fire under the state lab regarding the DNA.

Nathan now concentrated on the vehicle: the SUV Colby identified. Looking for an SUV owned by a Hanna Keyes fan who might be a serial killer. Going through the number of Chevy Tahoes registered in the county was daunting, according to Manny.

"Concentrate on the local ones first," Nathan suggested.

When Manny produced a list, he was happy to see that there weren't that many. A few notable owners caught his eye. Everett Buckley had four. Jude Carver had one. Marcus Marshall also had one. Nathan and Manny split up. Nathan headed for Dry Oaks to check out the Tahoes there, and Manny went to handle those in Sonora.

Thinking of Hanna brought the barrels to mind. What a find, after thirty-five years. He prayed that Hanna would get all the answers she needed regarding what had happened with Joe and the Carsons. Nathan also hoped that by returning to Dry Oaks, he could talk to Hanna again and apologize for being so distressed about Jared Hodges. They'd talked about having lunch. He hoped the time opened up in both their schedules.

The car slowly emerged from the water. "That's an old Mustang," Jared said. He'd been at the lake when Hanna returned. "Probably from the 1990s."

"You sure?" Hanna asked.

"I'm a bit of a car guy, remember?" He grinned.

"I remember. But the Carsons didn't have a Mustang. In all the crimes Joe is accused of, there is no mention of a car."

"Not related?"

"It can't be. But if it's from the 1990s . . ." Her voice trailed off. What on earth was going on?

When the dripping, rusted vehicle was placed on shore, it was clear that it was indeed a Ford Mustang. Asa walked around the vehicle, noting the plates. "This is a government car." He relayed the plate number to dispatch. A few minutes later, they got the return that had everyone scratching their heads.

"That plate returns to a missing vehicle and missing person: Brett T. Gilly. There are alerts attached, and the FBI is requesting notification."

Keys still in the ignition, there was a soaked, packed suitcase in the trunk, but nothing else in the car—no body, no indication where Gilly might be.

Reporters were everywhere, asking for comments. Hanna had none.

"What a mess," Hanna said to Jared. "The Feds will be here."

"Didn't they search for him thirty-five years ago?"

"They did. According to Everett Buckley, they tore the town apart. There was a federal presence here for six months."

"Obviously they didn't search hard enough."

Hanna asked the county team to do one more thorough search of the lake.

"It's unlikely that we'll find a body if it wasn't placed in a barrel like the first two," the head diver told her. "Or wrapped and weighted. Sonar picks up those objects more reliably. We'll do our best."

Hanna thanked them, and after the Mustang was loaded up on a flatbed, it was time to head back to the office to deal with the press. The PD itself didn't have a press office; that was handled by the county. She had to put something together for them.

"I wish there was something I could do for you, Hanna," Jared said. "This is a circus, isn't it?"

"It is. You've wasted your day off here at the lake."

"Hey, you know me; I always enjoyed the circus."

Hanna relaxed, thankful for the distraction and the lightness of the moment. "Enjoy your time off." She smiled. "Maybe I should have been a firefighter."

He laughed. "No, Hanna, you're right where you should be. In the circus there is always one great lion tamer; that's you. Go get 'em."

It was her turn to laugh. "That conjures up an image of a whip and a chair. Sometimes I wish the press could be handled that way." She turned from Jared, a little bit of the stress gone. Yes, she could handle this. It was what she'd signed up for.

"I promise to have a statement for you all in the next couple of hours," she said as she made her way back to her car. "I'll issue a statement from city hall." She got in her car and eased away from the crowds.

Back on the road, Nathan came to mind. He'd not yet discovered where Edda's vehicle was, but now they knew it wasn't in the lake. The jealousy situation with Nathan still bugged her. In spite of everything going on around her, she hoped there was a way they could straighten out things between them.

She called him using hands-free and the call went to voicemail.

"It's just me, wondering how your investigation is going. Call me when you have a chance."

✿

At the station, the preliminary autopsy report on the bodies from the barrel was in her e-mail. Both Carsons died from gunshot wounds to the head with a 9mm caliber weapon. Both wounds were through and through, there were no slugs or bullet fragments in the barrels. Death would have been quick. They were likely killed elsewhere and then placed in barrels to be concealed. As best as the coroner could estimate, the bodies had been in the barrels, in the water, for at least thirty-five years.

Hanna wished that there was one law enforcement person she could talk to from that time who'd been involved in the investigation. If there had been a PD here when the murders happened, she might have more information. But the Carsons were killed in a different time on a different watch. Nothing was even computerized back then.

The sparseness of the reports still bothered her, though. She could think of no reliable resource from that time, save Everett Buckley and—her father.

Fatigue enveloped Hanna, and she stepped up to the coffee station to make a fresh pot.

"Knock, knock."

Turning, she saw Mayor Milton. "I've come to help you with the press release. There sure are a lot of news outlets in town. My phone has been ringing off the hook."

"Yep. We've stepped on a hornet's nest, haven't we?"

"Maybe not. Maybe we're just closing the books on some old mysteries."

"Yeah, but there will still be a lot of questions."

"I don't think so. We know who murdered the Carsons; now we can guess that he killed Gilly as well."

"Can we?" Hanna stared at Mayor Milton. She was certainly confident. "Joe confessed so easily and quickly to the Carson murders. Don't you think that if he had killed Gilly, he would have confessed to that as well?"

"Not necessarily. Killing a federal agent would have likely made him eligible for the federal death penalty. Joe's confession was self-serving, so he would not face the state death penalty. If they could have pinned Gilly's murder on him, he would not have avoided a federal death sentence."

Hanna considered this. The mayor wasn't wrong. Joe confessing to local crimes kept everything local. But so much of this was bothersome. The timing, how did Joe get the Carsons into barrels and into the water before his arrest? He was picked up at the hospital right after the fire was put out. The tip was anonymous; the tipster never deposed or identified. When did Joe drive the car into the lake?

"Are you okay, Hanna?" Mayor Milton looked worried.

"Yeah, yeah, mind's wandering, I'm tired. Coffee is ready. Would you like a cup?"

"Sure. Then let's hammer out this press release."

CHAPTER 38

By Friday afternoon the press release was written and distributed. Hanna read it on air but didn't take any questions. The news outlets were satisfied for the time being. Hanna didn't know how long that would last, considering that two FBI agents and an evidence team arrived to process the Mustang. National news outlets were now starting to take notice. Circus indeed.

Hanna felt a second wind coming when her phone rang. It was Manny, Nathan's partner.

"Have you seen Nathan?"

"No, I haven't." Hanna looked at the office clock, trying to remember how long ago she'd left the message for him. "I called him and left a message; he hasn't called me back. We talked about having lunch together, but I hadn't heard from him. I assumed he is busy."

"I've called him too. And I've tried to locate him. His GPS is turned off. He was on his way to Dry Oaks to check out some SUVs. Why would he turn his GPS off?"

"SUVs, related to the homicides?"

"Yeah. There were some black Tahoes registered in Dry Oaks. I've been working on vehicles in Sonora."

Uneasiness roiled in her gut. It was not like Nathan not to check in or return phone calls.

"Who was he going to check on here?"

"There were six Chevy Tahoes registered in Dry Oaks, among them one to Jude Carver, four to Everett Buckley, and one to Marcus Marshall."

Hanna chewed on her bottom lip and considered this information. She knew where Marcus Marshall had been most of the day. She'd just handed him a press release. And Everett, his Tahoes were work vehicles. Would Nathan have checked on those? That left Jude Carver.

"You still there, Hanna?"

"Yeah, yeah, just thinking. Marshall has been just about everywhere I've been today, and I haven't seen Nathan come talk to him."

"That leaves Buckley and Carver."

"Right. I can check with both of them."

"I've tried calling Buckley; I got his answering service," Manny said. "He's not available. The last communication they had was that he was on the fire line."

"Did you call Carver?"

"His voicemail is full. That's as far as I got."

"I will go check on him."

"I'm leaving Sonora shortly. I'll meet you at his place."

Hanna tried Nathan again. It immediately went to voicemail. Putting her gun belt on, she stepped into the squad room. Asa was eating his lunch. She could go to see Carver by herself, but that was not good officer safety. And with his lawsuit hanging over the city, it wouldn't be wise.

"Asa, I've got to go check on Jude Carver."

"Why?"

She told him about Nathan.

He folded up the remains of his lunch and tossed it in the trash. "I hope it's just a matter of a dead cell phone."

"It probably is."

They took two cars. Hanna pulled up first. Carver's SUV was in the drive. The front fender was dented and held together with duct tape.

Carver came out onto the porch with a beer in hand. "You're trespassing." He slurred his esses as he spoke.

"We just came to ask you a question, Jude."

"Do I need my lawyer?"

"No. We're looking for Nathan Sharp. He was on his way here to ask you—"

"He was here. Your boyfriend was trying to connect me to those murders. Was that your doing? You so afraid you're going to lose that lawsuit that you're trying to pin those murders on me?"

Hanna ignored the dig. "How long ago was he here?"

Jude drank his beer and stared.

"Left a couple of hours ago," a voice behind her said.

Hanna turned. Jared was out on his porch. "He pulled out as I pulled up."

"Yeah, yeah, there's your other boyfriend. Is he spying on me?" Carver stumbled down his front steps, drunk and angry. Dropping his beer can, he came straight for Hanna.

"You'll always be the no-good spawn of Satan. I can't believe you're chief!" He swung a fist, which Hanna dodged easily. Unstable on his feet, Carver immediately lost his balance and went down.

Asa stepped between them. Jared also jumped off the porch and ran to help. Hanna and Asa were able to get a hold of the struggling Carver and handcuff him before Jared got involved.

"I don't want to arrest you, Jude. I only wanted to ask about Nathan."

Carver squirmed and cursed.

"Wow," Jared commented when he reached them. "We might get drunk just from his breath."

Another car pulled up. Manny got out and hurried to them, face tense with worry.

Hanna and Asa pulled Carver to his feet. "Let's get him to the porch and sit him down," Asa suggested.

Between the two of them they accomplished that feat. Technically, Carver could be arrested for assaulting Hanna, but that wasn't her goal. If he would just calm down, she'd be happy to leave him home to sober up and continue looking for Nathan.

"What is going on?" Manny asked as he jogged up.

"Do you have this?" Hanna asked Asa, who nodded. Carver did seem to be calming down.

She stepped back to speak to Manny, conscious that Jared was at her side. Briefly, she explained what had happened.

"You saw him leave here?" Manny asked Jared.

"Right as I got home, he was leaving."

"He had to be on his way to talk to Everett," Hanna said, but there were so many questions swirling in her head. Not just about this killer Nathan was tracking, but her father's case as well. The ugly thought that maybe Joe had not killed the Carsons would not go away. And if it wasn't Joe, did that leave Chase, or was someone else involved? The unnamed tipster? Or was it worse than that? Was Everett also involved?

Something was seriously wrong.

"Hanna, are you okay?" Jared took her arm, a concerned look on his face.

"No, I'm not. Nothing is adding up." She turned to Asa. Carver sat down hard on his porch stairs. "Can you get him inside to sleep it off? If he won't cooperate, book him."

"You got it, boss."

To Manny she said, "I have to go check something out, then I'm going to talk to Everett. Can you meet me there in about half an hour?"

He nodded. "I'll give Asa a hand and then let you know when I'm en route."

Hanna started for her car, Jared on her heels.

"I'm going with you."

"You don't know where I'm going."

"I don't. Wherever it is, I can help."

"Jared, this is something I need to do on my own."

That stopped him.

Her tone softened. "I need to talk to Joe. He's the only one who can clear things up for me."

"I'll pray that you get your answers."

Hanna got in her car and headed for her home. It was time to force Joe to tell her what he knew.

❉

Jared watched Hanna go, a nagging feeling that he should have gone with her, that she was in danger running through his thoughts. He was distracted when Jude Carver decided to act up as Asa and Manny were trying to get him into the house.

"Get off me," Carver hollered.

"Settle down, Jude. We're just trying to get you to bed." Asa was the picture of patience. He was on the left, Manny was on the right. They tried to guide Carver up the stairs and into his house.

Carver twisted away from Manny, shoving his chest into Asa.

As Jared stepped forward to help, Carver kicked out his foot, hitting Manny's knee.

"Ahh!" Manny screamed in pain and fell over onto the porch. Jared went to Manny as Asa twisted Carver's wrist, jacking him up into the porch post.

"All right, Jude. You just bought yourself a night in jail."

Manny moaned as Jared checked out his leg. "Oh man, Detective. He dislocated your kneecap." Jared turned back to Asa. "Are you okay?"

Asa answered, a little out of breath. "Fine. Let me get this guy in the car and I'll get medics rolling." He jerked Jude away from the house and toward his patrol car. As typical of drunks, Jude had shifted from being belligerent to whiny.

"Hey, man, why you being so rough?"

In a few minutes, Asa had him belted into the car and called for medics. Manny was in a lot of pain. By the time he was loaded into the ambulance, it was late afternoon. Was Hanna at home or on her way to talk to Everett Buckley? Since he still had a bad feeling about what she might walk into, when the ambulance left, followed by Asa and his prisoner, Jared climbed into his truck and drove to Hanna's house.

CHAPTER 39

JOE COULD BARELY BREATHE. He felt his time was short. In the bed, raised up to a sitting position, he wanted to do more than watch a local news feed on TV all day. He'd watched footage of the barrels being removed from the lake. They finally found Blake and Sophia, Hanna had told him. He wished he could tell her that he was just as surprised as she was.

He watched and listened as Hanna read her press release about what was taken out of the lake, and his heart swelled with pride. She was special. But as he watched, fear started. A truth had come to light, and certain people would be angry about that. He'd had nothing to do with it, but he doubted that would work as an excuse. As events unfolded, he'd have to do everything in his power to protect Hanna. He had nothing to give for her except his life.

Using hand gestures, he asked the caregiver to give him a pad of paper and a pen. He'd written a bundle of letters to Hanna over the years. He'd brought them with him. The instructions were that they be given to Hanna after he died. They were just about his life in prison, how he'd come to faith, what he hoped for her—all the things he'd have told her if she'd ever visited. He'd never written about what put him there. Holding the pen, he steadied his hand and began to write all the words he wouldn't have the breath to say.

⌘

Hanna called Everett as she headed home. It went to voicemail. That was weird. Not even the service answered. They or Grover usually answered if Everett couldn't. It only increased her worry about Nathan. Had he walked into some danger he never expected?

She parked in her driveway and jogged into the house. Joe was in bed. The back was raised, and he had the TV on. He turned to face Hanna when she walked into the room. She turned her radio down, not wanting to be interrupted by anything.

She saw him watching her, eyes moist, his chest rising and falling, breathing labored. A pad of paper rested on his chest.

"My colleague Nathan Sharp is missing. I don't have time for games or lies. Joe, you didn't kill Blake and Sophia Carson, did you?"

He held her gaze for a long minute and said nothing.

"He can't get his breath," the caregiver said. "It's a progression of the disease. He won't be able to talk to you."

"You can listen, can't you, Joe?"

He nodded.

"The timing doesn't work. There is no way you could have dumped those bodies—unless you were working with someone else and you covered for them. But I don't see any other names. I don't believe you had an accomplice. I don't think you killed them. I'm at a loss."

He gave a slight nod and tried to speak. Nothing came out. He held the pad out to Hanna. He raised a bony finger, pointed at the pad.

"You want me to read this?"

He nodded.

It was a couple of pages. "I don't have time to read everything."

Joe pointed at the pad.

She read the first line.

Hanna, please read. I hope this answers your questions was printed across the top.

She held the pad in both hands. Joe tried to speak and couldn't. There was only one word Hanna could understand. *Read.*

Hanna stepped to the door, leaned against the frame, and began to read. After the admonition to read, the next line was, *Hanna, all I've ever wanted to do is keep you and your mother safe.* It was written in bold capital print. She paused and saw that Joe was watching her. Hanna continued reading.

I told them I did the murders. I was backed into a corner. That night was the worst night in my life and the best night. In spite of the ugliness of what happened at the cabin, you were born, and you were the best thing I ever had a part of.

I went to the cabin that night to cook meth. That much is true. I tried to quit cooking for your mother and you. Chase wouldn't let me. He promised me it would be the last time. I agreed to one last time, but I never trusted Chase. He set up the kitchen in Beecher's cabin.

It was getting dark, and I was late. I drove your mom's car to the highest spot I could, without using the Buckley's trail. I parked to walk in and surprise Chase if he set me up. I had a gun just in case, an old .38, and started for the cabin.

Chase was always trouble. He never got arrested because his granddad owned the sheriff and the courts. The man was a Tasmanian devil when he was angry. I hurried up the steep trail, sorry I brought the gun because it rubbed against my hip. It was hot and I was sweating. It took me about twenty minutes to get up into the tree line where I could catch the trail to the cabin.

The writing became shakier and harder to read as she went on.

On my way up, I saw a car parked on an old logging road. Few people knew about that road and fewer used it. I knew that no one should be up there. It spooked me. I kept low and carefully moved closer to see if I recognized the car. When I caught a glimpse of the front end, I almost had a heart attack. It was Gilly's car.

Hanna stopped at this point and looked up at Joe. "Gilly was there?"

Joe shook his head and indicated with his hand that she keep reading.

I thought that the Fed was there. My first instinct was that it was a setup and I needed to run and not look back. I almost did that, but then I thought of Sophia. Maybe the Fed was after all of us. I wanted to warn Sophia, if she was there. I didn't really care about Chase or Blake. I didn't want to see pretty little Amanda without a mother. I felt like I had the element of surprise, and I could sneak up on the cabin. If the Fed was already on them, I could still make a break for it and be in the clear. After all, it was just the one guy.

As quick as I could, I hurried for the cabin. When I got to where I could see the roofline, I stopped and listened.

When I didn't hear anything, I kept walking. I pulled the gun; I wanted to be ready. As I got closer, I could smell something like burning plastic. I knew that they'd already started cooking, and there was no sign of Gilly.

There were no lights blazing and that was a good thing. They had the windows covered.

Then I heard two gunshots. I almost turned around and ran. They came from inside the cabin.

Did Gilly just kill them? Or did they kill Gilly?

Bang, bang, bang! Three more.

I was shaking by then, thinking, What do I do?

I turned to run away, but my curiosity wouldn't let me. I jogged forward. I could hear Chase talking, cursing, not making sense. Only Chase's voice, like he was talking to himself. I tiptoed to the front door, pushed it open a smidge, and peered in. Chase's back was to me. He had a gun in his hand and was waving it in the air. Looking down at something.

The putrid smell in the place made me gag. They'd tried to separate the elements from the cold tablets to get down to the meth, but they hadn't done it right. Everything was just burning. I pushed the door open farther, then stepped inside and tried to see what Chase was looking at. He was oblivious to me. Two more steps inside and I almost screamed. I couldn't believe it.

Blake and Sophia were on the floor, both tied up and shot in the head.

Chase jerked around and faced me, pointing a gun straight at me. "There you are! You stood me up! You sicced that Fed on me and then didn't show!" A wild look glinted in his dark eyes. He was higher than a kite.

I pointed my gun at Chase and stepped back, hoping for a standoff. "Whoa, whoa, I just came to warn you. The Fed is here somewhere. I saw his car in the forest."

"I took care of him and I just took care of the other traitors. Now it's your turn."

He fired at me and missed. I tried to shoot him, but man, that gun I had was old and frozen. It wouldn't fire. I threw it and hit Chase in the head, making him madder than a rattlesnake. He shot at me again and missed again.

All I wanted to do was get out of there or I knew I'd end up like Blake and Sophia. I reached for something to hold him off, grabbed the closest bottle, and threw it. My aim was off. The bottle hit the corner of the table and shattered, liquid and glass spraying all over Chase.

Hanna squinted down at the last paragraph. The writing was barely legible.

He screamed, the worst sound I have ever heard in my life. He dropped the gun, fell to one knee, and brought his hands to his face. I turned and ran out of the cabin, through the forest and back to my car, the echo of Chase's bloodcurdling scream ringing in my ears.

CHAPTER 40

BY THE TIME SHE WAS ABLE TO make out the last bit of the letter, Hanna's heart was pounding. She stood still, the room quiet but for the sound of Joe's oxygen feed and his labored breathing. She rubbed her temple and looked up at Joe.

"Chase said that he took care of Gilly?"

Joe nodded.

"Did that mean he killed him?"

Joe's thin shoulders shrugged.

"Why did you confess? Why did you let Chase get away with murder?" She asked the questions knowing Joe couldn't answer. He indicated that he wanted to write something. She flipped the page over and handed the pad back to him. She leaned close to the bed while the shaky hand began to scrawl again.

No choice. I wanted you and your mom to live.

Hanna felt as if her heart constricted.

Joe shifted in his bed, tried to lean forward. Tears fell from his eyes. His face flamed red with the effort. He spoke in a whisper.

"In—the—short—time—I—had—to—think—the deal— only way."

He caught his breath.

Hanna could barely hear him. "You trusted them to keep their word." Hanna tried to process everything.

"Trusted—Everett. He's—no—killer."

"What about Gilly?"

He shook his head. "Never. Saw."

Hanna considered this. If Joe had told the truth, the federal authorities would have paid more attention. There would not have been a simple three-person tribunal. The more she thought about it, the angrier she got.

Thirty-five years in prison.

Joe was writing, rather scrawling, more words.

My only leverage. Big Al—would have hurt you both. Keep you and Mom safe. Couldn't talk to Feds. Only way—keep you safe. Good trade.

Joe had sacrificed his life for hers.

She couldn't take her eyes off the dying man. Thoughts of all the years lost paralyzed her, then anger swelled. She sniffled, her throat tight. But there was no time for emotion, no time for recrimination. They had to find Nathan. She'd been here too long.

"Now that we've found the bodies, it casts doubt on your story, your confession. And if Chase thought Nathan was coming to talk about Blake and Sophia . . ." Her voice trailed off.

Her father's head turned slowly from side to side.

"If this happened like you say, there is no way Chase could have dumped the bodies. He was injured, in the hospital. Who put the bodies in the lake?"

A knock on the door made her jump. It was Jared. "What are you doing here?"

"Manny Pacheco is in the ER with a dislocated kneecap. Asa

had to arrest Carver. I wanted you to know, and I didn't want you to run off by yourself and do something crazy."

"I can call on resources. I need to find Nathan." She turned her radio back up, certain Asa had probably tried to call.

"I want to help." He frowned. "What is it, Hanna? You're unsettled. Did Joe die?" He looked toward the bedroom.

"He's weak. I just found out that he was never the killer." She handed him the letter.

He glanced at it.

"You're sure he's being truthful?"

"He has nothing to lose. And it fits the evidence." She sighed. "I'm going to talk to Everett. I'll notify the sheriff's department and ask for backup."

"How does Nathan being missing figure into all this?" Jared asked. "Did Nathan think Chase was the one who killed Edda and the other women?"

"He knew that the guy who dumped Edda drove an SUV. He was trying to eliminate SUV owners. Everett has four. According to Joe, Chase killed Blake and Sophia. But he couldn't have put them in the lake. There are more people involved in this. If Nathan took a trip up there to ask about the current murders and Chase feared his past murders had been discovered . . ."

"Nathan could be in real trouble."

"I have to get up there."

Jared put a hand on her arm. "Hanna, however I can help, I will."

She held his gaze, memories of all the crazy stuff they did as kids flooding back. Rock climbing was life or death, and he was always fearless. No matter what they did, she felt safe with Jared. This was life or death as well, but they'd be facing bullets.

"You're not a cop." Her protest was weak.

"No, but I'm an EMT. I can do first aid."

Hanna didn't want to argue. "We're running out of time." She opened the front door. "Do what I say, clear?"

"Clear."

Hanna cast a glance back at Joe. He was still writing.

She headed for her car, with Jared on her heels.

CHAPTER 41

HANNA HOPPED IN HER PATROL SUV and started the engine, but Jared was nowhere to be seen. He'd been right behind her. She jerked around when he rapped on the back window, then unlocked the door. He opened it and tossed a bag in the back seat, then climbed in the front seat.

"You have your toys; I have mine."

Hanna nodded, backed out of her driveway, and then headed for the Buckley compound. She radioed her intentions and asked for county backup.

On the way she explained to Jared what was in the letter Joe had written, the details of how Chase killed Blake and Sophia. And possibly Agent Gilly.

"Why would Joe confess to a crime he didn't commit?"

"He told me why he did it," Hanna said. "The bigger question for me is about the prosecutor and the judge who accepted such a scant confession to lock a man up for thirty-five years."

"The Buckley money, is that what you're thinking?"

"What else? I'm sure they didn't want Chase going to prison for murder. That is so hard for me to hear." Hanna tapped on the steering wheel, fidgeting. "Everett was good to my mom, and he's never been anything but supportive for me."

"Maybe he had to be."

Hanna glanced at Jared. "You're right. He was holding up his end of the bargain, wasn't he?" She concentrated on the road.

Jared reached over and put a hand on her shoulder. "I can't imagine what you're going through right now. All these years without a dad and then to find this out. I know you're committed to rush up into the unknown, no matter the danger, and that I should try to talk you out of it."

"But?"

"I'm going to rush right in there with you, so don't try and talk me out of it."

Jared always had her back. Hanna's heart swelled. They'd traveled a few miles before Hanna felt she could speak.

"Thanks, Jared." She turned into the long driveway of the Buckley estate, preparing to input the gate code. Everett had given the code to law enforcement and fire personnel. When she rounded the corner, the gate stood open.

"Is that normal?" Jared asked.

"I don't know. I don't come up here enough. All the security was upgraded several weeks ago, so I imagine this being open is not an accident." She saw the fence off to the right was up and completely blocking the access road she'd taken when she'd driven up to tell Everett about Scott's death.

She made note of the cameras on either side of the gate. They would not be able to arrive unannounced.

It was another ten minutes before they turned the corner, and the main house came into view. Hanna stopped and took a careful survey. Everett always had ranch hands in residence, though only a skeleton crew was working right now. He'd moved most of his horses to a different ranch because of the Crest Fire. From the looks of it, he had not brought them back yet. There was no activity in the corral or the exercise ring. Would there be this late in the day?

Four black SUVs, two pickup trucks, and a van belonging to a local landscaper were parked in front of the house. And there was Nathan's car, off to the left, in between the landscaper and one of the pickups.

"Nathan's car." Hanna spoke half to herself and started to pull forward.

"Looks like everyone is home," Jared said.

Hanna got on the radio and let them know that she'd found Nathan's car.

"Can you give me an ETA on backup?"

"10-4, Chief. They are approaching the driveway now, ten to fifteen ETA."

Hanna acknowledged the transmission and went back to studying the scene. Goose bumps prickled her arms. It was so quiet here. Every other time she visited, it teemed with activity. At the very least there should be seven people here besides Nathan, Everett, his cook, a maid, Timmons, Braden, Chase, and Grover. Things were dead calm.

"Wait in the car, Jared. Better yet, walk around to the back with me and I'll give you a spare vest."

"Since this is very creepy, I think I'll accept that offer."

They both exited the SUV and met where Hanna opened the back hatch. She pulled a Kevlar vest out and gave it to Jared. Never taking her eyes off the front door, she said, "Will you wait here?"

"Will you wait for backup?"

She stared at him. His expression was calm and set. "Wherever you go, I go."

"Fine." She started for the door, then stopped. Broken glass littered the front porch and what looked like several bullet holes pierced the front door. The lock was shot off. She drew her weapon.

Jared stopped her. "Wait for backup."

"The door is all shot up, Jared. Something is wrong."

"All the more reason to wait."

"You're right, but every second we wait . . ." Hanna knew she should wait, but this went beyond Nathan now. A lot of lives were at risk.

She bounded up the five steps to the big double door. Pushing the partially opened door a bit wider, gun up, she called out, "Everett, it's Hanna. Everything okay?" Blood was smeared on the door and on the floor.

She shoved the door wide open. The first thing she saw was Grover's body.

"Jared, we've got a man down."

She hurried to Grover, hearing Jared's footsteps right behind her. Grover had been shot. There was an entry wound in his chest, and a lot of blood. Hoping against hope, Hanna checked his neck and found no pulse. Jared knelt and tried as well. He looked over at Hanna and shook his head.

Hanna surveyed the entryway. It looked as if there had been a fight. Broken glass, a shot-up wall. From the way Grover lay and the stains on the wall, he appeared to have been standing when he was hit. She'd been to this house several times, the first when she was a child. She tried to remember the layout, rooms, entries, and exits.

"I've got to clear the house," she said to Jared. "It's one level, ranch style. I don't hear anything, but I need to check. Can you stay here and let the deputies know when they arrive and make certain no one comes through that door to surprise us?"

"You got it." Jared stood and closed the double doors. "Be careful."

Gun up, Hanna went left, where she knew the living room and

Everett's study was. This should be done with at least two people, but she had to figure out what had happened. The big rooms were clear. She also cleared Scott's room; it looked no different than it had when she'd been here to search after his crash.

Hanna crossed into the kitchen. The place was a mess. If there had been a fight, it took place here. The window was busted, and as she walked into the room, her boots crunched on broken glass. The intercom on the wall had been shot up. She looked up where she remembered the camera was and saw that it, too, had been destroyed along with the monitors.

Quickly she crossed to the other side of the house. Braden's bedroom, Everett's bedroom, three bathrooms—no one else was in the house. It was so very quiet.

She lowered her gun and went back to the entryway, surprised the deputies were not here yet.

"All clear?" Jared asked.

"Yeah, this is so weird."

She thought back to when Everett had told her about his security upgrades. She tried to remember all that he'd said. Then it came to her.

"Panic room."

"He has a panic room?" Jared asked.

"Yes."

"Chief." Her radio crackled.

"I copy, we've got a 929, and maybe other people hurt. Roll medics."

"10-4, we have a problem. We can't get the gate open for access."

"What?" Hanna arched her eyebrows. "It was wide-open for me."

"It's shut now, and it's heavy-duty. None of the codes work. We'll get it open. Be advised, I don't have an ETA."

"So someone closed the gate after we came through," Jared said after Hanna acknowledged the transmission.

Hanna nodded. "Let's get down to the panic room and see if anyone made it there. It's in the basement." Everett had modified the original canning room to be a panic room.

Hanna went back through the kitchen to the door for the basement. She raised her weapon again, then slowly made her way down the stairs. Charlie's calm voice came over the radio telling her that Fire was en route with a way to breach the gate. Backup would get here. Would it be in time?

In spite of the questions peppering her mind, calm infused her. Dispatch was a lifeline for cops—and it helped in stressful situations to hear the calm steadiness of a dispatcher who would take care of you.

She continued down the stairs and Jared followed. In the basement there was more evidence of a rampage—bullet holes and shell casings were everywhere. But she did find a working intercom. Hanna hit the button. "Everett, are you in there? It's Hanna."

A few seconds later he answered, his voice weak, "Yeah, I'm here. Where's Chase?"

"I don't know."

"He's not out there anywhere?"

"Not that I've seen."

"How about Braden?"

Hanna and Jared exchanged glances.

"No, Everett, nobody is here."

There was a minute of silence, then she heard locks being disengaged. Mechanical gears rumbled as the thick vault-like door eased open.

A bloodied Everett stepped out. It appeared as if he'd taken a bullet to the shoulder. He was wrapped in bloody bandages. He leaned against the door, eyes shrouded in pain.

"Chase is on a rampage. He's got Braden."

CHAPTER 42

"Braden?" Hanna's animosity, which had been building toward Everett, dissipated. Whatever Everett had done to her father, Braden was not part of it.

Everett nodded. He closed his eyes and started to fall. Jared caught him. As he pulled Everett aside, she saw more people in the panic room. Two men, one she recognized as the landscaper; the other was Timmons. He was also bleeding, holding a soaked rag to his head. Behind them were Everett's cook and housekeeper. No Nathan.

"What happened?" Hanna asked.

Timmons answered. "Chase went crazy. Detective Sharp came to talk to him, and he just lost it. I've never seen him so mad, so crazed. Everett tried to calm him down, but he wouldn't have it. He shot Everett and grabbed Braden."

"What does he want with Braden?"

Pale, Timmons shook his head. He leaned against the wall.

"He ranted about so much, not really making sense. He's paranoid. Maybe high. Grover went back topside to try and save Braden."

"Grover is dead."

"I figured."

"Where's Nathan?"

Timmons shook his head. "Last I saw him, he was walking down the path to Chase's place. I don't know what happened down there. When Chase came up from his space, it was chaos."

"How long was Nathan with Chase?"

"Ten, fifteen minutes? Ma'am, we were running for our lives. Look around. Chase was shooting at everything. He's convinced the Feds will kick down his door and drag him away. He says that a cripple will never last in prison. We backtracked to the panic room."

What he said about Chase's frenzy was true, Hanna saw as she surveyed the room. Bullet holes were everywhere.

She looked down at Jared. "How is Everett?"

"He needs a doctor. He's lost a lot of blood."

"How about you?" Hanna asked Timmons.

"I was just grazed. I'll be fine."

"Can you open the front gate from here? We have backup and medics coming. The gate is closed."

"You're here."

"It was open for me. But it closed for them."

Timmons eyes went wide. "Oh my, Chase has control. He locked them out. We should get back in the panic room. He can't get in there." Timmons started to usher the women back into the room.

Hanna grasped his arm. Something was missing from his story. "None of this makes any sense. If he's afraid of the Feds, why did he kill Grover? Why try to kill all of you?"

Timmons jerked away. "He doesn't want to go to jail. He's not thinking straight. Drugs are probably part of it. Whatever Detective Sharp said to him, well, it set him off. Chase's grasp of reality is gone."

Jared stood and helped Everett to his feet. He was shaky but he stood on his own.

"Let them go back in there and hide," Everett said. "This is really about me, and you." He nodded at Hanna.

"It has to do with my dad, doesn't it?" She held Everett's gaze.

"Yeah. When Sharp got here today, Chase thought it was because your dad told him what really happened that night at Beecher's cabin. It scared him."

"What really happened?"

Everett closed his eyes. "Chase happened." He opened his eyes, held hers. His gaze was set in stone. "He's got to be stopped."

"Why take Braden?"

"He sees Braden as his future. The only one he can trust, the only one not out to get him." Everett gave a weak shake of his head, leaning against the wall. "He wanted to take us all out, but you most of all. He thinks Scott controlled him all these years to protect you."

"To protect me?"

Everett looked away. "You found the Carsons. You're smart enough to know now that your dad didn't kill them."

"I figured it out." Her anger ramped up again. So much had been lost by lies. "My dad is innocent."

"Chase was high on drugs then. Yeah, he killed the Carsons, but your dad almost killed him. No one in the cabin that night was innocent."

"But my dad took the fall."

"My father wanted to protect Chase at any cost. I agreed with him. I did what I had to do to protect my son. Scott kept Chase in check. Kept him from hurting himself and anyone else. But Scott is gone, and I can't control Chase. It only got worse when they let your dad out. You don't know how hard it was to keep him from driving down there and killing Joe."

"Did he poison Scott?"

"I don't know, I—" He closed his eyes again for a moment. "I can't see him doing that. He depended on Scott, but I have no other explanation."

"Did he kill Nathan?" Hanna asked the question she feared the answer to most.

"Maybe. If I'd have been here, I would have stopped him. But I'd just gotten back from the fire line. And Grover had Braden. Chase was wild, out of control. He might only have one leg, but he knows how to use a gun."

Nathan could have been the first casualty this afternoon. Her insides churned with a tsunami of emotions. Nathan was her friend and colleague. She made her decision.

"You all get back in the panic room. I don't know when my backup will arrive. Stay there until they do." She turned to Jared. "Will they be okay? Should you stay with Everett?"

"You're not getting rid of me. If they keep pressure on his wound, he'll be okay for the time being."

He helped Everett return to the panic room. Before the door closed, Timmons said, "Chase isn't very mobile. That's the only advantage you'll have."

The door closed and the locks reengaged.

Hanna bounded up the stairs.

"Do you have a plan?" Jared asked as he followed.

Hanna shook her head and radioed to her backup to find out their ETA.

"We're almost through the gate," Asa said.

"10-4. Everett and four others are in the basement panic room. They need medics."

"Where are you?"

"I'm trying to find Nathan; he's on the property somewhere."

"10-4, we'll be there as soon as we can."

Hanna clicked the mike in response and looked at Jared. "Chase must know we're here. He hasn't appeared. I'm going to go to him."

"Then so am I."

It was useless to try and make him stay. He had a vest on, like she did. *Oh, Lord, keep us all safe.*

"There's a path." She pointed to the right. A brick path was lit every few feet with garden lights. "I remember Grover telling us when we came for Scott's things. Chase has his own space down that way. I've never been down there, but it must be easy to get to because he isn't all that mobile." She started that way.

"Even though it's dark, this is a wide-open path. We walk down there, he'll hear and see us coming."

"We've lost the element of surprise. He opened the gate for me, then closed it. How long have we been here already?" She checked her watch. "Counting the drive up? Maybe thirty minutes and he hasn't shown his face."

"He's lying in wait?"

"You have a better idea?"

Jared stood, hands on hips. "I don't."

"Then let's go." She started for the path, and Jared stopped her.

"One minute." He jogged to the SUV and grabbed his backpack from the rear seat. "It's first aid and stuff. In case."

Hanna continued on the path, Jared at her side.

"Keep your world small."

She took a deep breath. She had to shut out the fear rising for Nathan and Braden—and the urge to run full speed down the path to confront Chase.

CHAPTER 43

THE SOUND OF MUSIC ASSAULTED Jared's ears as he reached Hanna and secured his backpack. He could see that she was on the edge. He was right there with her when he thought about a ten-year-old kid being at the mercy of a crazy man. A man who had already killed at least three people.

Jared needed to be clear about something before they continued. "Hanna, before we face Chase, I need to know."

She stopped, turned, stepping off to the side of the path. He did as well.

"Know what?"

"Did Chase kill Edda?" He kept his voice low.

"I can't tell you. Nathan was here to check into that. The guy who dumped Edda had a *Vote Keyes for Chief* bumper sticker on his SUV. Did you notice if any of Everett's SUVs have the sticker? Nathan was trying to eliminate Everett."

"Whoa, instead he stepped on a land mine."

"If Chase went right rudder because of what happened thirty-five years ago, he's a killer. Does it matter if he also killed Edda?"

"I just want to know."

"I'm not sure. All I want to do is find Braden and Nathan. Are you okay?"

"I'm mad. It still hurts about her."

Pain and understanding crossed her features. Then just as quickly, her face was a mask of resolve. "Me too; let's keep going."

They kept walking, staying to the side of the path. The music got louder. It was hard rock from the seventies and eighties. They were moving toward the source. The closer they got, the louder the blaring music became. They rounded the corner to a wide-open doorway. Lights blazed, the music now deafening. Chase was nowhere to be seen.

"Stay behind me," Hanna spoke directly into his ear, and he barely heard.

She brought her gun up, and Jared did what she asked. But he was ready to push her out of harm's way.

It was difficult to think, the music was so loud. The walls seemed to vibrate with the drumbeat.

The front door opened to a narrow hallway. At the end of the hall was a light, and from the sound, that was the location of the music.

Hanna proceeded down the hall. She was calm and steady. Because of that, Jared was calm.

She walked slowly, but she slowed even more the closer she got to the doorway opening. To Jared it looked as if it was the kitchen. The smell of stale bacon grease wafted in the air.

Hanna poked her head into the room. Then she moved fast. It startled Jared and he was two steps behind her. He rounded the corner in time to see Hanna grab a gun from Chase. He was seated at a table littered with beer cans. His arm was splayed across the table and his head rested on it. The gun made it look as if he'd been sitting with the weapon, ready to shoot anyone who came through the door, but he'd fallen asleep instead. Pills were strewn all over the table along with a baggie of weed.

Hanna holstered her weapon and unclipped her handcuffs. Jared caught up with her but was too late. She already had the man cuffed.

"Is he drunk or high?" Jared asked, and then realized with the music blaring she couldn't hear. He looked around and saw the source of the music and shut it off. The silence was heaven.

"Drunk or high?" Jared repeated.

"I think he's a lot of things."

Jared checked Chase's pulse. His breathing was shallow and pulse very weak. He checked an eye, saw the pinpoint pupil, and answered his own question. "He overdosed with something." The pills looked to him like stuff he'd seen on calls. "Probably fentanyl."

"Is he going to die?" Hanna asked.

"I can't say how long he has."

Hanna looked around the kitchen, then hurried to the next room. When she came back in the kitchen, she looked at Jared. For the first time stress and fear showed on her face.

"Where are Nathan and Braden?"

CHAPTER 44

HANNA WENT THROUGH ALL of Chase's living quarters, turning on the lights. It was small, with a kitchen, living room, and bedroom. Her ears still rang from the deafening music. The fear she'd kept at bay had breached the wall she'd put up. There was no sign of Braden or Nathan anywhere, and she was in that space where every bit of her hope was being darkened by a shadow of terror. She had Chase secured, but he wasn't even conscious. Guns, shell casings, and unspent bullets were everywhere, but no blood and no bodies.

Hanna stepped to the table and shook Chase's shoulder. "Chase, come on, wake up."

His head lolled back and forth, and he gave no indication that he'd heard.

"He's more than three sheets to the wind," Jared said. "Only Narcan will help him."

"He's—" Her radio beeped.

"Chief, we've been trying to raise you." Charlie's voice was uncharacteristically stressed.

"10-4, I copy you now. There was a lot of background noise."

"10-4. Asa and the deputies are in the main house. Requesting your 20."

"I'm down the path, to the right of the house, where Chase stays. Care for the people in the panic room first. They need medics. I have Chase in custody and am code 4."

"Acknowledged."

Hanna looked at Jared. "I'm open to suggestions."

"I've been thinking. Suppose Chase has a panic room like his father."

"Good thought." She looked around. Where could that be?

"Chief, Chief." Asa and two deputies burst into the room, interrupting her search.

"I'm okay." She pointed to Chase. "He's in custody. But I haven't found Braden or Nathan."

"Everett said to look in the mine."

"Look in the mine?"

Asa nodded. "That's what he said before he passed out."

"This place was a—"

"Do you hear that?" Jared held up a hand and interrupted.

Hanna couldn't hear anything. "Everyone, quiet your radios and stay still for a minute."

They complied. In a few seconds, Hanna did hear something. It sounded like yelling, far away.

"I hear it. It's coming from over here." She stepped to a door that was padlocked. For some reason, she'd not noticed it before and credited that to tunnel vision.

"We've got a key for that." Asa got on the radio and asked for someone to bring it down.

While they waited, Hanna put her ear against the door. Someone was yelling; it sounded echoey and far away.

A few minutes later, a firefighter jogged in with a set of bolt cutters. In short order, the lock was cut and the door opened.

It exposed what looked like an enclosed back porch. Hanna

flipped the light switch. She could see that the porch gave way to a cave.

"It's a mine shaft," Jared said.

"I hear Nathan." Hanna hurried forward. Ten or fifteen feet away, the floor opened to a gaping hole.

"Hey, we're down here," could be heard echoing up from the opening. The boy's voice was also audible. "Here, here, we're here."

Hanna got down on her knees and peered down into blackness, shining a flashlight Asa had handed her. "Nathan?"

"Hanna! Thank God. I'm here, but I'm all busted up."

Hanna's fear dissipated, relief rolling over her. "What about Braden?"

"He's okay. And Pancho."

The deputies shone their lights into the inky blackness as well. About eighty or ninety feet down, she could see Braden looking up and Nathan waving his hand.

Hanna stood and looked around the dank, smelly place. There was no way to descend. No ladder was in evidence. There weren't even any ropes. She shone her light along the wall. There had been ropes at one time. Anchors were embedded in the stone wall; she counted at least five. "We need to get them out."

"I've got this." Jared took the backpack off his back and opened it up. He had climbing gear.

"You can't go down there."

"Why not? I can anchor up here and go down there to check on them while you let Fire know we need a rescue team. I have a first aid kit and some lighting."

Hanna could not think of any reason why not. Jared was an EMT, and he was a climber. He was perfect for the job.

He climbed into his harness, and Hanna checked each of the

anchors. They all appeared set and secured. In the meanwhile, Asa radioed to Fire to explain what they needed.

Jared picked an anchor and set up his belay device. He put his backpack back on and prepared to descend.

Hanna gave him a radio. "This is so we don't have to yell. Be careful, Jared."

He took the radio and shoved it in his pack. "I got this." He reached over and squeezed her hand, holding her gaze. Hanna held her breath when he let go and backed up to the side of the shaft, then proceeded to rappel into the darkness.

❈

Jared was in his element, even though it was dark. Climbing was one of his passions. The wall of the mine shaft was slippery but navigable and he was at the bottom in no time. He unclipped himself and turned, shining his light against the wall first where Braden sat, cradling his dog, and then at Nathan. Down this close to him, Jared could see the pain in his eyes. His right leg was bent at an unnatural angle.

He radioed to Hanna. "I'm down safe. Tell Fire we'll need a basket for Braden and a backboard and splints for Sharp."

"I got it." Jared recognized the voice of Fire Captain Darling. "Is the boy injured?"

Braden sat a few feet away from Nathan. He still had a cast on his wrist. It was dirty but intact.

Jared knelt. "Hey, buddy, are you okay?"

He nodded. "I'm afraid of the dark." He was shaking. It was dank and cold in the tight space.

Jared smiled, took his backpack off. "Me too." He handed Braden his flashlight and pulled out another from his bag. "You hold on to the light. They're going to send a ride down for the two of you, okay?"

Braden nodded. "Where is Papa Everett?"

"Up there somewhere. You'll see him soon."

"Braden and the dog are not injured," Jared told Darling before he turned his attention to Nathan. Why were they so far apart? When his light hit Nathan, he saw why.

Moving to Nathan, keeping his back to Braden, his light picked up the bones, the remains of someone or something just beyond Nathan.

Jared knelt in front of Nathan. "The kid looks fine. What happened to you?" He ran his light over the detective. His face was bruised. Tomorrow he'd have a wicked black eye.

"Chase, he let me down on a rope, then cut it about halfway down. I fell the rest of the way." Nathan winced. "When he lowered Braden, he did it slowly. I heard him tell the boy that he was protecting him."

Jared shone his light on the bent leg. "I'm going to have to splint that to get you out of here."

Nathan nodded, groaning some. "My wrist too. Do what you have to do. Just get me out of here."

Jared moved the light across Nathan's body and saw that the wrist was busted too. "We'll get you something for the pain. You didn't hit you head or hurt your back?"

"No, my leg and my arm took the brunt of the fall. I had a flashlight; the battery died. There are other guests down here."

"I see that. Let me tell them what we need and get Braden out of here. Hang on, okay?"

Nathan gave a weak nod.

Jared stood and let Darling know the situation. The first thing they lowered were more lights, then a basket for Braden and the dog with splints and pain medication for Nathan. Jared hurried to get Braden set. The light illuminated a lot of unpleasantness in the shaft.

"Keep your eyes closed and hold on to the dog," Jared told Braden. The boy nodded, hugged the dog, and the men above drew the basket up and out. Jared turned his attention to Nathan. He had medication and splints, so he went to work. Nathan was going into shock, and he needed to get out of this damp hole.

Once he was medicated and splinted, Jared laid out the backboard. "I've got to strap you down on here. You good to go?"

"Yeah, I feel a lot better now."

Jared pulled as Nathan slid and lay on the board. Carefully, Jared secured his head and neck, belted him down, wanting to make it as secure as possible because any jerky movement would be agony for Nathan on the way up.

As he was double-checking the belts, Nathan tried to grab his arm.

"What, too tight?"

"No. I need to know. Do you love Hanna?"

Taken aback, Jared rocked back on his heels. "We don't need to talk about this now."

"We do. I think she loves you. Before I back off, I want to make sure you won't hurt her again. If you do, you'll answer to me."

"I think that's the medication talking." Jared jerked the rope, which was the signal for the guys above to bring Nathan up.

Jared stood, staring up at the backboard ascending the shaft.

"Do you love Hanna?"

"I think she loves you."

The two phrases jolted Jared to the core. Of course he loved Hanna. He'd never stopped. If it were true, that she loved him as well—Jared wanted to believe it—he wanted to climb up out of the hole, grab her, and never let go.

CHAPTER 45

BRADEN EMERGED FROM the shaft dirty but uninjured.

"Hey, bud," Hanna said as she helped him out. "We have to stop meeting like this."

He wrapped her in a hug, and she felt his body shaking.

"Where's Papa Everett?"

"He had to go to the hospital, but he's okay." She looked to Asa. They needed to call Children's Services for Braden, but she balked, preferring to find someone he knew. He had a lot of great-uncles.

"Asa, have medics check Braden out and then see if Mayor Milton has an emergency contact, someplace we can send Braden."

Asa nodded. "Will do." He took Braden's hand. "Come on, sport, let's get you taken care of."

They left and Hanna paced until Nathan appeared at the top of the shaft. The waiting medics gently pulled him up and placed him on the gurney.

"Nathan." Hanna stepped forward and set a hand on his shoulder. A hug would not be appropriate, but the relief Hanna felt knowing he was okay made her want to hug him. He was pale and dirty. His eyes clouded with pain.

"Hey, I'm okay. I knew you'd find me."

"We need to get him out of here," Stokes said.

Hanna stepped aside and let the medics push Nathan toward the ambulance. She returned to the mine shaft and watched Jared pull himself up out of the hole.

"Hanna, there are more bodies down there." He unhooked his harness and started working with his ropes. "I looked around a bit, at least three human skeletons."

"Three?"

"Yeah. The first thing I thought was that one could be Gilly. I didn't poke around the bodies, but just in what I saw, I don't think they all died at the same time."

He bent down to wrap his things up and put them away in his backpack.

"Thank you, Jared, for going down there and getting them."

He looked up, surprise on his face. "Hey, you know me, any excuse to climb." He shoved his hands in his pockets. "And I'm a firefighter-EMT now, so technically, it's my job." He smiled his crooked smile and Hanna felt her heart skip. The emotional roller coaster of the day took a toll on her self-control.

Jared was always the only one for her, wasn't he?

It felt so right at this tension-filled moment that he was here, with her, and they were a team.

She stepped forward and threw her arms around Jared, holding him close and relaxing in his arms when he returned the hug.

❋

Besides sheriff's investigators, federal authorities also descended on the Buckley compound. With Everett in the hospital and Grover dead, two lawyers from San Francisco arrived to handle everything that was happening concerning the Buckleys. A thorough search of the mine cavern revealed three skeletal remains. Brett Gilly was one. A badge and an ID still survived on his decayed frame. The other two had no ID. One belonged to a woman, based on the deteriorating clothing and bone structure; the other appeared male.

It was late Saturday morning before Hanna was able to leave the crime scene. By then she'd heard that Everett was recovering after surgery on his shoulder, and his prognosis was good. Nathan also had surgery on his lower leg. It was a bad break made worse by the fact he'd sat on the floor of the mine shaft for hours without treatment.

Mayor Milton had taken Braden into her home and then notified his mother. Perhaps the only good news of the whole day was that Kelly planned to fly home from Hollywood to come take custody of him.

At least Hanna hoped that was good news. Poor Braden had been through so much. And he was very worried about his great-grandfather, a man he obviously idolized.

She pulled into her driveway tired and drained. There hadn't even been time to think about what to do about Joe. He deserved to have his name cleared. But did he have the time to see that process through? More importantly, could she find the hard evidence that she needed to find?

Hanna pulled herself out of the car, longing for a shower and bed. The caregiver met her at the door.

"Chief, you look exhausted."

"I am, Arthur. It's been a long night."

"I'm sorry to make it worse. Joe passed about ten minutes ago."

Hanna stared. "He . . ." She couldn't finish the sentence.

"His body just gave out." He held out the writing pad. "Joe finished writing this, and he wanted to make sure you kept his box of letters. They are all addressed to you. I called for the funeral home. Not sure when they will arrive."

He was still talking when Hanna walked past him to the guest room. The oxygen machine was silent. Joe looked as if he were sleeping. It was as quiet as death. She sat next to the bed and looked at the piece of paper in her hand. No neat block writing; it was difficult to read. Made more difficult by the tears that clouded her eyes.

I had to take the deal. No choice. Big Al said they had holes to drop you and your mom in that were so deep, no one would ever find you. Don't cry for me, Hanna. I'm not sure the man I was then would have been able to take care of you, raise you right. I think I took care of you better than I ever could by going to prison, finding Jesus, and praying for you every minute of every day. I took the path God had for me. It seems wrong and sad and hard, but God chose to be with me through it, not take me out of it. Please continue to be happy and live good. Your father loves you, and he is so very proud of you.

Hanna wept.

CHAPTER 46

"My father is dead," Hanna told Everett. It was Sunday afternoon, and she was the first person he agreed to see after his surgery, while he recovered in the hospital. Everett was so pale. For the first time since Hanna could remember, he looked every bit his age and then some.

He looked away. "Sorry for your loss."

"I don't think that you really are. I want to clear his name."

Everett fiddled with the pulse monitor on his finger. "What does it matter?"

"It matters to me."

"You don't know the whole story."

"I know enough. You can fill in the blanks. Chase killed the Carsons. Did he kill Gilly as well?"

Everett closed his eyes and leaned back in bed. "I honestly don't know about Gilly. It was so very long ago. None of it was my idea. I've been afraid of Chase since he was ten years old. My father could control him, so could Scott. But I couldn't."

He swallowed and paused. "That night we found him at the cabin, acid-burned face and leg, I thought he would die. When he survived, I hoped he'd become more manageable. But he didn't. He was less mobile, but he was still Chase." Everett held up a hand. "The Carsons were not at the cabin when I found Chase. I never knew they were in the lake until you found them."

"If you didn't help dispose of their bodies, it had to be Scott."

"No. It had to be my dad, not Scott."

Hanna considered that answer. It was easy to blame the dead guy. "Did Chase kill Scott?"

"I told you, I don't know for sure. Scott controlled Chase, but he was tired of it. He warned me that Chase might be into bad things. I didn't want to hear it. There have been many times in the last few months when Chase took off and no one knew where he was."

"He was more mobile with the prosthesis."

Everett gave a slight nod. "Scott planned to marry Valerie and take Braden and raise him in Corte Madera. He wanted the boy to grow up right, away from his crazy grandfather. I tried to find a way to deal with Chase, figuring for the day Scott would move, then . . ." His voice trailed off.

"You don't have to deal with him anymore, not if you tell the truth. He shot you, tried to kill you, and he did kill Grover. If you add the other murders my father confessed to, Chase will never see the light of day."

"Your dad wasn't innocent. He cooked meth."

"He didn't murder anyone in cold blood."

Everett went quiet. After a minute he said, "Where's Braden?"

"With his mom. Kelly flew back to town last night." Hanna let him think about that for a few seconds. "Agent Gilly was down in the hole. And he wasn't alone. They found the remains of two other people down there. Who else did Chase murder?"

Everett looked at her. "What?" There was genuine surprise in his face and voice.

"Chase killed more than the Carsons. You didn't know that?"

"No. Three more bodies?"

For a minute, Hanna felt sorry for him. But that dissipated quickly when she thought about her father spending over three decades behind bars for something he didn't do.

"Yeah, I'd think long and hard about what you want to tell the FBI. They swooped in last night, and they're handling the shooting at your house, and the dead bodies. Chase is a serial killer. He may even be the Lonely Heart Killer. I hope for your sake you weren't helping him. I don't think even you can pay the FBI off." She turned to leave.

"Where is Chase now?"

"He's in medical custody. He overdosed on fentanyl. Paramedics brought him back with Narcan on the way to the hospital. He's not talking, but we have his weapons and everyone's statements from that night, so he's got a no-bail hold on him."

Everett considered this.

The door opened and in walked Mayor Milton and a couple of men Hanna recognized as Everett's attorneys.

"Chief," the mayor said with surprise.

"I was just leaving."

"Nothing Mr. Buckley said is admissible without his attorneys present," one of the suits said.

Hanna ignored them and left the room. It was time to go visit Nathan. He was in intensive care now. He'd picked up some kind of infection from the mine shaft, and doctors were worried about his leg. Both bones in his lower leg had shattered, and his ankle was a mess. From everything Hanna had heard, he had a lot of surgeries and rehab ahead of him. He was down one level, so she got on the elevator.

His mother and father were there. Only one visitor was allowed at a time, so Hanna waited with his mother while his father was with Nathan.

"Hanna, Nathan has told me so much about you."

"I'm sorry that we have to meet this way."

"So am I. But I'm thankful that you found my son when you did. Doctors say that he would not have survived much longer in that hole. I'm grateful for the firefighter who splinted his leg and gave him first aid. I'm told that helped a great deal as well. Maybe saved him from amputation."

Nathan's dad came out and indicated that Hanna could go in.

"I'm not sure that I want to cut into your time."

"Go," he said. "Nathan wants to see you."

She had to gown up and put on a mask. Hanna pulled the mask up as the nurse told her she only had five minutes. She walked into the dim, quiet room, the sound of monitors beeping.

Nathan smiled when she came in. Both eyes were black now, though he looked better than the night she watched paramedics pull him from the shaft. His eyes were more alert, less pain filled. His left wrist was in a cast, and his left leg was wrapped and raised, resting on pillows.

"Hey, thanks for stopping by." His voice was strong.

"I hate to take time from your mom."

"She understands. I need to know what happened. Why Chase went nuts. He was so angry."

"He never said anything to you?"

"No. I knocked on the door. He opened it and jammed a gun in my face. Then he hit me in the head." Nathan shifted in the bed. "Next thing I know, I'm being pushed down a mine shaft. He let me dangle for a few minutes, asking me what Joe told me. He didn't believe me when I said I hadn't spoken to Joe." Nathan took a breath and shifted again in the bed. "Did Joe talk to you?"

"It's a long story, longer than my five minutes. I'll just say that Chase killed the Carsons thirty-five years ago."

"Not Joe?"

"No."

"How is he?"

"My dad died yesterday."

"Hanna, I'm sorry." He reached out to grip her hand, but no touching was allowed.

"Hey, it was a forgone conclusion, right?" She surprised herself by how steady her voice was. "I only hope I can clear his name. Enough about me. What is next for you?"

"More surgery after they are sure I've beat the infection. And then a long period of physical therapy. My partner is one floor up. We might rehab part of the time together. My only regret is I didn't catch the Lonely Heart Killer."

"You left a lot for the new team to follow up on. They'll get him."

"Thank you for sending Jared down to help me. He did a good job."

"He's a good guy."

"I know he is. And I know you still have feelings for him."

"Nathan—"

"Let me finish. Don't worry about me. I'll always care for you, but I don't think you're being honest with yourself about him. Work that out. I'm not going anywhere. I want you with the right guy."

The nurse poked her head in the room. "Chief, couple more minutes."

"Nathan, I'll always care about you as well."

"But not in the way you care about Jared."

"It's complicated . . . We have a history." Hanna swallowed a lump. It was time to be honest not only with herself, but Nathan as well. She wished she could hold his hand, let him know that she had felt something for him—until Jared returned.

"I've been lying to myself. I, uh, I do still love Jared. I tried not to, because he did break my heart when he left. It was a pain I never thought I'd get over. But I truly thought I was over it when I met you."

"But you weren't." His tone was calm, resigned.

She shook her head. "I'm sorry if I hurt you. I didn't mean to."

"I only want the best for you, Hanna."

"Likewise. Now, get better."

He saluted and she left.

CHAPTER 47

HANNA LEFT THE HOSPITAL WITH Nathan's words ringing in her thoughts. *"I know you still have feelings for him."* It's funny how he knew. He'd made it easy for her to stop lying to herself. She waded through so many emotions right now—about Joe, about Jared, about Nathan. Added to everything was the bunch of letters Joe had written and left for her. He'd written them over the span of twenty-five years. Each one was dated and addressed to her. After the state had cleared all the hospice equipment from her house, they'd left Joe's valise, saying that he'd wanted her to have it.

Hanna didn't have the emotional energy to look in it or read the letters right away.

She wanted to talk to Jared but he was at work.

The rest of Sunday involved resting and decompressing. She heard from one of the FBI agents in charge that Gilly had been officially identified by dental records.

"His neck was broken and his skull fractured," he said. "Coroner thinks Gilly was dead before he was dropped into the shaft."

Hanna shivered at that thought. "What about the other two corpses?"

"Both of the other bodies showed evidence of gunshot wounds. They were probably killed sometime after Gilly. Hard to be exact right now. Neither of them had any identifying documents on them. We found a purse and a wallet during the search of Buckley's residence. The purse belonged to Ellen Fargo. The wallet to Alister Driscoll. I read somewhere that Ellen was Chase's girlfriend years ago, but I can't place Driscoll."

Hanna's jaw dropped. "He was Joe's public defender." She'd forgotten that she had called the court asking about Driscoll but had not received a response yet.

"We'll start with these two IDs. Maybe they belong to our Does. I'll keep you updated, Chief."

Chase had killed Devon's mother, Braden's grandmother. Hanna had to sit and digest this new information. Was Chase the Lonely Heart Killer? The agent had not mentioned any other purses or IDs. This reminded Hanna that she wanted to find out who had taken Nathan's place on the Lonely Heart murder case.

Asa stopped by her house to see how she was doing.

"I'm exhausted," she admitted. "I may take tomorrow off."

"You deserve it. Try to relax."

"Who took over the Lonely Heart case?"

"Mason and Trejo."

"Oh, they're good."

They talked briefly about the FBI findings. Asa was as surprised as Hanna about Ellen and the PD Driscoll.

"Interesting about him," he said. "The court in San Francisco just answered your query regarding Driscoll."

"Yeah? What did they say?"

"He went missing from San Francisco. He left Dry Oaks after Joe's conviction and began working there. He was there for at least five years before he disappeared. No one ever considered he'd come back here. He quit and left. Since he was a loner, no report was ever filed."

"I wonder why he came back here."

"Could have had a change of heart. He did a poor job for Joe, and maybe he knew Joe was innocent. Something was going on there."

"We may never know everything. Thanks for all of your hard work."

"My job. You rest. We have things handled. Chase is well enough to be transferred to jail. His arraignment is set for Tuesday."

"I'll be there for that, for sure. Is he talking?"

"Not that I've heard."

After Asa left, Hanna took Gizmo for a walk. She sent off a text to Jared to see how he was.

Good. Work today, off tomorrow. Coffee in the morning? Maybe somewhere with real chairs and a table?

Hanna laughed, feeling a little darkness lift. She did care for Jared, a lot. And she was tired of crying. Laughter was good.

Sure, The Beanery?

He sent a thumbs-up with **9:00** after.

The house was so quiet, and her father's valise seemed to call out to her. She picked it up and brought it into the living room. Looking inside, there was nothing but the letters and his Bible. Hanna couldn't bring herself to open any of the letters or look through the Bible. Everything was so raw.

She put everything aside, made dinner, took a nice long bath, and went to bed early.

❀

Jared looked forward to coffee with Hanna more than he could say. The station had been quiet most of the night. They responded to two traffic accidents, nothing major, and he got a good night's sleep. He got off work on time and headed for The Beanery.

Hanna stayed on his mind all night. More specifically, the hug after he'd come up from the mine shaft. Sure, she was relieved about Nathan. But she sure held on tight. Maybe she still had enough feelings for him.

"Do you love Hanna?"

"I think she loves you."

Nathan might have been shocky and dopey, but his words were clear.

Jared arrived at the coffee shop first, ordered two cups of coffee, and found a table. He had to wipe his palms, smiling because he was so nervous. When Hanna arrived, he stood, praying that today would be the day they could start a life together—a second chance for him. Maybe a chance he didn't deserve—a realization of a hope that hadn't died over the years.

❧

Hanna saw Jared and her heart skipped a beat. He had broken her heart ten years ago; she couldn't deny it. In spite of that memory, she knew she still loved him. They'd been together too much, grown up together. No matter the years, he was still the guy for her.

She remembered the sentences Joe had written: *I took the path God had for me. It seems wrong and sad and hard, but God chose to be with me through it, not take me out of it.*

When Jared left that day, so many years ago, Hanna knew, though she didn't like it, that he had taken the road God had for him.

"Jared." She stopped at the table, not sure how to proceed.

He solved her dilemma when he stepped forward, taking her in his arms. Hanna buried her head in his shoulder. It felt right. So many years ago, Jared was her best guy. Time hadn't changed anything but their age.

"Hanna," he whispered in her ear. "I'm so sorry I left. I never forgot you. I never could."

His warm breath on her ear gave her goose bumps. She breathed deeply the scent of his aftershave.

After a minute, he pulled back, their eyes met.

"I'm so sorry—" he started to say, and Hanna put her finger on his lips to quiet him.

"Don't, Jared. You're back now and we have faith in common now. Don't apologize. As hard as seeing you leave was ten years ago, I know that it was a journey you had to take."

He gripped both of her hands in his. "Maybe so, but I can still lament the wasted time. And make up for it. What about Nathan, is he okay?"

"He's in for a lot of rehab. He knew how I truly felt about you before I admitted it to myself. He's a good guy."

"I agree. And us, can we go forward here?"

An inexpressible feeling of joy rippled through Hanna. "I want to. You've always been the one for me."

He smiled, brought her hands to his lips, and kissed her knuckles. "I got you a cup of coffee." He released her hands.

They sat at the table and Hanna sipped her coffee. After a few minutes, she filled him in on the progress in the investigation.

He shook his head when she told him about Ellen. "Ellen Fargo. I don't remember the name. I remember the story was she left Chase because he was maimed."

"There are a lot of stories we've always heard that have turned out to be lies."

"Yeah, sorry about your dad."

"Me too. But I know that he's in heaven."

"Can you clear his name?"

"I don't know. There is so little evidence. Everett would have to come clean and, in the process, incriminate himself and Big Al."

"Not likely he'd do that."

"No, and Chase isn't talking either."

"We'll pray." Jared reached across the table to grip Hanna's hand.

"Thanks, Jared." They bowed their heads and Jared prayed.

"Lord, I pray you lead us the right way, that the truth, which is precious to you, comes out, and Joe's name is cleared. He wasn't a perfect man, but no one is. We all need your forgiveness, whether we know it or not. And you are a forgiving God. Amen."

Hanna looked up and smiled. "Betty said that to me a long time ago. We all need forgiveness, whether we know it or not."

"Betty has always been a tower of faith. I saw that even when I was dense about things of faith."

"True. When I was a kid, Betty always helped me understand when things went wrong or life was hard. Her house was a safe space for me." Thinking about Betty, Hanna remembered her saying, *My house will always be your safe house, Hanna.*

Suddenly it occurred to her that Betty would be a good person to talk to now about Joe, and Chase, and all the history.

"Do you have plans today, Jared?"

He shook his head and smiled. "Only planned to hang out with my girl."

"I want to go visit Betty. Come along?"

"You bet."

CHAPTER 48

BETTY STILL LIVED IN THE SAME HOUSE Amanda had grown up in. The same house that Hanna had always loved and saw as her safe house.

Hanna had texted Mandy before she and Jared left The Beanery, asking if Betty was still with her. Hanna knew Brody was home.

"She moved home on Friday. What's up?"

"Nothing big. I just wanted to talk to her. Think that's okay?"

"Yep. She loves company."

"We good to go?" Jared asked.

"Betty's moved back home. She must be mobile enough after her hip surgery."

Since Chuck passed, Hanna knew that it had been difficult to keep up the place. Mandy wanted her grandma to downsize, to move to a smaller place, but Betty refused.

Hanna parked in front and strode up the walk. Betty must have been watching because she opened the door when Hanna reached the first step. She had come with the help of a cane and not a walker.

"Hanna, it is always so good to see you." Betty wrapped her in a tight hug. Hanna loved Betty's hugs.

"It's always good to see you, Aunt Betty." Hanna hugged back, struggling mightily to contain the emotions swirling inside.

Betty let go and turned to Jared. "You are a pleasant surprise. Mandy called me, but she didn't say anything about Jared coming too."

He got a hug as well.

When she let go, she took Hanna's hand and led her and Jared into the house, back to the kitchen.

"I'm sorry about Joe. I hope it wasn't too hard for you, having him home and then three days later . . ."

"It was expected, Betty, you know that."

"*Expected* doesn't mean *easy*."

Hanna thought. She and Jared sat at the table while Betty brewed the coffee. Though they'd just had coffee at The Beanery, Hanna didn't want to turn down Betty's hospitality. Since Jared didn't say anything either, she felt they were on the same page. Betty chatted on about Amanda and her wish for great-grandchildren.

Since Hanna wasn't certain Mandy was ready for kids, she simply nodded and smiled.

When the coffee finished, Betty poured the drink and set cups in front of Hanna and Jared before sitting down herself. "So, what brings you by today?"

Hanna sipped her coffee and cast a glance at Jared before she answered. "Something I discovered, and I thought you should know. Joe didn't kill Blake and Sophia."

"What?" Betty's brow furrowed.

"It was Chase." Hanna barely kept her voice steady. "Joe was forced to confess."

Betty reached across the table and gripped Hanna's hand. "Oh, honey. He told you this?" Disbelief filled her tone, and Hanna didn't blame her.

"The evidence doesn't fit." Hanna swallowed and tried not to sound as if she doubted her own story. "I saw that myself. After we found the oil drums, I reviewed the original case. If only I'd looked through the case sooner, I would have seen the inconsistencies, the holes. Maybe I could have . . ." Surprised, tears sprang to her eyes, and all the wasted years registered again.

"Stop, Hanna, don't do this to yourself. If this is correct, there is nothing in the past we can change now."

"I know." She wiped her eyes. "But so much was lost. My mom was so angry my whole life, and it was drummed into me what a horrible man Joe was. He's not just Joe to me anymore; he's my dad. And I'm not even sure if I'll be able to clear his name."

Betty handed Hanna a box of Kleenex, and Hanna blew her nose.

"Why do you say that you won't be able to clear his name? If this is the truth, it should be out there."

"I don't have any evidence. I can see that Joe would not have had time to kill two people and put them in the lake, but the crime scene is gone, all the main players are dead, and there is no physical evidence." Hanna wiped her eyes again and composed herself. It helped that Jared put a comforting hand on her shoulder—his support fortified her.

"I hate to be devil's advocate," Betty said, "but what if Chase and Joe were working together?"

"The evidence doesn't fit that either. Chase was injured by my father. Someone got rid of the bodies after Joe was arrested and Chase was in the hospital. Everett wants to place the blame on his father, Big Al. But what if it was Everett and Scott?"

Betty nodded slowly. "I can't see Everett helping with something like that. I can, however, see Big Al orchestrating the whole thing."

"Big Al?" Jared asked.

Betty nodded. "He was a difficult man. Your father had a run-in with him many years ago."

"My father?" Jared looked perplexed.

"Big Al wanted your father's farm. He tried to take advantage while your mother was sick. That's why Ben lost his landscaping business."

"I always thought that was because of my mother's sickness."

"Partly, yes. Big Al tried to bankrupt your dad. A few of us couldn't believe it. He already had lost so much. Edda Fairchild organized a group of people to help your dad. We couldn't save the business, but we made sure your father kept his farm."

"I never knew this."

Jared looked as stunned as Hanna felt.

"Neither did I," Hanna said. "I thought Big Al died after the murders; Everett claimed he passed because of the stress."

"No, he died just before the vote for the police department. He'd been sick since the murders. At least, that's what we heard. He helped Everett form the PD here, mostly because he wanted control. I do believe the vote passed because he was dead. We trusted Everett, not Big Al."

"Getting a history lesson here," Jared said.

"You two were kids. Things were bad here before the PD was formed. Big Al's money bought people and arranged outcomes. Chase was wild; we all knew Al kept him out of jail. Yes, I can see Al framing Joe. But not Everett. When Al died and Everett took over, everything improved. He was never as controlling as his father."

"Still, Everett never set the record straight. Clearing my father will put the spotlight on him and Chase. Without evidence, it's my word versus theirs, and I was just a baby when all this happened."

Betty sat back in her chair and shook her head. "I confess, I always wondered about Joe's confession. Chuck questioned Sheriff Peterson at the time."

"What did Peterson say?"

"To trust him. He would never arrest an innocent man. Everyone knew Joe cooked meth. It was easy to convince people that Joe killed Blake and Sophia, and we should be happy that the killer was caught so quickly. We trusted him. Of course, Peterson was certainly beholden to Al." She sipped her coffee, and to Hanna it looked as though she had more to say.

"Years later, Marcus published his book. He never claimed to have interviewed Joe, yet he had a lot of details. I always wondered where he got all the information. He seemed to know so much about Joe and how he operated."

"Did you ever ask him?" Jared asked.

"Chuck did. Marcus gave a flippant answer about a reporter not revealing his sources. We never pressed him on it. Rather, we prayed. We have always prayed for Joe and for Chase and his family as well."

"Some of it, I think, he got from my mom. I never read the book."

"You should. I know it's all old news, but Marcus tells quite a tale. He claimed that Joe planned the murders, that was why he was able to hide the bodies."

"The confession makes no statements that could be construed as premeditation."

Betty drank her coffee. "Thinking back to those days, there was such a big problem with meth." She tsked. "It got a hold of Edda's son, Bobby; it got my Sophia. Back in the 1990s meth was everywhere, and it was so addictive. Like fentanyl is today. We tried to help Sophia, for Amanda's sake, get off the drugs, but she was hooked."

"Probably didn't help that my dad was her friend."

"Before the murders, I thought Joe was cleaning up his act. There was an incident. Sophia was badly burned when a trailer with a drug lab inside exploded."

"Did my dad have something to do with that?" Hanna asked.

Betty shook her head. "I don't know for sure. I always blamed Blake. I never cared for him. He was a bad influence all the way around. But he was Amanda's father, so we tried to accept him."

"That DEA man, Gilly, he came by and asked about it. He talked to us. He hated meth as much as we did. His brother was hooked. He thought Joe was involved in the trailer explosion, but he couldn't prove it. And after the incident, Joe tried to change, we saw that." She nodded toward Jared. "He worked for your dad for a while."

"Really?" Jared perked up. "Doing what?"

"Landscaping. I paid attention to what your dad was doing, Hanna, because I thought if he got off the meth, maybe Sophia and Blake would too." Betty shook her head sadly. "It wasn't to be. Blake would never give it up, and Sophia would never give up Blake. Even with the burns, she held on to that guy."

"Where was Marcus when all of this was happening? Was he friends with Blake and Sophia? Part of the druggie crowd?" Jared asked.

Betty frowned. "That's testing the memory. I vaguely remember him hanging around, always on the periphery. He was Blake's friend more than anything. I remember Sophia didn't like him. I was friends with his mother. I don't believe he was a drug user. If he was, he kept it well hidden from her." Betty paused as if trying to remember. "She thought the world of her son, spoiled him, really."

Looking at Hanna, she said, "You were seven or eight years old when Marcus self-published his book. That was around the same time his mother passed away. He inherited her house, but I don't remember what year that was. He was an outsider, I think, desperately wanting to belong somewhere but not really belonging anywhere. Does that make sense?"

"Yes. The house he lives in, he inherited from his mother?" Hanna knew the beautiful Victorian house at the edge of town. Town lore said that the home was one of the first homes built in Dry Oaks in the 1850s.

"Um-hmm." Betty tapped on her chin with an index finger. "His ancestors built that house. It's been in his family since day one. For a time, it got a little run-down, but his parents restored it. He's kind of let it go a bit, which is sad to see. It's really a beautiful place."

"I knew it was a historic home but not that it was his family's."

"It might have been in probate when your mother dated him."

"All I remember about Marcus was the books. He always had a lot of books."

"You should talk to him about that time. He probably will remember more than I do."

Betty was right. Hanna hadn't thought about talking to Marcus before because what happened when she was a kid made her prefer avoidance. Her mother had bad-mouthed Marcus almost as much as she bad-mouthed Joe. His book did more to blacken her father's reputation than the actual investigation.

Betty continued. "He tries so hard, but I don't think he's going to achieve his goal. Will you two be going to Edda's celebration-of-life service?"

"What? Oh, I'd almost forgotten. That's tomorrow, isn't it?"

"Yes."

"We'll be there," Jared said.

"It was good to talk to Betty," Hanna said as she and Jared walked back to her car.

"I'm glad that she impressed upon you how useless it is to beat yourself up over the past that you can't change."

"She did. I'd still like to try and clear my dad's name."

"How do you plan on doing that?"

Hanna started the car. "First, I'm going to the library to read Marcus's book. You want me to drop you back at your truck?"

He shook his head. "We used to spend a lot of time at the library. I'd love to join you."

Hanna smiled, glad he was coming along, and drove to Dry Oaks Library. The talk with Betty helped her thought process. She agreed with Jared and knew it was futile to lament the past. It just dug into her like a spur how much both she and her father had lost because of a lie. The lie would never end because there were so many copies of Marcus's book out there. As much as she hated the thought of reading it, Hanna knew that she had to.

Together, she and Jared found two copies. Sitting across from one another, she began to read exactly what had been written about Joe.

CHAPTER 49

MURDERS AT BEECHER'S MINE CABIN WAS a difficult book for Hanna to read for a lot of reasons. Marcus had a clunky way of writing, and he was very wordy.

> The nineties were a time of excess—excess greed, excess rock and roll, excess partying, and excess drugs to fuel the parties. Joe Keyes was the chef du jour of the meth trade in Tuolumne County.

He went line by line through Joe's early arrest record and talked about Blake and Sophia being his partners. Most of the descriptors he used for Joe were harsh: *opportunistic, crafty, unscrupulous, corrupt, evil.* According to Marcus, Joe was also very jealous, threatening any guy who looked at Paula in what he considered "the wrong way."

Her mother was also mentioned a lot, and not in a great light. According to Marcus, Paula was a heavy drug user until she found out that she was pregnant. Besides that, he alleged that it was Paula who pushed Joe to cook meth because it was so lucrative.

Hanna found it hard to believe that about her mother. When

Hanna was growing up, Paula was strict about a lot of things. One item she drilled into Hanna's mind was how bad drugs were for everyone. She liked her alcoholic cocktails, but her mother was not into drugs. What Marcus wrote clarified for Hanna why Paula was so mad when the book came out. Marcus the Muckraker fit.

The nineties were a drug-crazed period; Hanna knew that from her own law enforcement training. Like Betty said, during the nineties meth or crack was the drug of choice, and many clandestine labs sprung up in a lot of rural areas. They were dangerous cesspools of hazardous materials.

The only pages of the book that really caught her attention was a chapter titled "The First Attempt." There, Marcus alleged that Joe had tried to kill his partners Blake and Sophia six months before the incident at Beecher's Mine cabin. It was the trailer incident. Marcus saw it as intentional. Joe blew it up on purpose and fled, leaving Blake and Sophia to die.

In the book, they survived because of Blake's quick thinking, but Sophia was badly burned. Hanna sat back after she read the chapter. This was the incident Betty referred to.

Jared looked up. "What?" he whispered.

"Marcus asserts that Joe murdered Blake and Sophia in a premeditated fashion." She pointed to her open page. "Supposedly he'd missed once, so he made sure of things at Beecher's Mine cabin. I'd heard a version of the story before, and I saw the crime report in my father's file about the meth lab fire. Blake, Sophia, and Chase were mentioned tangentially in that report."

"Yeah?"

"But Joe didn't kill Blake and Sophia. The way Marcus writes this account, the detail about the trailer, makes me think that he did have inside information. I can't believe he got this from my mom."

"Do you think he played a bigger part in the drug scene than anyone knows?"

"He had to, Jared. Betty said that he was friends with Blake. Even though Betty didn't think so, druggies tend to hang with other druggies."

"We have questions; let's go to the source."

Hanna sat up. "Yes, let's. I just want to look at a little more of this."

Jared nodded. "You got it."

Hanna skimmed through the rest of the book. After about fifteen more minutes, she decided she'd read enough. She wanted to hear it clearly from Marcus.

While she'd never seen evidence that Marcus was a drug user, she did know that he had a record. Misdemeanor stuff like obstruction and one DUI a long time ago, nothing drug-related.

She closed the book, then she and Jared replaced them back on the shelf. It was time to talk to Marcus. She wasn't on duty, she was driving her personal vehicle, and she was with Jared. When not out irritating law enforcement, Marcus worked out of his home. Hanna decided she'd pay him a surprise visit and turn the tables and interrupt his life this time.

CHAPTER 50

WHILE NOT AS HIGH AS the Buckley compound, Marcus's house sat at an elevation overlooking the valley.

"He sure has a beautiful view," Jared commented as Hanna neared the house.

"He does. I haven't been out here in a while. He used to tell my mom that when his book became a bestseller, he'd buy us a great big house. He never mentioned that he would inherit one from his mom."

Surrounded by large pine trees, with a few water-starved shrubs for privacy, the Victorian had seen better days. Unlike most people who lived close to the forest, he had no clear defensible space between his house and the greenery.

Jared gave a long low whistle. "All the trees and shrubs are horribly dry. His yard is a tinderbox. If we'd been here for an inspection, he'd have been cited."

"Betty said that he has let the house go. Stands to reason he'd ignore the yard as well."

From her car window, she could see the top of Marcus's SUV at the far end of the driveway, so she assumed he was home.

Hanna made a U-turn in the cul-de-sac and parked in front of the house.

"I saw his car," she told Jared. "Let's go talk to the author."

They got out, crossed the sidewalk, and walked up five stairs to the narrow paver path that led toward the front porch.

"The house looks worse the closer you get," Jared noted.

Hanna nodded. The paint was peeling, one front window was cracked, and a board on the front porch was broken. The whole scene reminded Hanna of the old horror movie *Psycho*. It was simply creepy.

Carefully stepping up on the porch, Hanna approached the door, moved to the side, and then knocked. She waited, knocked again, and got no response.

"Not home, or doesn't want company?" Jared cupped his hands around his eyes and tried to peer in a window.

Hanna stepped carefully across the creaky porch and tried to look into the window on the other side. It was dirty and the shades were drawn.

After a minute or so, she turned to Jared to suggest that they leave.

A dull thud sounded from somewhere inside.

"Did you hear that?" she asked.

Jared nodded. "Sounded like someone fell on a hardwood floor."

"Someone is here." She knocked again. "Marcus? Are you in there?" Again, she waited. Then she thought she'd try a different tack. "It's Hanna. I've got some news for you, news about my dad and Chase."

Was Marcus there and he just didn't want to talk? That in itself was odd. Marcus always wanted to talk.

"He doesn't seem to want to engage." Jared stepped off the porch to the front yard and looked up at the upper stories.

"Someone is here." Hanna suddenly felt uneasy. Was it just the unkept nature of the house that bothered her? Or the noise that indicated Marcus certainly was at home? She glanced back at her car. She should have brought her phone, her gun.

"Do you have your phone?" she asked Jared.

He shook his head. "I hate dragging my phone around with me. Want me to go get it?"

She thought for a second. "No, let's just check his car out. Maybe he's not avoiding us. He could be in the garage. If he's not around or he doesn't want to talk now, I'll catch up with him some other time."

Hanna really had no idea why Marcus would not want to talk to her. In fact, she thought it odd that with all that had happened with Chase, she'd not heard from Marcus. Another oddity, he'd not been around pestering the FBI or at the hospital sniffing after a statement from Everett.

She joined Jared in the front yard, and they turned right to walk around to the back of the house. Hanna realized that she knew nothing about Marcus's personal life. Over the years, she'd seen him with a girlfriend here and there, and at police incidents where he pressed for quotes and insights for his podcast, but they were not friends. Ever since her mother had thrown him out, Hanna had been wary of Marcus. He lied to and used her mother, and that always colored her opinion of the man.

Shoes crunching the dead grass in the front lawn, they continued toward where she'd seen his car. The SUV was backed in, the rear a few feet from the garage.

"The garage was built later than the house," Jared said.

"What?"

"It's partly made of brick, and it's a tad lower than the house, though it looks as if it's attached."

"It still looks old."

"It's not a recent addition. If the house itself was built in the 1800s, the garage looks more like the 1940s. It's maybe a one-and-a-half-car garage, not big enough for two cars."

Now, Hanna could see the difference. The brick walls gave way to wood about three-quarters of the way up, and the roof had different shingles on it. The garage door was closed, and off to the left, a side door was also shut.

Out of habit, she touched the hood of the SUV to ascertain if it had been driven recently. It was warm to the touch, but not overly so.

"Still warm?" Jared asked.

"Hmm." Hanna nodded and stood for a minute as an uncomfortable feeling washed over her. Was Marcus hiding? If so, why? She walked around his vehicle, and her eye caught the *Vote Keyes for Chief* bumper sticker. She froze. It couldn't be, could it?

"What's the matter?" Jared asked.

"Look at the bumper. I just got creeped out."

Jared eyes got wide. "Don't blame you. You're not thinking . . . ?"

"Could be a coincidence."

"That combined with a house that would fit in perfect with any horror movie would give anyone the creeps. Added to that, it's totally private back here. Marcus could be the Lonely Heart Killer and a mad scientist, and no one would know."

The fact that she and Jared were on the same page made Hanna smile.

Curiosity aroused, she walked around the SUV, saw a shed farther back where the lot ended in a hillside, and another vehicle. This was a small SUV, a newer Honda. She'd never seen Marcus in any car other than his Tahoe. Next to the Honda was a third car, under a tarp. She couldn't see the car, but something about the shape triggered her instincts.

Walking to the car, Jared at her side, Hanna lifted the edge of the tarp. Her jaw went slack.

"That looks like Edda's car." Jared's voice was tight with tension. "My goodness, what have we walked into?"

"I don't like the answer that comes to mind."

"Find what you were looking for?"

Hanna dropped the tarp. She and Jared jerked around to see Marcus. He must have come out of his garage—and he was pointing a gun at them.

CHAPTER 51

HANNA WORKED TO CONTROL her shock, anger, and fear. Before she could say anything, Jared stepped around her and faced off with Marcus.

"You killed Edda?"

"Back off, Water Boy. I'll shoot you where you stand." Marcus made a menacing gesture with the gun, and Hanna grasped Jared's arm, stepping even with him.

"What are you doing here?" Marcus demanded. "Your father finally start talking?"

"The evidence has. Chase killed Blake and Sophia, not my dad."

Marcus chuckled. "Joe must be clearing his conscience."

"He's dead."

Marcus gave a rakish tilt of his head. "Oh, too bad. He'll always be remembered as a killer anyway."

"You already knew it wasn't him. You still published a book of lies."

Marcus's face reddened. "I hated your dad. I had a chance to mess him up so I took it. He got what he deserved."

"You were the unnamed witness." For Hanna it all fell into place. Why hadn't she seen it sooner?

Marcus nodded and chuckled. "Big Al's idea. I was at the right place at the right time. I wasn't able to save Blake and Sophia, but I saved Chase, most of him anyway. The acid had burned into his face and eaten away half his calf. My dragging him out of the mess was something Big Al never forgot."

He waved the gun toward the garage. "That way. Into the garage, both of you."

Hanna saw where he pointed, the side door to the garage now open. She started walking that way, Jared's and her arms touching. Her mind churned with scenarios about Marcus.

"Chase killed everyone: Blake, Sophia, and Gilly, I'm guessing. You just stood and watched?"

"Keep guessing."

She and Jared stopped at the door, and Marcus shoved her shoulder. "Go on, through the door."

Hanna stepped over the threshold and into the semidarkness of the garage. The concrete floor was old, cracked, and uneven. Rather than housing a car, the garage had boxes piled in the center of the space, and there was a lot of dust and cobwebs. One naked light bulb shone in the far corner.

Marcus prodded them to move farther into the back. After he came through the door behind her, she heard him close it and two locks engage. Hanna wanted to keep him talking. If he was talking, he wouldn't be shooting. She stopped moving forward and faced him.

"Okay, I'll keep guessing. Chase told me you were soft. You didn't kill Edda; you don't have it in you. Chase killed her. That's what he is: a killer. You're not."

His eyes narrowed to slits, his voice clipped with anger. "Shows how much you know. Soft? I took care of Gilly, a big bad DEA agent. He was snooping around the cabin that night. I hit him over the head. I didn't mean to kill him, but Big Al was grateful to his dying day for everything I did. I got rid of Gilly, helped clean up Chase's mess. No one has any idea what I'm capable of. No one ever has. Edda included."

"She was a sweet old woman who never hurt anyone." Jared's voice vibrated with anger.

"That was just a game. Like the other women, I toyed with her for the fun of it. I guess she was smarter than I gave her credit for. She figured me out, demanded to know why I was pretending to be someone else."

Marcus spit off to the side. "She had the nerve to threaten me. 'I'll tell Hanna,' she said. The biddy got what she deserved. She underestimated me. Everyone underestimates me. You'll see my abilities firsthand. Keep walking toward the light."

The dark garage smelled musty and old. To the left a short stairway led up to a door, she guessed to the main house. Marcus directed them to the right. A dim, naked light bulb hung from the rafters. Hanna's eyes adjusted to the semidarkness and saw what looked like a work area, with a vintage bench and a tool cabinet that looked antique. But what was lying between the bench and the cabinet stopped her in her tracks, with Jared running into her heels.

There lay a woman—bound, with duct tape across her mouth, her eyes filled with fear—staring up at them.

"Meet Rita. She drove all the way from Jamestown to meet me. She was as surprised as Edda." Marcus let out a maniacal laugh.

The irritating laughter threw Hanna back over the years when she used to be taunted by bullies while walking to and from school. Sometimes if she jerked around quickly and unexpectedly, catching them by surprise, it would scare them off.

True, Marcus had a gun and he wasn't a boy, but if she didn't do something now, she and Jared would end up like the woman on the floor.

Concentrating, Hanna tensed. She'd only get one shot. And she didn't want Jared or the terrified woman on the floor hurt. She and her police force practiced gun takeaway methods in their routine training sessions. She needed her move to be spot-on.

Remembering that Marcus held the gun in his right hand, when Jared knelt to help the woman, Hanna jerked to the right, grabbing the gun's slide with one hand and Marcus's wrist with the other.

"Umph." A grunt escaped his lips, and his eyes widened.

Hanna twisted his wrist to the right with all the force she could muster, then pulled.

"Ow!" He let go, and the ease of the release startled Hanna. She stumbled back with the gun in her hands, running into Jared and tripping over the woman on the floor.

Marcus cursed and backpedaled, while Hanna settled on her butt, then aimed the gun at Marcus. She tried to fire, but the safety was still engaged. Rookie move. She clicked it off and balanced herself. "Stay where you're at, Marcus, it's over."

"No, it's not." He reached for some empty cans and hurled them at Hanna, some of which Jared deflected. Marcus turned and sprinted up the steps and through the door. She trained her gun on his retreating back, but Jared jumped in front of her line of sight when he leapt after Marcus.

Hanna scrambled to her feet and stumbled after Jared. Marcus opened a door at the top of the stairs, slipped out, and then slammed it shut behind him. Hanna reached the door as Jared rammed his shoulder into it. It held and he stepped back.

"It's solid wood," he said. "They made them to last back in the day."

"Try the other." She pointed to the door they'd come through. "I'll check on Rita."

She retreated to the woman on the floor while Jared checked the other door.

"It's dead-bolted." Jared rammed his shoulder into it. "No give at all."

Hanna carefully pulled the tape from Rita's mouth.

"Is he gone? Please tell me he's gone."

"I think so. Let's get you untied."

Hanna heard Jared push on the large garage door. He kicked at the bottom.

"Don't hurt yourself, Jared. There must be implements down here we can use."

"It will have to be heavy. The wood here is old and solid, with strong locks." He rubbed his shoulder and joined Hanna and Rita. "This place was well built."

Hanna turned to face the door, listening for any sound that would indicate Marcus was coming back. She set the gun down and took the small folding knife she always carried in her pocket and cut Rita's bindings.

Jared knelt to help. He tapped Hanna's shoulder.

"What?" She turned her head and saw him smiling at her.

"I'm glad to see you still have the knife."

Hanna smiled back. "A really good friend gave this to me years ago." She held his gaze until Rita reminded her that they were in quite a bit of danger at the moment.

"Oh, thank you so much." Rita rubbed her wrists and tears fell. "I thought I was dead. Did you meet him on Mix and Match too?"

"That's where you met Marcus?"

"He told me his name was Perry."

"Can you stand? We have to get out of here."

"I think so."

Hanna helped her up, noting that she'd dressed for a date and was wearing high-heeled shoes.

Jared went to the cabinet and opened it. "We're in luck. Crowbar and sledgehammer. One of them should work."

"Great." Hanna picked the gun back up. It was a 9mm, same caliber that killed the three Lonely Heart victims. Hitting the magazine release, she saw that the mag was full, and there was a round in the chamber. She jammed it back into place. Marcus had not disengaged the safety earlier. It made her wonder how familiar he was with guns.

"We need to get out of here before Marcus gets far. Come on, Rita, get ready."

"You don't have to tell me twice." Rita rubbed her wrists and followed Hanna as she followed Jared to the side garage door.

He held the sledgehammer in both hands and turned to Hanna. "The way we came in or up through the house?"

"I don't want to go through the house. Marcus could be waiting to ambush us."

"He might be outside as well," Jared pointed out.

Hanna thought for a minute. "There are no windows in this garage, are there?"

Jared shook his head. "No garage door opener either." He pushed the old, heavy wooden door with his hip and it budged not an inch. It was sunk into the ground, probably hadn't been opened in years.

"It's the side door or nothing," he said.

"I wish I'd thought to put my phone in my pocket," Hanna lamented.

"My phone is in my purse," Rita said.

"Is it down here?"

"I don't know."

"Jared, try to open the door, and I'll try to find her phone."

He nodded. Rita stumbled back to the workbench where she'd been restrained.

Jared raised the sledgehammer. Just then the acrid odor of gasoline permeated the air. Hanna heard liquid splashing all along the garage door. Then Marcus snickered. With a whoosh, fire ignited, the sound of the flames moving along the door, up toward the roofline to the edge of the house.

"Whoa." Jared stepped back. "I'd rather try another way. The walls might be brick, but the door, roof, and roof joists are dry wood. So dry, this house will go up like a Roman candle."

As if to prove his point, fire flashed through the crack between the top of the door and the frame, across the ceiling.

"Enjoy the barbecue, ladies." A car door slammed, and an engine started.

Jared hopped back to where Hanna stood.

Smoke began to flood the area, along with heat.

Marcus meant to burn them to death.

Jared was right. As dry as everything was and with smoke quickly growing thicker, Marcus might just be successful.

"We got to get out of here. Where do you think the purse is?" Jared asked.

Hanna turned to Rita, who searched the ground around where she had lain. "Did he bring it in here with you?"

"I'm not sure. He dropped me on the floor and then I think he walked over here." She indicated the back wall. "But he was behind me."

Jared joined them in searching the area. "Hurry, fire burns up, but smoke and heat will soon be a serious threat to us in here."

Hanna stood next to Rita and considered the back of the garage.

"This is an old house," she said, half to herself. "It looks like a solid wall, but is it?" Another whoosh flared behind them as the fire ramped up. The smoke got thicker, and Hanna coughed. So did Rita and Jared.

"What are you thinking?" Jared asked Hanna.

"Back when this house was built, they often had cellars. But the garage is newer. Maybe the new construction blocked off the old cellar."

"Maybe. After all, Everett's panic room was built in an old cellar."

Hanna saw that Jared still had the sledgehammer. She was about to ask him to smash the back wall when she saw a scrape on the cracked concrete floor.

"Jared, look, I think this is a door."

He followed her gaze. "I think so too." He dropped the sledgehammer and grabbed the crowbar. He picked a crack in the wood, slid the end of the crowbar in it, then leaned in. The wall slid open along the scrapes in the floor. Hanna could see the hinges and was able to push it open wider. Once opened, she saw the shelves. This was a canning cupboard, a cool part of the house where the food stores could be kept.

"There's my purse." Rita pushed past Hanna and grabbed a colorful flowered bag.

The purse was not all that was there. There were three more bags. Even in the dim light, Hanna recognized one of them as Edda's. And there was a dented and bent travel coffee mug. Hanna picked it up and saw the engraving. It was Scott's.

Rita found her phone. "He turned it off." She hit the power button, and it began to power on. "Should I call 911?"

"Let me." Hanna took the phone and hit the three numbers.

"911, what is your emergency?"

"Charlie, it's Hanna. 999." She gave him the code for *officer needs immediate assistance*. "I'm in Marcus Marshall's garage with Jared and another woman, and the house is on fire. I need Fire, and I need everyone on duty here now. And put a BOLO out on Marcus Marshall. He assaulted me; consider him armed and dangerous."

Thankfully, Charlie didn't hesitate. "10-4, Chief, I'll get Fire rolling. And all units to your 20—do you have his address?"

"I don't know the exact—it's at the end of Granite."

Just then part of the garage door exploded as the growing fire destroyed a support. Rita jumped and coughed; Hanna coughed as well. Jared was probing the back wall of the cupboard with the tip of the crowbar.

"Are you okay, Chief?" Charlie asked, for the first time the timbre of his voice changing to concern.

"For now. We need Fire ASAP." She ended the call.

"What are you looking for?" Hanna asked Jared.

"A way out. The side wall is brick. The porch is raised and wooden." He coughed and pulled his shirt up over his mouth and nose. "If we can get through this wall and out to the porch, we can get out."

Rita and Hanna both coughed again. The smoke and heat were getting more intense by the moment.

"We need to get down," Jared said as Hanna took Rita's hand. "Fire, smoke, and heat rise." They knelt as Jared continued probing the wall. It did sound hollow.

They'd found the phone and help was coming. Would it get here in time?

CHAPTER 52

JARED KNEW THEY HAD TO GET OUT into the fresh air soon. He could hear sirens now, but they could not afford to wait. The dry wood was burning hot and fast, and the fire was burning hottest by the door—the only way out was under the house, he was sure.

His eyes and throat burned, and Hanna and Rita were coughing too. It was getting harder and harder to breathe. He used the tip of the crowbar and found an opening. Success!

Coughing, he turned to Hanna. "Get all the way in and pull that door closed behind you."

Hanna did as he asked. With the squeak of nails protesting, he pulled a board free and then another. Cool air came through the opening. When it was big enough to step through, he knew they would get out.

"Okay, let's go." He helped Rita up and pushed her through the opening. He motioned for Hanna to follow.

Rita's cell phone rang. Hanna held it and answered on speaker.

"Chief, Asa wants you to stay on the line. Fire is almost on-scene. Where are you?"

A large crash sounded from the garage, and red-hot embers

exploded through the space under the door. Hanna ducked reflexively and almost dropped the phone.

"I think the garage is collapsing," Jared said. "We have to hurry." He heard Hanna's conversation with the PD.

"We're under the house, on our way to the front porch to get out," Hanna told dispatch. She coughed too much to suit Jared. They had to get out. Now!

"Have to move, Charlie, have to move."

Jared saw her end the call and then wipe her watery eyes, which probably burned, with her palm.

"Come on, Hanna." Jared pushed her through the opening behind Rita and then followed. It was dark and smoky but not as bad as it had been in the garage. They built things differently in the 1800s. Basement rooms were common then, though not now. This was an obvious passageway under the house. It was complete darkness here, but the air was better, and it was cooler.

Jared could hear sirens close and the sound of trucks coming to a stop. "Ah, help is here."

Just then Rita fell to the ground, coughing and sobbing.

"Let me have the phone." Jared reached out to Hanna, and she handed it to him. He found the flashlight function. Shining it on Rita, he saw that she'd cut her foot. She'd lost one of her high heels, and her skirt was black with dirt and soot.

"Sorry, Rita, but we have to move. There is not enough room in here for me to carry you. I guarantee that we're almost out."

Hanna cast a glance at him as she coughed as if to say, *"Are you sure?"*

He illuminated the path, then the ceiling. It was low; he could feel and see floor joists brushing his head.

"I can't," Rita coughed. "Let's wait—"

"We can't wait." Hanna took the words out of Jared's mouth

and pushed her along the passageway. She had one of Rita's arms and Jared took the other as they pulled her along as gently as possible.

"I'm afraid this will take us farther under the house," Jared said, "and not the way I want to go, toward the porch."

He could feel the heat increasing. Had he miscalculated?

"Look up," Hanna said.

Jared shone the phone light up and continued forward. *Just move away from the flames.* But were they heading out of the frying pan into the fire?

"There!" Hanna exclaimed.

They came to two steps. Above the steps was a trapdoor.

Jared handed Hanna back the phone. He pushed on the trap-door, but it held tight. He repositioned himself on the stair to increase his leverage. Putting his back into it, he pushed as hard as he could and felt the latch give. The door flipped open. He shoved his head through the opening. To him it appeared as if they were in a living room. It was smoky and hot but no flames. It was also packed with boxes, books, and paper. Was Marcus a hoarder in addition to everything else?

He looked back down at Hanna. "Can you get Rita to the steps? I'll pull her up and out."

Hanna looked down. "Come on, Rita, we're getting out."

Rita was still coughing, but she looked better. Once she was up with Jared, Hanna followed up the steps.

"Are we in the living room?" she asked.

"Not sure, let's find the front door."

Jared picked Rita up and followed Hanna though the smoky house to the front door. She turned the dead bolt, then threw the door open. They were met by two of his colleagues in full turnout gear.

"Hodges?" one of them said, surprise in his voice.

"Yeah, I don't think there is anyone else in the house, but I'm not positive." He coughed. "She needs first aid on her feet. We could all use some water and O_2."

One of them took Rita from him.

Jared put his arm over Hanna's shoulder and together they walked to the paramedic rig.

CHAPTER 53

"I FEEL AS IF I'VE JUST RUN A MARATHON," Hanna said to Jared as they reached the paramedic rig. One of the medics held out water bottles. She took one and so did Jared.

"With all the smoke we inhaled, we might as well have run a marathon in thick smog."

Hanna chugged the water as Asa jogged up. "What on earth happened?"

Hanna sat on the bumper and told him about Marcus and finding Edda's car.

"There are purses in the garage, I hope they survived because they're evidence. It's possible they belong to the other Lonely Heart victims. Marcus kept trophies."

"The guys are getting a handle on the fire," Jared told her. "The way it's burning, the house will be a total loss, but the purses might be okay."

"As soon as they let me, I'll go take a look." Asa shook his head. "Are you certain Marcus is not in the house?"

"What? Why?" Hanna stood and looked toward the garage. She could see the top of the SUV. "His SUV is still here."

"We heard a car leave," Jared said.

"Asa, can you check and see if there is a Honda still back there or a red VW? Marcus might have left in a different car. The BOLO that went out on his SUV needs to be changed."

Asa nodded and went to check.

Rita pulled the O$_2$ mask from her face. "Did he steal my car?"

"We'll find out."

Asa walked back. "Edda's car is still there. So, what kind of vehicle is Marcus in?"

Rita gave him the information, and Asa let dispatch know to change the BOLO.

"Oh, my mistake." Hanna slapped a palm into her forehead. "I never should have assumed Marcus left in his own car."

Jared placed a hand on her shoulder. "There was no way we could have seen what car he left in."

"I just wonder how far he could have gotten when everyone was looking for the wrong car."

"We'll catch him," Asa said. "I can't believe that Marcus is a killer. He's always been annoying, but a killer?" He turned to Rita. "Are you up to telling me what happened?"

She nodded and removed the mask again. "He told me his name was Perry. We met on Mix and Match a couple of months ago."

"What did he tell you about himself?"

"That he worked from home and was stuck overseas because of a passport glitch."

"Passport glitch? Did you send him money?"

"I sent him about five hundred dollars to help him with legal issues. Yesterday he texted and told me he'd made it home and asked me to meet him here." She frowned.

"What's wrong?"

"Well. I'm not sure that was Perry. Maybe this guy did something to Perry."

"What do you mean?"

"Can I have my phone back?"

"Sure." Hanna realized she still had the phone so she handed it back to Rita.

Rita played with the phone and then held it up so Hanna could see. "This is the profile picture I have for Perry. It doesn't look anything like that guy."

Hanna stared. The picture on the phone was not Marcus. It was Chase, a picture from thirty-five years ago, before his burns.

CHAPTER 54

PARAMEDICS TRANSPORTED RITA to the hospital just to be certain she was okay. She had a cousin in Twain Harte who would come and get her.

After drinking water and inhaling O_2 for several minutes, Hanna felt like she could breathe again. The fire was under control, and while the house would be a total loss, firefighters concentrated on saving as much of the garage as they could. Jared had taken it upon himself to talk to his colleagues while they battled the blaze. He explained where the purses were so when firefighters entered the garage to make it safe and hunt out any pockets of fire remaining, they would be mindful. And if there was any way the items could be salvaged, they would be.

Hanna waited. The 9mm handgun she'd taken from Marcus was in an evidence bag. It would be tested and hopefully matched to Edda and the other victims. The purses and the coffee mug were important evidence as well, but the fire had been so destructive, would anything survive? She wanted Marcus caught and tried in a court of law, using all the evidence possible.

While she waited, she listened to the radio. Tony, a reserve officer covering for Jenna because of her broken hand, stood nearby and Hanna heard the BOLO for Marcus broadcast a couple of times with the correct vehicle information. She prayed he didn't get far.

While the fire and cleanup were happening, several people stopped by to gawk and wonder about Marcus. The sheriff of Tuolumne County drove up.

"I was just at the hospital with Nathan when I heard the BOLO you put out. Marcus Marshall is a killer?"

Hanna explained to him everything that had happened. That Marcus had used Chase's picture was an odd mystery. Would they ever learn the reason? Of course, Chase was decidedly better looking than Marcus, especially thirty-five years ago. She repeated the story for Mayor Milton when she arrived.

The mayor looked as if she'd been hit by a truck.

"I can't believe what the past few days have brought. Detective Holmes and one of the men from the FBI have briefed me on the incident at the Buckley house. First Chase, now Marcus. And Hanna, I'm sorry about Joe. Were we really wrong all this time?"

"Yes, we were. He never should have been convicted."

"You don't think Everett had anything to do with, well, the subterfuge?"

"I don't know what to think. Big Al certainly had something to do with it."

Milton looked somewhat relieved. "Maybe so. I, ah, I just can't believe Everett was responsible. He is a good man."

Hanna said nothing. She was so eager to get home. Poor Gizmo had been cooped up all day.

When the firefighters made entry into what was left of the garage, Tony went with them, gloved up with an evidence bag. The outside walls were gone, but when Tony got to the closet, Hanna saw him take a couple of photos and then retrieve some items.

"Looks like they made it," Jared said with a smile. He threw his arm around her.

Tony looked pleased when he approached Hanna. "Everything is a little wet and sooty but intact."

"Notify the team handling the investigation now," Hanna said.

"10-4."

Deep inside she had doubts that Marcus acted alone. The only way to quell the doubts was to catch him. She knew that would happen eventually. She prayed that he wasn't planning a suicide by cop. But then that didn't really fit his personality. Knowing Marcus, he'd want to crow to the heavens about what he'd done. Hanna was ready to go home and leave the catching of Marcus to the competent officers she worked with and around.

She looked up at Jared. "I'm ready for a shower and a hot meal."

"You read my mind."

"You want me to take you back to your truck? We can decide where we want to go after we're both cleaned up."

"Sounds like a plan."

They walked hand in hand back to her car. Hanna relished the comfort and connection she felt with Jared. They drove in companionable silence to the coffee shop, where she dropped him off at his truck.

"I'll go home and shower," he said, "then come by and pick you up."

"Awesome."

They shared a tired kiss and Hanna continued home.

She felt fatigue hovering on the edges, waiting to descend on her like a dark fog. She fought it off. Her plans were to walk and feed her poor dog, shower, and change. Looking forward to dinner with Jared kept the fatigue at bay.

When she pulled into her driveway, she noted that the street was a little empty. No hospice workers anymore. A wave of emotion hit hard. Joe was gone. She wasn't sure who she needed to call about planning for burial. Or cremation. She wasn't even certain what Joe wanted.

She sat for a few minutes in her car, reflecting on everything that had happened in the past few days.

Oh, Lord, please bring the truth to light, and help me to process everything that's happening.

She got out of the car and walked to her front door. Gizmo attacked her with gusto when she opened the door. Hanna bent down and picked him up, enjoying a cascade of doggie kisses. She took him into the kitchen and fed him, then let him out into her backyard.

"Sorry, there's no walk right now, baby, but I've got a date." Thinking of dinner with Jared as a date made her giddy.

Gizmo pranced around the yard for a bit and then did his business. Hanna ushered him inside and went to shower and change, suddenly feeling less tired and very chipper.

CHAPTER 55

JARED WHISTLED AS HE SHOWERED and changed into fresh clothes. He felt light and happy. His second chance with Hanna was the reason. He thought back over the years, remembering how badly he wanted to get out of Dry Oaks. Now, it was his home and he looked forward to roots, and children. The thought of children brought on a chuckle. He was putting the cart before the horse.

Despite what he and Hanna just went through, he was not tired. He was excited. To have an evening alone with Hanna and talk about the future energized him.

He left his room to grab his car keys from the small table in his kitchen. Jubilation fled, and his reach stopped halfway there.

"You're in a good mood." Marcus Marshall stood in Jared's doorway, pointing a shotgun at him.

"How'd you get in here?"

"I guess you were so preoccupied, you forgot to lock the door. You have a hot date?" He laughed. "I thought you just came from one. I am surprised and a little impressed you got out of that. My mistake to try and burn a firefighter to death."

"What do you want, Marcus? The whole county is looking for you. You're not getting out of this. Give yourself up."

"Maybe I don't want to get out of this. Maybe I want to leave a mark, something people will still talk about thirty-five years from now."

"You'll get your wish, I think. If you really want to be remembered as a monster."

"Not a monster, a genius. Sit down." Marshall pointed at a chair with the barrel of the gun.

Jared hesitated.

"I don't want to shoot you yet. Don't test me. I will if you force my hand."

Jared sat and watched Marshall closely. Could he take him without getting shot?

"Where's your phone?"

Jared patted his pockets. "I don't know. I hate lugging it around. It's probably still in my truck."

"Are you lying?"

Jared held his hands up. "Search me if you want. I'm always leaving my phone somewhere. If I'd had it with me this afternoon, we wouldn't be having this conversation."

Marshall pulled a phone out of his pocket. "I didn't want to use mine because I know once I turn it on, it will be easy to track. It doesn't really matter now, does it? This is the endgame."

He set the phone on the table and turned it on. When it powered up, he pressed a button. The phone rang twice and then Jared heard Hanna's voice.

"Marcus."

"That's right. Here at your boyfriend's house. Listen quick and fast. I've got him. You have five minutes to get here, or I blow his head off. Anyone else shows up, I blow his head off." Marshall ended the call and shut off the phone. He grinned at Jared. "Now we see how much she really cares about you."

Anger poked at Jared and every muscle tensed. He wanted to jump Marshall and smash his face in. "I'd like to kill you for what you did to Edda. How does killing a sweet old lady make a mark?"

Marshall jammed the shotgun in Jared's face. "You wouldn't understand. No one ever treated you like dirt."

Jared leaned back with the shotgun barrel pressed into his cheek, Marshall's stale breath in his nostrils. The man raged.

"The people who never took me seriously have paid and will pay. Joe paid, Scott paid, and that old biddy paid. You and Hanna are next."

Jared held his tongue in the face of the other man's rage. He could now see Marshall as a killer.

After a minute, Marcus blinked and backed up, the pressure on Jared's cheek eased as he pulled the shotgun back. Marcus looked surprised at his own outburst and calmed somewhat.

"The women were Chase's idea; he called it big-game hunting. Stringing them along for money was mine. Scott caught on and tried to keep me away from Chase. I took care of him. Now you're in the way. I don't want to be distracted when your girlfriend gets here."

Marshall raised the shotgun again and Jared stiffened.

❇

Hanna froze for a moment, then heat enveloped her. It was as if every nerve in her body was on fire.

The face of her phone simply showed the time. Marcus had ended the call. In the time it took her mind to register what had just happened, one minute gave way to another.

Fear pushed her to sprint into her home office and grab her duty belt and vest. After she put the vest on and hitched on her belt, she picked up her car keys and sprinted for her car, speed-dialing dispatch on the way. When the night dispatcher answered, Hanna stopped dead at her car.

What could she tell them? That Marcus had Jared? Every cop in the county would come in blazing with lights and sirens, and Hanna believed Marcus would shoot Jared. "Sorry, accidental dial."

"Okay, Chief, you have a good night."

"You too."

The call ended and Hanna hopped in her car. She started the engine. Put the car in gear and then stopped again.

I have to think. But there was no time to think. She pounded her fist on the wheel, then backed out of her driveway, knowing she'd have to figure something out on the way.

If Marcus had Jared and he wanted her there, he meant to kill them both.

CHAPTER 56

HANNA ARRIVED AT JARED'S HOUSE in three minutes. She parked behind his truck, concentrating, watching his porch and front door. She found herself hoping that Jared didn't try anything heroic. After climbing out of her car, she walked to the front of Jared's truck and stood behind the front wheel well, watching the house, hand on the butt of her gun.

Despite the fear, a spark of hope struck deep. She remembered the handgun she'd recovered in the garage; Marcus had not released the safety. Was he really the killer he wanted everyone to believe he was? Chase had said Marcus was soft. To Hanna that meant that Chase was the only killer, not Marcus. They must have been working together.

Would Marcus be able to shoot to kill? Hanna had never discharged her weapon in the line of duty. However, she knew from talking to others that it was no easy thing to shoot a person, even when you feared for your life.

Her phone stayed quiet. She set it on the truck's hood and was about to redial when the noise of a slamming door to her left caught her attention. Jude Carver strode toward her. He must have gotten bailed out.

"I need to talk to you," he hollered.

Hanna couldn't look at him; she kept her eye on Jared's front door.

"Not now, Jude. I've got a situation." He should notice the gun and back off. He didn't.

"Don't put me off," he fairly snarled.

Jared's front door moved. She drew her weapon and stepped toward the front of the truck.

Jude reached her, grabbed her shoulder to make her face him, and stepped in front of her.

"Look at me."

In the split second Hanna took her eye off Jared's door and looked at Jude, Marcus emerged from the house and the boom of a shotgun sounded.

Hanna ducked.

Jude screamed and arched his back, twisting away from her and falling to the ground. Hanna brought her gun up, taking a step back to keep the truck between Marcus and her.

"Drop it, Marcus!"

He didn't drop it, but he fumbled with the shotgun, falling to one knee, pain on his face. He'd not held the shotgun properly, and the recoil had injured his shoulder. He tried to bring the gun back up and couldn't.

She stepped between Jude and the truck.

"Put the gun down!"

Marcus tried to raise it again and cursed when he couldn't.

"It's over. Drop the gun and get down on the ground. Now!"

He glared at her and tried one more time. She was about to ask where Jared was when he came bounding out of the house. His face was bruised and bloody. "Hanna!"

Marcus must have smacked him with something, but he was

okay. Jared hit Marcus in the back with a shoulder tackle. Marcus screamed and the shotgun went flying.

With Marcus on the ground moaning in pain and Jared on his back, Hanna lowered her gun.

"Hands behind your back, Marcus."

"Ahh, my arm is broken. Get off me, get off me!"

Hanna holstered her weapon. Jude also moaned and cursed behind her. She could see blood staining his hip and lower leg.

"Jared, can you check on Jude? I'll handle Marcus."

"You got it."

Jared got off Marcus and went to Jude. Hanna pulled out her handcuffs and dealt with Marcus.

"You are so sued," he whined as she pulled on his left arm. "My arm is broken and you're making it worse."

Hanna had a feeling he'd broken his collarbone. She'd seen that happen before with someone who didn't know how to hold a shotgun when he fired it. "Give me your right hand."

"I can't. It's broken."

"The sooner I get you cuffed, the sooner I call the medics."

He slowly brought his right hand back, and Hanna clicked on the cuffs. He fairly howled with pain. Hanna ignored him as her adrenaline spike dissipated. She just didn't know about Jude.

She helped Marcus to his feet. He stumbled along and continued to whine. She walked him toward where Jared looked after Jude. "Is he okay?"

Jared looked up, the shadow of a smile on his lips. "Looks like he took a load of bird shot in the backside. He's lucky Marcus was such a poor shot."

"I'll kill you, Marcus," Jude hollered. He tried to get up, but it was obvious that pain kept him down.

"Is it really bad?" Hanna asked Jared.

He shook his head. "I'm sure it hurts, but it's not life threatening. He got a bunch of pellets in his rump. Lucky Marcus didn't load the gun with double-aught buck."

All Hanna could do for him was call paramedics. Marcus was now in custody, and that meant to her, the nightmare in Dry Oaks was over.

CHAPTER 57

"EDDA'S LIFE WAS ABOUT SERVING OTHERS wherever the need was the greatest." Amanda paused in her remarks to wipe her eyes.

Hanna found herself doing the same thing. Edda's celebration-of-life service brought so many emotions to the surface. She grieved not only for Edda, but also for Joe and her mother.

"She served women struggling with unexpected pregnancy, she worked tirelessly to help those fighting addiction, and she was always available to pray with anyone who asked."

Hanna's sadness was tempered by the knowledge that Edda was in heaven, enjoying her eternal reward. And in saying goodbye, at least for now, she knew who was responsible for her friend's death.

❄

Hanna went back to work the day after Edda's celebration. Jared was off work and home recuperating with facial fractures. When Marcus hit him with the shotgun, it broke his nose and cheekbone. He'd attended the celebration of life but looked horrible as his face was black, blue, and purple with bruising. She planned on bringing him dinner at the end of the day.

At the moment, she was in Sonora for Marcus Marshall's arraignment. A great deal of media was present at the courthouse, and she had to walk the gauntlet.

"Chief Keyes, can you give a statement about the arrest of Marcus Marshall?"

"Care to comment on Chase Buckley?"

"Is it true that your father's murder case will be reopened?"

The last question stopped her. She searched for the reporter who had asked. It was a guy from the local paper. "Where did you hear that?"

"Can you confirm the rumor?"

Hanna studied the man for a minute, not hearing the other questions swirling around.

"I haven't heard it. But it should happen. My father didn't kill anyone." She continued into the courthouse as more questions exploded from the crowd.

Inside the door, Manny Pacheco leaned on a cane and smiled when he saw her. "Morning, Chief. I thought I'd join you."

"Of course, Manny, good to see you out and about." She asked him about the reporter's question, and Manny smiled.

"Nathan petitioned the sheriff to reopen the case. He said that in light of Chase Buckley's arrest, it would be a travesty to let Joe's conviction stand."

"Wow." All Hanna could do was shake her head. Nathan was a good friend. "I heard Mason and Trejo now have the Lonely Heart case."

"Yes, it's in good hands. Marshall isn't talking at the moment. He invoked his right to silence, but there is a chance Chase will talk."

"I think Chase is the one who killed Blake and Sophia, and maybe the three women. Marcus claimed he killed Gilly and Scott. And of course, he helped Chase."

"We'll see." Manny gestured to the wooden door. "Let's go listen to the proceeding."

They took their seats in the courtroom and watched the arraignment. Marcus was brought in, one hand shackled to a belly restraint, the other in a sling. He looked small, deflated, and old.

The judge read the long list of charges—kidnapping, false imprisonment, arson, attempted murder, just to name a few.

"Not guilty" were the only words Marcus spoke.

The judge placed a no-bail hold on him despite his attorney's protests.

After it was over, Manny invited Hanna back to the station to talk to Mason and Trejo.

"Good to see you, Chief." Mason was the only one in the office. He brought Hanna up-to-date on the investigation.

"We located the car Marcus stole about three blocks from Hodges's house. It was a treasure trove."

"Really?"

Mason nodded, a satisfied smile on his face. "It was all a homicide detective could ask for."

"His computer was there," Manny said. "Edda Fairchild's journal was also there. She'd guessed it was Marcus scamming her because of some phrases he'd used. She was afraid to say anything until she was absolutely certain. Edda didn't want to falsely accuse anyone. Marcus was the one collecting women online and taking their money. Tech is still pulling stuff off his device."

"There were messages from three different women waiting for him to respond," Mason said. "And"—he handed Hanna a flash drive—"he had a half-finished manuscript in his documents. I made a copy for you. I think you'll find it interesting. As soon as we finish collecting all the evidence we can and get a statement from Chase, Marshall will be back in court for more charges."

"Thank you."

"You did the hard part; you caught him. We will put him away."

�֍

Hanna headed back to Dry Oaks, eager to read what Marcus had written. She waited until her shift was over and she was with Jared.

"Marcus really was writing another book?" Jared's face was still horribly bruised, but the worst of it was fading. He couldn't go back to work until released by a doctor, and the doctor wanted the fractures to heal. He was already champing at the bit.

"I hate sitting around doing nothing. Do you think this would keep my interest?"

Hanna considered his question as she finished chewing. She had picked up dinner from Faye's.

"Let's open it up and see."

Jared grabbed his laptop and inserted the drive. The file was entitled *The Chess Master.*

They sat together on the couch and began reading, and it wasn't long before Hanna got the gist of the story. The manuscript was supposed to be a fictional tale of a serial killer who outsmarted every law enforcement officer who ever lived. It read like a confession of sorts, written in the first person. The characters had different names, but what she gleaned from the pages of Marcus's writing was that his current crime wave began years ago, when he caught Gilly at Beecher's Mine cabin.

The agent was behind a tree, concealed, or so he thought. So intent was he watching the cabin that he didn't hear my approach. I had in my hand a thick branch. I crept close, raised the branch, and just as he turned, I swung

316

it and hit him in the head with all my might. He went
down and stayed down.

He then warned Chase, who took the agent and dropped him
in a mine shaft, where he died. He also wrote about helping to
conceal the bodies of a man and a woman in a lake. Joe was written into the story as a hapless hanger-on who they set up to be a
fall guy.

From that point on, the story spanned years—a story of an
alliance between Chase and Marcus. Marcus painted himself as
a genius manipulator and Chase as his pawn. Marcus chose the
women to victimize, and he made Chase his little helper, like Igor
helped Frankenstein.

What was true? Did Chase kill the women or did Marcus?
Hanna wondered if the real truth in all of it would ever be known.

"I can't read any more of this." She rubbed her eyes after they'd
gone through about half.

"It is pretty sick."

"I think I'll head home."

Jared walked her to the door. He took her into his arms, and
she closed her eyes and rested her head on his shoulder.

"I know it's hard, but it's almost over," Jared whispered.
"Marcus and Chase will face justice."

She stepped back, smiled, and they shared a kiss. As she drove
home, she thanked the Lord for the great blessing of having Jared
back in her life again.

CHAPTER 58

HANNA'S PHONE RANG when she pulled into her driveway. It was Mason.

"Chief, hope it's not too late. I wanted to let you in on the latest development."

"It's not too late. What's up?"

"Chase is talking. He agreed to an interview, and when I read him excerpts from Marshall's book, he began to sing like the proverbial canary."

"Oh, that is good news."

"He mentioned your dad, said the idea to frame him came from his grandfather, Al Buckley. He paid everyone off to railroad your father. Back in the day, everyone was afraid of Al. They told your dad that if he ever tried to tell the truth, you and your mom would join Gilly at the bottom of a mine shaft. The public defender had a change of heart a couple of years later. Chase claims that he killed Driscoll. I wanted you to know."

"Thanks. My father told me what he could before he died. I'm glad his last words were verified."

"There will be more to come. Kind of sick, but Chase doesn't want Marshall getting credit for what he did."

The call ended, and Hanna got out of her car and walked to her front door. *Sick* was right, and it made her so tired. So much evil in the world and so much of it had shaped her life. Her faith had always kept her standing. She believed that her father's name would eventually be cleared.

There was some closure knowing that Chase and Marcus would both be tried and held accountable for their crimes.

But she grieved for her mother. Paula wasn't a victim of Joe but of a big lie, of evil secrets buried by evil men.

Hanna opened her front door and bent to pick up the squirming, happy Gizmo. She turned her thoughts to the positives in her life. The best thing to come out of this horrible situation was her rekindled relationship with Jared. He was her first love, a love that had not dimmed over the years. The next best thing to come out of it was the revelation that her father was not the cold-blooded killer she'd grown up believing that he was.

She wished that she'd had the chance to get to know him better. All she had was his Bible and the letters he'd written. She'd put off reading them for too long.

It was time.

Hanna set the dog down and picked up the valise from where she'd stored it the day after Joe died. She poured a cup of tea, sat in her recliner, and pulled out the bundle of letters. He'd numbered them all, and as she removed the rubber band, she pulled out number one.

For a minute, she held the creased and stained letter in her hands and studied the neat block printing. Then she carefully opened the envelope, unfolded the letter from inside, and began to read, slowly getting to know the father who'd truly sacrificed his life to save hers.

DISCUSSION QUESTIONS

1. Joe Keyes accepted a sentence for a crime he didn't commit. What do you think of his reasons for doing so? Can you relate to the decision he made?

2. Hanna's mother kept her from getting to know Joe. Do you agree with her decision? How does it seem to have impacted Hanna?

3. As Hanna struggles with whether to reconcile with her father, Jared suggests that she weigh the possible outcomes: saying no and never having the chance to talk to him about anything, or saying yes—risking other people's anger, but opening a dialogue with him. Jared says, "Same weight, but what can you live with?" If you were in Hanna's position, what would your answer be? How do you personally make tough choices like this?

4. Hanna also has to consider whether to forgive her father for his (assumed) egregious acts. Have you ever had to ask someone to forgive you, either for recent or long-past mistakes? How was it received?

5. Hanna says about Joe, "He's certainly not the big bad murderer Marcus or my mother always described." What do you think she expected? Does committing sins make someone a bad person?

6. Hanna loves Nathan, but at some point along the way, she realizes she's in love with Jared. What do you think of the way she—and Nathan—handle this realization? Do you think they'll be able to remain friends? How do you break up with someone gracefully?

7. Hanna lets Jared leave her because he doesn't share her Christian faith. Do you think she made the right decision, or should she have worked on breaking down that barrier and witnessing to him? Have you ever been in a similar situation?

8. Hanna was bullied as a child for the perceived sins of her father. How does this affect her life as an adult? Were you or someone you care about bullied? What were the effects on you or your friend or loved one?

9. Hanna feels confident about her decision to care for Joe, as "the Christian thing to do." Do you think she would have made the same decision if she hadn't been a person of faith? Why or why not?

10. In addition to committing heinous crimes himself, Marcus allowed his ambition as a writer to take over his life and destroy the lives of others. How could he have used his ambition for good? Do you think he can still be redeemed?

ABOUT THE AUTHOR

A former Long Beach, California, police officer of twenty-two years, JANICE CANTORE worked a variety of assignments, including patrol, administration, juvenile investigations, and training. She's always enjoyed writing and published two short articles on faith at work for *Cop and Christ* and *Today's Christian Woman* before tackling novels. She now lives in Florida, where she enjoys ocean swimming, golfing, spending time on the beach, and going on long walks with her Labrador retrievers, Abbie and Tilly.

Janice writes suspense novels designed to keep readers engrossed and leave them inspired. She has penned more than a dozen novels including the Line of Duty series, the Cold Case Justice series, *Breach of Honor*, *Code of Courage*, and *One Final Target*.

Visit Janice's website at janicecantore.com and connect with her on Facebook at facebook.com/JaniceCantore and at the Romantic Suspense A-TEAM group.

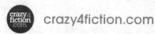